**Biblioasis International Translation Series**
**General Editor: Stephen Henighan**

Since 2007, the Biblioasis International Translation Series has been publishing exciting literature from Europe, Latin America, Africa and the minority languages of Canada. Committed to the idea that translations must come from the margins of linguistic cultures as well as from the power centres, the Biblioasis International Translation Series is dedicated to publishing world literature in English in Canada. The editors believe that translation is the lifeblood of literature, that a language that is not in touch with other linguistic traditions loses its creative vitality, and that the worldwide spread of English makes literary translation more urgent now than ever before.

1. *I Wrote Stone: The Selected Poetry of Ryszard Kapuściński* (Poland)
Translated by Diana Kuprel and Marek Kusiba

2. *Good Morning Comrades*
by Ondjaki (Angola)
Translated by Stephen Henighan

3. *Kahn & Engelmann*
by Hans Eichner (Austria-Canada)
Translated by Jean M. Snook

4. *Dance with Snakes*
by Horacio Castellanos Moya (El Salvador)
Translated by Lee Paula Springer

5. *Black Alley*
by Mauricio Segura (Quebec)
Translated by Dawn M. Cornelio

6. *The Accident*
by Mihail Sebastian (Romania)
Translated by Stephen Henighan

7. *Love Poems*
by Jaime Sabines (Mexico)
Translated by Colin Carberry

8. *The End of the Story*
by Liliana Heker (Argentina)
Translated by Andrea G. Labinger

9. *The Tuner of Silences*
by Mia Couto (Mozambique)
Translated by David Brookshaw

10. *For as Far as the Eye Can See*
by Robert Melançon (Quebec)
Translated by Judith Cowan

11. *Eucalyptus*
by Mauricio Segura (Quebec)
Translated by Donald Winkler

12. *Granma Nineteen and the Soviet's Secret*
by Ondjaki (Angola)
Translated by Stephen Henighan

13. *Montreal Before Spring*
by Robert Melançon (Quebec)
Translated by Donald McGrath

14. *Pensativities: Essays and Provocations*
by Mia Couto (Mozambique)
Translated by David Brookshaw

15. *Arvida*
by Samuel Archibald (Quebec)
Translated by Donald Winkler

16. *The Orange Grove*
by Larry Tremblay (Quebec)
Translated by Sheila Fischman

17. *The Party Wall*
by Catherine Leroux (Quebec)
Translated by Lazer Lederhendler

18. *Black Bread*
by Emili Teixidor (Catalonia)
Translated by Peter Bush

19. *Boundary*
by Andrée A. Michaud (Quebec)
Translated by Donald Winkler

# BOUNDARY:
# THE LAST SUMMER

# Boundary
## The Last Summer

Andrée A. Michaud

Translated from the French by Donald Winkler

BIBLIOASIS
WINDSOR, ONTARIO

FIRST EDITION

*Library and Archives Canada Cataloguing in Publication*

Michaud, Andrée A., 1957-
[Bondrée. English]
Boundary / Andrée A. Michaud ; translated from the French by Donald Winkler.

(Biblioasis international translation series ; no. 19)
Translation of: Bondrée.

Issued in print and electronic formats.

ISBN 978-1-77196-109-7 (softcover).--ISBN 978-1-77196-110-3 (ebook)

I. Winkler, Donald, translator II. Title. III. Title: Bondrée. English.
IV. Series: Biblioasis international translation series 19

PS8576.I217B6613 2017 C843'.54 C2016-907966-X
C2016-907967-8

Edited by Stephen Henighan
Copy-edited by Cat London
Typeset by Chris Andrechek
Cover designed by Chris Tompkins
Front cover image by Steve Ginn
Back cover image by Tobias Sheck

Canada Council for the Arts Conseil des Arts du Canada

Canadian Heritage Patrimoine canadien

Published with the generous assistance of the Canada Council for the Arts and the Ontario Arts Council. Biblioasis also acknowledges the support of the Government of Canada through the Canada Book Fund and the Government of Ontario through the Ontario Book Publishing Tax Credit. Biblioasis also acknowledges the financial support of the Government of Canada through the National Translation Program for Book Publishing, an initiative of the *Roadmap for Canada's Official Languages 2013–2018: Education, Immigration, Communities*, for our translation activities.

PRINTED AND BOUND IN CANADA

MIX
Paper from responsible sources
FSC® C004071

**Translator's note**:
Phrases in italics are in English in the original.

*To my father*

Bondrée is a place where shadows defeat the harshest light, an enclave whose lush vegetation recalls the virgin forests that covered the North American continent three or four centuries ago. Its name derives from a deformation of the word "boundary," or frontier. No borderline, however, is there to suggest that this place belongs to any country other than the temperate forests stretching from Maine, in the United States, to the southwest of the Beauce, in Quebec. Boundary is a stateless domain, a no-man's-land harbouring a lake, Boundary Pond, and a mountain the hunters came to call Moose Trap, after observing that the moose venturing onto the lake's western shore were swiftly tripped up on the steep slope of this rocky mass that with the same dispassion engulfs the setting suns. Bondrée also includes several hectares of forest called Peter's Woods, named after Pierre Landry, a Canuck trapper who settled in the region in the early 1940s to evade the war, to flee death while himself inflicting it. It's in this Eden that ten or so years later a few city-dwellers seeking peace and quiet chose to build cottages, forcing Landry to take refuge deep in the woods, until the beauty of a woman called Maggie Harrison drove him to return and roam around the lake, setting in motion the gears that would transform his paradise into hell.

The children had long been in bed when Zaza Mulligan, on Friday 21 July, stepped onto the path leading to her parents' cottage, humming "A Whiter Shade of Pale," flung out, in the bedazzlement of that summer of '67, by Procol Harum, along with "Lucy in the Sky with Diamonds." She'd drunk too much, but she didn't care. She loved seeing objects dancing about her and trees swaying in the night. She loved the languor of alcohol, the odd gradients of the unstable ground, forcing her to lift her arms as a bird unfolds its wings to ride the ascending winds. *Bird, bird, sweet bird*, she sang to a senseless melody, a drunken young girl's air, her long arms miming the wings of the albatross and those birds of foreign skies that wheel over rolling seas. Everything around her was in motion, all charged with indolent life, right up to the lock on the front door into which she couldn't quite manage to insert her key. *Never mind*, because she didn't really want to go in. The night was too lovely, the stars so luminous. And so she retraced her steps, crossed back over the cedar-lined path, and walked with no other goal than to revel in her own giddiness.

A few dozen feet from the campground she entered Otter Trail, the path where she'd kissed Mark Meyer at the start of summer before going to tell Sissy Morgan, her friend since always and for evermore, for life and 'til death do us part, for now and forever, that Meyer frenched like a snail. The slack memory of that limp tongue wriggling around and seeking her own brought a taste of acid bile to her throat, which she fought off by spitting, barely missing the toes of her new sandals. Venturing a few awkward steps that made her burst out laughing, she moved deeper into the woods. They were calm, with no sound to disturb the peace in that place, not even that of her footsteps on the spongy earth. Then a light breath of wind brushed past her knees, and she heard something crack behind her. The wind, she said to herself, *wind on my knees, wind in the trees*, paying no heed to the source of this noise in the midst of silence. Her heart jumped all the same when a fox bolted in front of her, and she started laughing again, a bit nervously, thinking that the night gave rise to fear because the night loves to see fear in the eyes of children. *Doesn't it, Sis*, she murmured, remembering the distant days when she tried with Sissy to rouse the ghosts peopling the forest, that of Pete Landry, that of Tanager, the woman whose red dresses had bewitched Landry, and that of Sugar Baby, whose yapping you could hear from the top of Moose Trap. All those ghosts had now vanished from Zaza's mind, but the sky's moonless darkness revived the memory of the red dress flitting through the trees.

She was starting to turn off onto a path that intersected with Otter Trail when there was another crack behind her, louder than the first. The fox, she said to herself, *fox in the trees*, refusing to let the darkness spoil her pleasure by unearthing stupid childhood terrors. She was alive, she was drunk, and the forest could crumble around her if it wished, she would not shrink from the night nor the barking of a dog that had been dead and buried for ages. She began to hum "A Whiter Shade of Pale" among the swaying trees, imagining herself in the strong arms of someone unknown, their dance slow and amorous, when she stopped short, almost tripping over a twisted root.

The cracking came closer, and fear, this time, began to steal across her damp skin. Who's there, she asked, but silence had fallen upon the forest. Who's there, she cried, then a shadow crossed the path and Zaza Mulligan began to retreat.

PIERRE LANDRY

I remember Weasel Trail and Otter Trail, I remember Turtle Road, Côte Croche, and the loons, the waves, the docks suspended in mist. I've forgotten nothing about the Bondrée forests, and their green so intense that it seems today to have emerged full-blown from the radiance of a dream. And yet nothing is more real than those woods where the blood of red foxes flows still, nothing is truer than the fresh water in which I swam long after the death of Pierre Landry, whose presence in the heart of those woods still haunted the surrounding area.

Many stories circulated concerning this man who it was claimed lashed out with a mystifying rage, stories of bestiality, savagery, and madness, all to the effect that Landry, rejecting the war, had signed a blood pact with the forest. Some drew on these absurd legends to explain why Landry had hanged himself in his shack, but the most plausible version spoke simply of a love story and a woman Landry called Tanager, associating her red dresses with the flight of those scarlet birds. Recollections of this woman, whose name was linked inexorably to that of Landry, had bit by bit worked their way into Boundary's collective memory. She had become a ghost to whom children cried out at dusk as they stalked the shadows dancing on the shore. Tanager, they whispered, fearful, Tanager of Bondrée, hoping to see the silhouette of this bird woman, born of a few shreds of red silk tossed together in Landry's deranged mind, rise from the thin fog licking at the shoreline. I dared not, myself, conjure Tanager, fearing in my own muddled way that her ghost might materialize before me and give chase. I preferred, perched in a giant tree, to watch for the spectacular emergence of the tanagers in Bondrée's dense forest cover, barely compromised by the construction of the road leading to the lake.

It was that road, they said, which had forced Landry to retreat deep into the woods, a road soon followed by cottages, and then the men, the women, the voices seconding the din from shovels and motors. Soon after these disturbances, patches of colour appeared in the still-virgin landscape, creating a small province where for a few months each year the colour took on life, to encroach on the greenery at the heart of which Landry had established his derisory empire.

Despite the relatively small number of vacationers, the human presence, while it lasted, detracted from the wildness of that place. From the beginning of June doors began to slam, radios to crackle, and sometimes you heard a child cry out that he'd caught a minnow. But it was in July that Bondrée really came alive, with its share of teenagers, tired mothers, pets, and family vehicles so loaded down with belongings that you could almost see them sending off fumes at the last turn onto Turtle Road, the gravel road circling the lake, which followed, it was said, the trail marked out by the slow exodus of turtles come from ancient rivers. All those people who were jolted along Turtle Road formed a mixed community of English speakers and French speakers from Maine, New Hampshire, or Quebec, living side by side and barely talking to one another, often content with a wave of the hand, a *bonjour*, or a hi!, signalling their differences, but acknowledging the bond they shared in this place they'd chosen to assert their remote connection to a nature that excluded them.

As for us, we arrived right after the Saint-Jean Baptiste holiday and the end of classes, whatever the weather. That summer, however, my father treated us to three days of rides, cotton candy, hot dogs, and space travel at Expo 67, before, our heads crammed full of Africa and Sputniks, we got on the road for Bondrée and the familiar rituals that awaited us, without which no summer would be worthy of the name.

They never changed, and smacked of a freedom known only to a life that's free from care. While my parents unloaded the car I went down near the lake to drink in the smells of Bondrée, a mix of water, fish, sun-warmed conifers, and wet sand, along with the slightly mouldy odours that permeated the cottage right into September despite the open windows, the aromas of steak and fruit pudding, and the pungent perfumes of the wildflowers my mother gathered. Those odours, which lasted from June until the nights grew cool, have no equal beyond the wetness in the air when it comes to unearthing my childhood memories, shot through with green and blue, with grey overtopped by foam. They are the custodians, beneath sunlit surfaces, of those summers' humid essence during the years when I was growing up.

I was only six years old when my parents bought the cottage, built from cedar logs and surrounded by birch and spruce that shaded a windowed room from which we could admire the lake. That's why they'd acquired the property, for the veranda and for the trees that gave them renewed access to a utopian dream that life had taken from them. They were only twenty years old when my brother Bob was born, twenty-three when I arrived, twenty-eight when Millie came on the scene, and even if they weren't old their idea of happiness had contracted, had been reduced to a veranda and a cockeyed garden where parsley and gladiolas grew pell-mell.

I knew nothing of those dreams that had vanished along with my mother's virginity, dreams sacrificed to the scrubbing of diapers and the many unpaid bills piled up on my father's desk, squeezed into a corner of the living room. I didn't realize that my parents were still young, that my mother was beautiful, that my father laughed like a child when he could forget that he had three offspring of his own. Saturday mornings he jumped onto his old bicycle and did the tour of the lake in forty minutes, more or less. My mother timed him, watched him dart through the trees and take the turn at Ménard Bay, and she gave a yelp of victory if he beat his own record. Thirty-nine minutes, Sam! she exclaimed with a delight whose ardour escaped me, because I didn't know that my father was an athlete converted to hardware, and that he could have left in the dust that handful of adolescents coming down Côte Croche, Snake Hill to the English, feet perched on the handlebars of their bicycles, trying to impress the girls.

My parents' lives began with me, and I couldn't conceive that they had a past. The little girl posing in black and white on photos stored in a Lowney's chocolate box that served as our family album didn't at all look like my mother, no more than the boy with the shaved head chewing on a wisp of hay near a wooden fence looked like my father. Those children belonged to a universe that had nothing to do with the adults whose immutable image kept the world on its steady course. Florence and Samuel Duchamp's entire purpose in life was to provide, to protect, and to impose limits. They were there and would always be there, familiar figures for whom I was the only reason to be alive, along with Bob and Millie.

It was only that summer, when things got out of hand and I began to lose my bearings, that I came to see that the frailty of those little people shut up in the Lowney's chocolate box had endured down the years, along with the fears buried at the heart of every childhood, fears that resurface as soon as it becomes clear that the world's solidity rests on a foundation that can be swept away with a single gust from an evil wind.

Sissy Morgan and Elisabeth Mulligan, called Zaza, the two girls who would prove to be the conduits for this calamity, were still only children when we moved to Bondrée, but they were already inseparable, Zaza always dressed like Sissy, and vice versa. You would have thought they were twins, one head red and the other blond, tearing down Snake Hill crying *Sissy, look! Run, Zaza, run!* pursued by who knows what creature making them race until they were out of breath. *Run, Zaza, run!* My mother called them the Andrews Sisters, even if there were three Andrews Sisters and they sang a hundred times better than Sissy and Zaza.

My mother, whose maiden name was Florence Richard, loved everything old-fashioned, including the Andrews Sisters, and sometimes she even tried dancing to "Boogie Woogie Bugle Boy." In the rare moments when she let herself go with what seemed to me a sort of exhibitionism, I did my best to remove myself as far as possible from the Andrews Sisters' voices crackling away on the old cottage turntable, because I was ashamed to see my mother showing herself off. Dancing was not for mothers. Nor was youth. They were only for the LaVernes, the Maxines, and the Patty Andrews, for the kind of girls Zaza Mulligan and Sissy Morgan would become, like Denise Lachapelle, one of our neighbours in town, who dressed provocatively and had loads of friends who came by to pick her up on Saturday night in their convertibles or on their motorcycles, Kawa 750s that roared away in the mild air and made my father envious, he who couldn't even afford to replace his old '59 Ford.

Sissy and Zaza were, for me, Denise Lachapelles in the making who would turn boys' heads and paint their faces on Saturday night. But for most people they were only spoiled children, spoiled rotten in fact, obnoxious kids for whom nothing was out of bounds, tilting whichever way the wind blew, goading each other on, and riding for a fall. Not bad seeds. Just wild plants, that's all, whose weakness for the sun you could do nothing about. I would have loved to be the one to turn their duo into a trio, but they wouldn't have anything to do with a little twerp four or five years younger than they were, trying to impress them with her collection of live insects or by catching toads. *Yuk*! they cried, *is this your brother?* Then they burst out laughing and gave me a candy or some bubble gum because they found me cute, *she's so cute, Sis*. And they took off and left me with my toad, my grasshoppers, my crickets, and my treats. Sometimes I asked my mother the meaning of "frogue," "foc," or "chize." "*Fromage*," cheese, she replied, with her smile widening around the word "cheese," and she executed a mother's pirouette over the word "foc," a wimpish pirouette that didn't risk hoisting her skirt up over her thighs. She gave me a lesson on "*phoques*," or seals that lived at the North Pole and spoke Eskimo, anything at all, answers for big people, adults, who'd forgotten how much a word divorced from its meaning can unsettle a childhood.

I never ate the candies. I put them away in my treasure chest, a rectangular tin box decorated with a Christmas tree, and also containing stones, feathers, twigs, and snakeskins. I did, however, save the bubble gum for special occasions, when I'd just spotted a raccoon rummaging in a garbage can, or a trout snagging a fly on the surface of the lake. The smallest rabbit dropping stuck to my red running shoes became a pretext to run and hide under a Virginia pine whose branches touched the ground, a shaded space I called my cabin, where I unwrapped the bubble gum, repeating *here, a baby yum for you, littoldolle*. With my tomboy air I was anything but a doll, but I was proud of projecting an image in the eyes of Bondrée's two most fascinating creatures, grasshoppers and salamanders included, as perfect as their gilded universe. I squeezed the baby yum with my fingertips until it was nice and soft, and stuck it to my palate with a smile: *here, littoldolle*. Those globs of bubble gum were in some sense the ancestors of the Pall Malls I would later crave, the distinctive trademark of Sissy and Zaza, who were able to pop enormous bubbles without ever having them stick to their faces. In my cabin I practised bursting bubbles like you practise blowing smoke rings, then I buried the gum under pine needles and went back to the lake, to the squirrel paths, to everything that then delighted me, to those simple things rich with odours that would later help me to resuscitate my childhood and renew contact with a simple joy every time a rustling of wings stirred up a scent of juniper.

The last summer we spent at Bondrée was, however, suffused with another odour, one of flesh, both sex and blood, which rose from the humid forest when night fell and the name Tanager echoed on the mountain. But nothing hinted at that tenacious perfume when the campfires, one by one, were lit around the lake, those of the Ménards, the Tanguays, the McBains. Nothing seemed able to cloud the sunstruck indolence of Boundary, because it was the summer of '67, the summer of "Lucy in the Sky with Diamonds" and the Montreal World's Fair, because it was the summer of love, as Zaza Mulligan proclaimed while Sissy Morgan lit into "Lucy in the Sky" and Franky-Frenchie Lamar, with her orange hula hoop, danced away on the Morgans' dock. July offered up its splendour, and no one suspected then that Lucy's diamonds would soon be reduced to dust by Pete Landry's traps.

But the springing of those traps would resound as far as Maine, because Zaza Mulligan and Sissy Morgan, who were considered the sort of girls to be forgotten after one night, would brand Bondrée's memory with a red-hot iron, and make it clear to all that people like Pete Landry, bound too tightly to the woods, never quite died. Like Landry, they headed down the tortuous paths of a forest well trodden by man to become legends in their turn, in tales where the redhead and the blonde would in the end be confused, since there where you saw Sissy, you were sure to encounter Zaza. The urchins of the time even made up a silly song they chanted to the tune of "Only the Lonely" every time the two girls flounced by, but what did they care, they were Boundary's princesses, the red and blonde Lolitas who'd made men drool ever since they'd learned to lure their eyes with their well-tanned legs.

Most of the women didn't like them, not only because they'd one day or another caught their husband or fiancé ogling Zaza's navel, but because Sissy and Zaza didn't like women. Zaza tolerated only Sissy, and vice versa. The rest were just rivals whose potential for seduction they appraised, elbowing each other and sniggering. Neither did the men like those girls, who seemed to have no better goal than to excite in them what they thought only lurked in others.

They were for them just fodder for their fantasies, conjuring the worst obscenities, Zaza with her thighs spread wide, Sissy on her knees, cock-teasers they would discard along with their Kleenex, ashamed, when their wives called them in for supper, of having behaved like all other men.

So they weren't surprised to learn about what happened to them. Those girls had been asking for it, that's what most of them couldn't help thinking, and those thoughts sparked in them a kind of treacly remorse that made them want to pound themselves with their fists, to slap themselves until they drew blood, because the girls were dead, good God, *dead, for Christ's sake*, and no one, not them nor anyone else, deserved the end that had been reserved for them. It took this calamity for them to think of those girls as anything but schemers, for them to understand that behind their rancour was only a vast emptiness into which they'd all stupidly thrown themselves, seeing nothing but the tanned skin camouflaging that emptiness. If life had not pulled the rug out from under them, they might have filled that gaping hole and loved other women. But it was too late, and no one would ever know if Zaza and Sissy were rotten to the core, destined to become what they called "bitches" or "old bitches." And so they resented them, almost, for being dead and for instigating that soul searching where you took the measure of your own ordinariness and pettiness, of the ease with which you were able to damn and judge others without first taking a good look at yourself in the mirror.

Fortunately September had arrived, because by the end of summer no fewer than half the members of the small community despised themselves enough to have to acknowledge it, while the other half, in taking stock of themselves, were learning to value the merits of mendacity. As for me, I was sheltered from the guilt gnawing away at the adults. I did not know the true meaning of the word "bitch," nor the burden of sin contained in a simple thought, the awful temptation that can poison one's mind as much as a done deed. If I avoided mirrors, it was not because of Sissy or Zaza, but because I was twelve years old and I found myself ugly. But I revered those two girls with silky hair who smelled of peach and lily of the valley, who read photo-novels and danced rock 'n' roll like the groupies who waggled their hips on TV to songs translated by the Excentriques or César et les Romains. To me they represented a quintessence of femininity to which I hardly dared aspire, a magazine femininity reserved for girls who had long legs and lacquered nails. I observed them from afar, and tried to mimic their moves and their poses, their way of holding a cigarette, all the time dreaming of the day I would exhale into the air around me the smoke from a Pall Mall the way Zaza Mulligan did, tilting my head back and making an "o" of my lips out in the midday sun. I picked up a wisp of straw and held it delicately between my index and middle fingers, saying *foc, Sissy, disse boy iz a frog*, until the cry of a loon or the hammering of a woodpecker brought me back home to the lake, the river, and the trees.

I dreamed of also having a friend, to whom I could say *foc* while swinging my hips, but the only adolescent my age at Bondrée was a girl from Concord, Massachusetts, who took herself for Vivien Leigh in *Gone With the Wind*, and who spent her days fanning herself on her parents' porch. Taratata! In any case, I could only manage a few words of English in those days, *see you soon, racoon*, and other such fooleries, and I was sure that Jane Mary Brown—that was the name of the girl—couldn't even translate "yes" or "no" into French. *Franky, I not gave a down*, I'd retorted the day she shut the door in my face, cheerfully butchering Clark

Gable's famous comeback to Vivien Leigh in the dimming light of a Virginia in flames. *"Frankly, my dear, I don't give a damn."* Jane Mary Brown had been dealt with.

Françoise Lamar, whose parents had bought the cottage next to us the year before, spoke for her part an English as impeccable as her French, despite a first name that drove her crazy every time an anglophone tried to pronounce it. It was her mother, Suzanne Langlois, who'd insisted that her daughter have a suitably French name, even if Franky was born of an anglophone father right in the heart of New Hampshire. At the beginning of summer 1967 she'd risen from the chaise longue where she baked herself from morning to night, to cozy up to Sissy and Zaza, and she'd begun to smoke Pall Malls she concealed under the elastic of her Bermuda or polka dot shorts when she left the family cottage, slamming the screen door. I don't know how she managed it, but it only took her a few days to be accepted by the Sissy-Zaza duo, which I'd thought was impregnable. From that point on there were no longer two pairs of legs stretched out on the rail of the Mulligans' motorboat, but three, wrapped in a cloud of white smoke, as the radio blared out the hits of the day.

So began, long after the tale of Pierre Landry, the story of the summer of '67 and "Lucy in the Sky with Diamonds," starting with that friendship and the three pairs of legs you saw everywhere, that you saw too much of, that were omnipresent, with the dirty jokes and guffaws that followed in their wake, dropping with the Kleenex into the open drains.

For the merchants of Jackman and Moose River, to whom he sold his pelts, Pierre Landry soon became Peter or Pete *Laundry*, a wild man jabbering a rudimentary "franglais" and scenting himself with beaver oil. And that's what he was, a wild man, an exile, but one who had not yet severed all ties with his fellows. Near Moose Trap he sometimes received visits from a hunter in October, a fisherman in June, with whom he shared a forty-ounce Canadian Club, but he spent the winters on his own, taking pleasure in the frozen beauty of Boundary, which, with his Canuck accent, he'd rebaptized Bondrée, the rough country of Bondrée. Among his more loyal visitors there was a young man who went by the name of Little Hawk, a rangy type with a nose like an eagle's beak, to whom Landry had taught the rudiments of trapping, which he himself had learned from his father and grandfather, both of whom had lived off what the Beauce had to offer in furred and feathered creatures. Little Hawk was his friend, the only man he allowed to tend his traps, the only human being, in fact, with whom he was prepared to share the reality of death. He and Little Hawk didn't speak the same language, except for a few words, but they shared a language all the same, that of the gestures and silences survival demands. When Little Hawk stayed for the night they sat on Pete's shaky deck and listened to the forest, the growling and squealing of animals devouring each other. It was from the way Little Hawk then inclined his head that Pete had seen that they were the same, two people acknowledging the sad necessity of what some called cruelty, but which was just an echo of the earth's primal breathing in and out. Then one day Little Hawk stopped coming. Landry waited for him, and concluded by his absence that he'd fallen into the trap that he himself had avoided by leaving Quebec, refusing to be thrown into a war about which he knew nothing, and where death for him had no meaning. Little Hawk hadn't been so lucky. Like thousands of other young Yankees, he'd won Roosevelt's lottery for a one-way trip to Europe, called up along with all those who were deemed fit to fight and who didn't question their aptitude for dying or for rubbing shoulders with death.

With no one to talk to about the beauty of the forest and the wildlife procreating there, Landry walled himself off in silence. At first he still talked to the trees and animals, and addressed the limpidity of the lake. He also talked to himself, commenting on the weather, describing the storms, even telling himself some lame jokes, stories of fishermen tangled in their own lines, but speech bit by bit abandoned him. He thought in words, but they stayed inside him, melted into his thoughts, lost themselves in the shapes of things there was no more point in naming. If the idea survived, it no longer expressed itself in sounds. During the time when Little Hawk paid him visits and shared his speckled trout, he'd rediscovered the true meaning of speech in the nights punctuated by silence. Little Hawk was not talkative, but he'd revived in him the desire to say things about the sky, to utter the word "blue" or "cloud," *midnight blue* or *thunderclouds*. Once Little Hawk left, the blue no longer had any reason for being, nor did the smiles he tried to muster in the little mirror over the mottled basin where he washed himself and his pots and pans.

Then the blue was suddenly back with the arrival of the picks and shovels, the throbbing engines putting up cabins and putting down a road, blue and all the colours of creation, what with the sudden appearance of Maggie Harrison running along the lake in her scarlet dresses, dancing beneath the moon, and setting the skies to reeling. If he'd had the power Landry would have sent packing those infernal machines that seemed to have no goal other than to destroy everything that belonged to him, the silence, the clear water, the ethereal flight of the loons, but Maggie Harrison's long black hair soon muffled the constant din. He instantly fell in love with this woman whose skin was too pale, and harbouring her in his mind, he rebaptised her Marie in a stream's pure water. Right away he began to watch her, swimming out from shore, striding along the beach with her dog Sugar, *Sugar Baby my love*. Concealed behind trees, Landry saw her dance with the waves, and whispered *Marie, Baby, my love*. Softly he repeated the words that expressed his love, softly, not to startle her, *my love*, because Maggie Harrison, along with the colours of creation, had given him back the longing for rapturous words, *Marie, sweet bird*, Tanager of Bondrée.

The honeymoon lasted for a time, then other, brutal words silenced Pierre Landry's love song, obscene words, *bastard, savage*, uttered by men who'd seen him step out of the woods to walk on the beach. *Bastard, savage*, when he'd only wanted to come near, when he was just trying to stroke the contours of what had restored to him the spoken word. He'd stretched out his arms and Marie had pushed him back, *get away from me*, just when he was going to touch her hands, her eyes, her red lips that said *don't*, her glistening lips that gave onto a great black hole and cried *don't, go away, don't touch me!*

That same day Pierre Landry buried himself in the woods, and he was never again seen near Boundary Pond. It was Willy Preston, a trapper people called The Bear, who found him in his shack a few weeks later, probably dead about the time of the new moon, his corpse eaten away by flies and maggots. Near the shack lay the body of Sugar Baby, *Sugar Baby my love*, disappeared that morning, disembowelled by a trap. A little after sunset Preston was seen coming out of the woods, holding to his body Sugar Baby's remains. Maggie Harrison's lament was then heard tearing through the ethereal flight of the loons, its echo merging with their complaints and sending shivers down the spines of even hard-working men. After two or three nights the echo went silent on the slopes of Moose Trap, and Maggie Harrison left Bondrée, leaning her shadow on the stooped shoulder of her husband. Like Landry, they were never again seen in the region, neither him nor her, crying out the name of Sugar Baby.

Among all the people who visited Bondrée at the time, only Don and Martha Irving, along with the Tanguays, Jean-Louis, Flora, and old Pat, had known Pete Landry, as far as you could know a man who came out of the woods only to melt back into them. They'd seen him not there but in the bay later called Ménard Bay, grumbling as he demolished his shack in order to rebuild it farther on, where the shovels and machines would not reach. They'd also seen him at the mouth of Spider River, stark naked, scrawny, his hip bones forming a bowl for his hollow belly, washing his clothes in clear water, without any soap to dislodge the grime.

Some people had hounded Don and Martha Irving, urging them to relate whatever they knew about Landry, but

Don just mumbled that it was no one's business, *none of your goddamn business*, while Martha blew smoke in their faces from her fortieth Player's of the day.

The same thing for Pat Tanguay, who refused to talk about Landry out of respect for the dead, he said, his basket of dead fish in his arms, and because he hated the inevitable gossip born of what people said, whatever it might be. Flora, his daughter-in-law, however, enjoyed circulating stories about Landry. She'd one day paid him a visit at his shack, neighbours had to get to know each other after all. Met by Landry's cold gaze she'd retreated as far as the door, where she'd torn her pink cotton dress, a few threads of which stayed behind, caught on the door frame. Flora Tanguay never missed an opportunity to talk about that expedition, describing the beaver skins hanging on Landry's walls like so many cadavers staring at you with their milky eyes. She imagined them with the heads of lynx or wolves, and talked only of blood, excess, and bestiality. She was the source for the story of Tanager, which she embroidered every which way, and altered according to her listener's degree of captivation.

Several people claimed that Flora Tanguay ought to have been gagged for running off at the mouth and further sullying the good name of a man who, as far as was known, had never done any harm to anyone, not to Maggie Harrison or Sugar Baby, whose death was no more than a deplorable accident. Landry was just another of the forest's victims, lost in his fascination for the beauty of flowers and birds. There was just one point on which everyone agreed with Flora Tanguay, and that was Landry's feral behaviour, which got worse during the freeze-ups of his last winter, and brought disarray and disorder the following summer.

Still, no one thought after Landry's death that anyone around the lake would turn deviant just from consorting with animals. The few oddballs still on the loose in the area were not really dangerous. There was old broken-down Pat Tanguay, of course, who spent all his life in his rowboat, most likely to spare himself the endless prattling of his daughter-in-law, who could herself qualify as one of the local eccentrics. There was also Bill Cochrane, a veteran who heard the roaring of war engines on stormy nights, and Charlotte Morgan, who walked around in her pyjamas all day long, and, to preserve her white skin, only went out at dusk. But there was no one with an affliction similar to that of Landry, who'd ended up at one with the forest. As for Zaza Mulligan and Sissy Morgan, they were just different. Yet it was through them that the savagery had returned, because of them, they thought, without daring to say it out loud, because those girls were dead, good God, *dead, for Christ's sake!* It was thanks to their beauty and Maggie Harrison's, and to that of all happy and desirable women, that Pete Landry's traps had emerged from the dark earth, and with them the violence of other men.

# ZAZA

*Who's there? Who's fucking there?* Zaza Mulligan cried, before a man's shadow, enormous to her eyes, crossed the path, its back bent. For a moment she felt the coolness of the ground numb her legs, like a long wet animal rubbing against her skin, and she sought support nearby, a tree to hold on to. This was not the time to faint, not now, Zaz, *not now, please.* She dug her nails into an oak's bark, took a deep breath, and again cried *who's there? Who's fucking there?* trying to keep her cool, so the man wouldn't sense the fear oozing from her every pore, but her voice was already cracking and tears were burning her eyes, tears she wiped away with the back of her hand, to restore to the dark and eddying night some semblance of brightness.

*Who are you, for Christ's sake?* And the shadow remained silent, mute and motionless. All that reached Zaza was the sound of her own breath, which she tried to connect with that of the fox that had burst out in front of her a while ago, *wind on my knees, fox in the trees*. This kind of thing couldn't happen to her, not to her, not now. *It's a fox, Zaz, you're drunk, it's a fucking fox, or a bear, that's it, a damned bear,* because Zaza would have much preferred to face a bear than this unseen and silent man. *Talk to me, please! You're not funny!*

Warding off the images flashing through her mind, one more frightening than the next, she clung to the idea that someone just wanted to give her a good scare, *that's it,* a bloody scare. *Mark, is that you? Sissy? Frenchie?* But the shadow stayed mute, shrouded in its own slow breathing.

Keeping her eyes on the dark, hushed stillness where the animal's shadow had slunk away, *it's a fox, it's just a bear,* Zaza Mulligan began to retreat, silently, one step following on another, over the spongy soil. *It's a fox.* Then a hand came down on her shoulder and Zaza Mulligan screamed.

It was Gilles Ménard, who lived down by the water, who found Zaza, her leg severed by an old bear trap overgrown with vegetation. The rusted iron had torn into the limb and bared it to the bone, to the long white tibia of a leggy young girl.

There had been no sign of Zaza for almost forty-eight hours, but with her parents absent, no one was concerned except Sissy Morgan, whose voice echoed around the lake for two days, from Saturday morning to Sunday noon, while the men mowed their lawns or sipped beer while reading the newspaper. The two girls, along with Françoise Lamar, called Franky-Frenchie, had spent Friday evening at the campground. They'd left at about eleven o'clock, after having shared a twenty-sixer of gin pinched by Frenchie from her father's liquor cabinet. Marcel Dumas, whose cottage bordered the campground, heard them laughing as they passed under his bedroom window, then one of them tripped, he didn't know which, and their laughter got even louder.

Sissy came in through the back door, preferring not to run into her parents, who were entertaining the McBains, and she climbed right up to her room. She lay down without getting undressed, holding onto the sheets to stop the bed from rocking, then fell into a deep dreamless sleep from which she was wrenched by a violent nausea. As she ran to vomit in the toilet, a barn owl outside began shrieking like a woman being raped. A chill ran through her just as pink spray splattered the bowl. Zaza, she murmured, and the owl went silent.

Seeing her sheets on the floor, Saturday morning, she wondered where she was, then the owl's complaint came back to her through the hissing of the waves. Zaza's image loomed up before her in the room's semi-darkness, and she rushed to the telephone her father had just had installed so Sissy could reach Zaza. Getting no answer, she charged outside despite her headache, without taking the time to have breakfast or brush her teeth, and went to hammer on the door of the Mulligans' cottage, almost kicking it down. She finally got into the cottage through the kitchen window, the little window over the sink, tipping over a pile of dirty dishes, *goddamn, Zaza, you could have washed your dishes,* then she called out Zaza, Zaz, passing through the cottage's rooms one by one, a huge living room, four bedrooms, a sitting room, a dining room off the kitchen. *Zaza, where are you, dammit?* Finding Zaza nowhere, she circled the lake on her bicycle shouting out her friend's name, threatening to tear out her fingernails, her hair, her eyes, everything a girl flipping out might think of extracting. Several residents saw her coming down Turtle Road, out of breath, with her face on fire. *What's happening?* Stella McBain asked, dropping a stitch in her knitting. Ed, her husband, answered that it was Sissy, Victor's daughter, chasing her shadow.

After two hours of fruitless searching, Sissy swallowed her pride and, with a view to dragging her along, went to get Frenchie Lamar, who slept until the cows came home, out of bed. Frenchie also had a throbbing headache, and, not in the mood to be rushed, she took the time to swallow a Nescafé. She must have gone to join her parents in town, she told Sissy, adding sugar to her cup as the coffee level went down, or maybe she treated herself to a nighttime walk with Mark Meyer, the campground guy, teasing him just to get his goat. But Sissy didn't believe it. If Zaza were going into town, she would have told her. Zaza told Sissy everything, and vice versa. Neither did she believe that Sissy would have taken off with Mark Meyer. Meyer was a pretentious idiot, who frenched like a snail. She'd tried him too, before Zaza, after Zaza, who cares. Zaza would never have gone off with *this stupid guy*, never without telling her, *never!*

Frenchie shot back that Meyer wasn't as stupid as all that, that she and Zaza didn't even know him, and the two girls walked as far as the campground in a sour mood. Busying himself around the attendant's shed, Conrad Plamondon, the owner of the campground, reminded them that Meyer was off that day, and Frenchie called herself stupid for having forgotten that Mark didn't work on Saturday. *I told you, she's with him*, she added, giving a kick to a deflated ball, *she's with him, that bitch. It's impossible,* Sissy replied, *totally and fuckingly impossible. And Zaza's not a bitch!* She kicked the flattened ball in her turn, and Frenchie left her there to go and tan herself. *Zaza would have told me,* she shouted after Frenchie, then she spent the next hour tossing stones in the water, stones big as a fist meant alternately for Franky-Frenchie Lamar, Mark Meyer, and Zaza Mulligan. *You would have told me,* she repeated every time she pronounced Zaza's name, adding the word "bitch" to underscore her frustration, *you would have told me, bitch!* Only she had the right to insult Zaza, she alone, her friend for always and forever, only she: *bitch!* Now she was angry as well as worried, because whatever the reason Zaza had vanished, she'd lied to her or hidden something. Unless there'd been an accident, unless Zaza had decided to take a midnight swim and had been surprised by a stomach cramp, a spasm that tied her in knots so her moans couldn't be heard on shore. Sandra Miller had almost drowned that way the year before, trying to catch her breath between waves. If old Pat Tanguay hadn't been fishing that morning, Sandra would have gone under and been gobbled up by the pike. But Zaza wasn't Sandra Miller, and Zaza wasn't dumb. She swam like a bloody mermaid, and could cross the lake both ways with her hands tied behind her back.

But Zaza was drunk, but Zaza reeked of gin, Sissy thought, weighing in her hand the warm stone she was getting ready to throw at the first goddamn little minnow swimming by. And Pat Tanguay, despite his old crock bull-headedness, still didn't fish in the middle of the night. *Run, Sissy, run!* And Sissy ran, other vacationers saw her fly by, her hair dishevelled and tears, perhaps, in her eyes reddened by dust. She tossed down the stone she was holding, and sped home to her mother's arms, because where could a lost child take refuge if not in the arms of her mother, who'd brought her into the world to dry her tears and console her.

Charlotte Morgan was preparing her first cocktail of the afternoon when Sissy burst in, but she was too distracted placing one of the little wood and rice paper parasols into position to take note of her daughter's distress. *Bloody hell, Sissy, go have a shower,* she said calmly, a bit put off by her sweat-dampened hair, her dirty hands and feet, her tank top stained with who knows what. Under other circumstances Sissy would have left, slamming the door, but she needed an adult, there, now, someone who'd call the police and Zaza's parents, who'd have the lake dragged, who'd rouse the neighbours and phone her father to ask him to come home right away.

Charlotte Morgan did none of that. She sipped her daiquiri while listening with half an ear to her daughter, and replied that there was no reason to panic, that Zaza was just the kind of girl to disappear and reappear without warning. *That kind of girl,* she let drop, and Sissy felt as if she'd been slapped. *That kind of girl,* her mother repeated, knowing perfectly well that Sissy and Zaza were the same, that they took themselves for twins, blood sisters, babies found in the same damn basket. *That kind of girl, you know?* And Sissy drew back. She left her mother to her daiquiri and set out to question the neighbours, who all said the same thing, *that kind of girl,* but in terms more polite, more insidious. She even interrogated the little kid who stuck her nose in everywhere, little Aundrey something-or-other, *Aundrey Whatever*. Uncharacteristically, she'd seen nothing, heard nothing, but she was troubled by Zaza's disappearance. So Sissy recruited her to forage around at the edge of the forest, in the backyards, to check out the lakeshore. Sissy would search near the campground and Ménard Bay, the kid would take care of the northern sector, from the McBains' cottage to that of Brian Larue, and they would meet two hours later at the same place, below Snake Hill. As the kid had no watch, she lent her her own, she'd go by Frenchie's to pick up another, and they separated. The afternoon was winding down when they got back together, empty-handed. Aundrey had picked up a bunch of objects, a bag of vinegar chips, a crow's feather, a matchbook, and a mother-of-pearl button. She'd even put her hands on an earring lost by Zaza at the beginning of summer, all excited to show her discovery to Sissy, who clutched the jewel in her fist while fighting back tears, stroked the kid's hair, full of pine needles, and told her to go back home.

It was the hour when the men lit their barbecues, the mothers called home their children, *Michael, Marnie, Dexter, suppertime,* Julie, Bernard, your hot dogs are going to burn, *come on.* Conversations, the noise of dishes and utensils overlapped, filtered through the smells of charcoal, sausages, and buttered bread sizzling on the grills. The Morgans ate later, like civilized people in the words of Charlotte Morgan, who'd visited the Côte d'Azur four years earlier and ever since had taken herself for Grace of Monaco. Sissy had swallowed nothing all day and was dying of hunger, but she was too proud to make herself a sandwich under the scornful gaze of her mother. *No way!* She'd rather die or mooch a burger from Don Irving, going into ecstasies over the hairdo of his wife, a washboard with a perm who smelled of vinegar and smoked two packs of Player's a day. But Sissy wasn't in the mood. Instead she'd make her way over to the Mulligans' cottage and wait for Zaza on the veranda after digging out something to eat in the art deco kitchen of Sarah Mulligan, Zaza's mother. She got in again through the kitchen window, landing in the dirty dishes, and asking herself why she'd not unlocked the front door earlier on. As usual the refrigerator was empty and the pantry not much better, but she was so hungry that she could have downed a jar of mustard with a spoon. She fell back on a box of Froot Loops that she brought out onto the veranda, as the closed-in odour of the cottage was making her queasy.

She was ashamed to be eating while her best friend was maybe gathering white pebbles at the bottom of the lake, those magic pebbles they'd once piled on top of each other to make their own Himalayas, but hunger, and its gurgling echoing in a vacuum, was for the moment stronger than shame. The hunger was seconded by a voracity born of dread, driving her hand compulsively into the Froot Loops box, as she recalled the mornings when she and Zaza, centuries earlier, used to write on the tablecloth, lining up letters picked out from their Alpha-Bits.

As memories jostled each other in her head, the pillow fights, the awful air guitar concerts, the badminton matches, Sissy gave vent to a resounding *Jesus Christ* and hurled the Froot Loops as far as she could. The box ended up propped against the screen door, and Sissy rushed over to crush it, squash it, to demolish Toucan Sam's damned face, the idiot smiling bird on the package, which lost none of its jolly demeanour despite the blows from her heel raining down on it. She was behaving like an idiot, as if Zaza were not coming back, dredging up treacly memories that she tarted up with stupid sunlight, stars, and birds that never even existed. She gave one more kick to the toucan, right on the beak, and went back inside, determined to phone the Mulligans in Portland. After fifteen rings she hung up with a curse, then tried again, once, twice, three times, begging the Mulligans to answer, to come home, to finally pick up the receiver. Around her objects wavered, liquid and grey in the shadows, and the ringing resounded every two seconds in George Mulligan's office at the other end, in the sitting room with its lacquered furniture, in the kitchen, and in Zaza's room, near the Paul McCartney poster on which were stamped thousands of Zaza's lip prints, pink or white, Dazzling Pink or Everlasting Snows. Every two seconds the phone vibrated in front of the grimy poster, awaiting the growling of an engine, the clicking of a key in the front door, and it seemed strange to Sissy that she was listening to the one audible noise in the Mulligan house about two hundred miles away, while the Mulligans could not hear her sniffling. It was hard to take in that the sounds, on either side, did not follow the invisible wire linking her to the empty house. She stood there, hoping for a sign of life beyond the electrical connection. She redialled the number until darkness fell, in vain. The Mulligans were not in Portland, nor was Zaza. As for Jack and Ben, Zaza's older brothers, they had to be tanning themselves somewhere in Florida or Virginia, waiting to go back to college.

Zaza had just barely disappeared, and already Sissy didn't know who she was. Without the image sent back to her by Zaza, the smiling reflection deep in the vast flawed mirrors around her, without this confirmation of her reality, she felt deprived of her identity. Zaza filled the void, and gave meaning to the world's instability. For a moment, to feel less lost, she wanted to go and get Frenchie Lamar out of bed again, but Frenchie, besides being an idiot, was just a copy of Zaza, a tracing whose lines wandered wide of the mark. She couldn't hope for any consolation from this girl who thought the coolest thing in the world was to raise your index and middle finger and shout *peace and love, man!* A bit queasy, she butted out her nth cigarette in the shell-shaped ashtray, and went down to the beach.

A little before midnight, as she paced the shoreline, telling herself that she would at least have found Zaza's towel if she'd taken a midnight swim, her father appeared. She saw the glow of his flashlight coming around the cottage, and wondered whether the man casting that beam of light before him was arriving as a friend, or if he was one of those faceless monsters you saw at the movie theatre, looming up out of nowhere and dragging behind him the poor imbecile who'd ventured out alone at night. Transfixed by the man's silence, she imagined herself in the presence of one of those hideous creatures who made off with young girls, totally drunk Zazas, and then she recognized her father, his features coarsely highlighted by the yellowish ray that lit only the bottom of his face. *Dammit, Dad!* she cried, *You scared the hell out of me. Sorry,* Victor Morgan replied, lowering his light, and he took Sissy's hand to bring her back home. But Sissy resisted. No question of leaving when Zaza needed help. *Something's happened to her, Dad, I know it, I know it*, she moaned, challenging her father to make her budge. And Sissy knew, in fact, that there'd been some kind of accident, because the bond that linked her to Zaza was stronger than blood. It was rooted in the lonely nights of little girls, huddled together in the pink sheets of Zaza's bed, while the music down below, and the alcohol, were oblivious to their stomachaches and the monsters hiding in the closet. Their bond was forged from that music's indifference, from the warmth of little bodies clinging to the pink sheets. If one suffered, the other felt her pain, there, right in her heart, in some mysterious way. If one wept, the other couldn't laugh, not even smile. She'd take a handkerchief and dry the wet face, her own or that of the other, it made no difference.

On her knees in the bathroom the night before, Sissy knew immediately, hearing the barn owl's cries, that Zaza was in danger, that Zaza was in trouble, that Zaza was afraid, and now she blamed herself terribly for having waited until morning to run and knock at the Mulligans' door. So there was no question of her leaving their cottage. *No way, Dad!* Still, reasoning with her, her father managed to persuade her that there was no point brooding away in a dark and empty house. If Zaza were to reappear before dawn, she wouldn't come here, but to them, the Morgans, to seek comfort in Sissy's arms, as in times past, two young girls sharing their hopes and fears. But Zaza would not return that night. *Young ladies, young girls*, her father murmured, did not venture out in complete darkness. Those simple words broke down Sissy's resistance, *young girls, young ladies.* Aware suddenly of the night's chill, she took hold of her father's arm, shivering. They'd find Zaza the next day, he promised, *I swear to God*, thus lightening Sissy's terrible solitude in Zaza's absence, and allowing her to lean, for a few hours, on a shoulder where the reassuring scents of Aqua Velva and fresh cotton blended together.

Around the lake, all the windows were dark. Only a few bulbs on the porches were still lit. You could also make out two camping lights, behind the trees, whose weak halos were wrapped in fog. A dismal prospect. *Gloomy*, Sissy murmured, and she huddled up to her father.

She only slept a few hours that night, dropping off and waking with a start, certain of having heard Zaza's voice, Zaza's footsteps under the window, *open the fucking window, Sis!* And fatigue swept her away, opened up the corridors of dream. Zaza danced to "Lucy in the Sky," sang her head off with Frenchie, but the sky was dark, and the waves were drawing the boats towards the open water. Heavy breathing coiled about Zaza, *run!* but Sissy had no more voice, there were hands closing around her throat, and she screamed silently, her eyes wide open on a night that wouldn't end.

With the first light of dawn, she slipped into the kitchen and made coffee and ham and mustard sandwiches, her father's favourite, which they would take with them. There was still no one outside except for Pat Tanguay, who would end up emptying the lake of all its fish. His boat was anchored in Ménard Bay, and you only saw the old man's head peeking over the edge, sporting the same dirty hat he'd worn for the last ten years. No longer able to contain her distress, she wanted to go and toss stones at his hat, to wake him and ask him if he'd seen Zaza in the water along with the pike, but finally she heard the shower. She left old Pat to his fish, took the sandwiches out of the fridge, and waited, again, for the scent of Aqua Velva to precede her father into the hallway. Coming into the kitchen, he kissed her on the brow, *good morning, Sis,* swallowed a cup of black coffee in one gulp, then, like the night before, took her gently by the hand, *come.*

Victor Morgan hadn't slept well either. In fact, he'd only dozed off here and there, transfixed by the crystal flask shimmering on the chest of drawers, staring at it while he asked himself if he shouldn't have paid more attention to Sissy's fears and acted immediately. Because Sissy was right, Zaza would never have left Boundary without telling her, without calling or leaving her a note: *Hi Sis! Gone to town with Dad. Back tomorrow. Zaz.* Now he could feel his daughter's anxiety in the dampness of her hand, in the faint trembling it passed on to him, and he didn't know what to say to reassure her, because the sense of foreboding that had crept over him during the night was only magnified in the morning light.

For most of the day, Victor Morgan and his daughter made the rounds of the cottages, talking to people who didn't dare any more say *that kind of girl,* but who shook their heads when Morgan asked them if they'd seen Elisabeth Mulligan two nights ago. About three o'clock they were finally able to reach Zaza's mother on the phone, back from a trip to Boston with her husband. No, Zaza wasn't with them, Zaza was in Boundary, Sarah Mulligan replied, then, after a heavy silence, she added that she'd be there with George before nightfall.

Contrary to what Pete Landry thought, Little Hawk did not really win a one-way trip to Europe. He won a trip there, and, you might say, half a trip back, because he left behind him more than his blood. In the midst of the killing, he lost the faculty most men have of distinguishing good from evil, and acquired something more rare, the rage of a man ready to kill anyone who would threaten his son, his daughter, his brother, his dog.

On Tuesday 6 June, 1944, after a tense crossing on the *USS Augusta*, Little Hawk took part in the first wave of the Operation Neptune assault on Omaha Beach in Normandy. A few harrowing minutes after his barge landed, he was thinking about Moose Trap's cool forests while clutching to his chest the bleeding body of his barracks chum, Jim Latimer, the best poker player in the 1st Infantry Division of Uncle Sam's army, whose cries were still echoing in his ears, *shut up, Jim, shut up,* as the crazed cacophony of the dying answered back to the detonations of weaponry. It was Latimer who saved his life, the broken body of Latimer, jiggling in Little Hawk's arms, convulsing under the impact of the bullets. Latimer had been dead for some time when Little Hawk laid him down on Omaha's cold and blood-drenched sand in the middle of dozens of other boys pitting their fair-haired America against the blond Aryan youth, but Little Hawk kept talking to him as he ran through the projectiles, swearing he would avenge him, would free him from the carnage, promising him life and what was impossible, resurrection and happiness in the bosom of a nature that would never die.

Officially Little Hawk didn't die that day, only his vision succumbed and a kind of blindness took its place, with the same pictures flashing by over and over, red and deafening. Thanks to this sightlessness he later survived the battle of Caen, escaping the German Tigers' roaring maws by heaving himself into mud-filled holes that the war machines blew open, growling, roaring in his turn, a maddened animal daring anyone to get near him without putting his life on the line.

Sent back to America because of his psychic trauma, Little Hawk was interned in a military hospital, among syringes and white blouses that were as threatening to him as so many Gewehr 43s and Wehrmacht uniforms. Then one day, encouraged, perhaps, by the surprising calm that came in the wake of his agitation, the doctors released Little Hawk into the world. He wandered for a while, lost in the alarming tumult of thc city, and then set off for Peter's Woods, where, despite the silence, a roiling anger erupted within him when he found Pete Landry. The man was a wreck, a slobbery ruin reduced to a shell by a woman in no way obliged to offer him her body, but who, worse than that, refused his gaze. Little Hawk instantly developed a hatred for this woman, fed by the fury he had contracted in Omaha Bay, and the long-suppressed howl finally burst from his breast the day when, a few weeks after he'd tried to rouse Landry from his torpor by taking him to gather up his abandoned traps, he found him hanged in his shack.

The night following this discovery a wolf bayed until dawn in Peter's Woods, then the animal took off on a hunt around the lake and caught Sugar Baby, Maggie Harrison's beloved, who howled in his turn, two wounded beasts blind to the fate of the damned. Cured for a time of his rage, the wolf then came out of the woods, leaving Landry's body suspended in his shack at the heart of this kingdom whose clown he had, despite himself become. Came out of the woods, swearing that no one, ever, would lay a hand on his son, his daughter, his father, his brother.

I was coming back along the lakeshore when Gilles Ménard, wearing an undershirt, arrived at a run, his face white, and burst into the cottage without even knocking. Then I heard his voice, and my mother let out a mouse's squeal, like those she emitted when she was insulted or got bad news. Three minutes later my father came out with Monsieur Ménard, two ashen faces that left in the direction of the McBains' cottage, where my father never set foot. They're English, he said, we don't understand each other, or they're rich, we're not part of the same world. This visit to the McBains meant something serious had happened. Right away I thought of Zaza Mulligan, who hadn't answered Sissy's calls, and was nowhere, except no one could be nowhere. If you existed, you were sitting, standing, on all fours, or lying down somewhere, and you were talking. It was Zaza's silence, her nowhere silence, that had panicked Sissy Morgan. I'd seen it in her cat's eyes when she'd taken my hands and begged me to look everywhere, giving me a golden watch that made a soft tick-tock up against my ear. *Look, Aundrey, look everywhere,* and I took off running, telling myself that there must be a place that was Zaza's somewhere, a cabin, a ditch, a clearing where she couldn't hear Sissy, unless she'd become completely deaf. Still I cried Zaza, Zaza Mulligan, picking up every object that might show that she'd been there recently. I'd been given a mission from which nothing could distract me. But neither the stuff I gathered nor the pride I felt in becoming Sissy Morgan's accomplice led me to Zaza's somewhere.

I still had the watch in the back pocket of my jeans, which reminded me that Zaza was doing something in some unknown place. I'd forgotten to give it back to Sissy at the same time as the earring that looked like a tear or a raindrop that had fallen from a crow's nest. Sissy didn't want any of the other things, but I'd saved the matchbook and the bag of chips in case Zaza had dropped them when her red hair vanished into the greenery of a tree. Every chance I had, I patted the bump the watch made in my right buttock, telling myself that Sissy would never have entrusted this jewel to the little snotnosed kid who'd replaced the *littoldolle* of once upon a time if she hadn't feared the worst, which I couldn't help associating with Gilles Ménard's waxen face, transfixed by some terrifying tableau in which Zaza played a part. It was Zaza's inexplicable lack of response that had set Gilles Ménard running, I would have sworn, and that had flung my father after him as if he were being pursued by an icy wind.

I wanted to catch up to them when they came around the cedar hedge separating our cottage from that of the McBains, but my mother ordered me not to move, you don't leave the yard, Andrée Duchamp, and told me to play with my sister, who was trying to build a sandcastle with a twisted plastic shovel. Unlike the two men, my mother had red cheeks, and the little purple circle that appeared in the middle of her forehead when her mind couldn't contain everything stirring inside her began to show itself, a sign that you'd better not get on her nerves. I asked what had happened, but again I just got an old person's answer. Supposedly, nothing was going on. My father had gone to the McBains' because only a few of the English, and the Maheux across the lake, had telephones. As for the reason for this urgent call, that was none of my business.

No point in pressing the matter. When my mother sealed her lips, they were welded together. I went to join Millie on the beach, and helped her shore up her castle, while glancing over at the McBains' and straining my ears in case I could catch a bit of conversation thanks to the echo over the lake. My father and Monsieur Ménard reappeared on the McBains' porch while Millie was telling me she was going to put butterflies in her castle, yellow-orange and edged in black. Papa and Monsieur Ménard shook McBain's hand, exchanged a few words with the aid of signs to make up for the linguistic deficiencies on either side, and went back to the cottage with their ghastly faces. My mother rushed out as soon as they stepped into the yard, with a clean shirt for Gilles Ménard, whose undershirt was covered with sweat stains, and she urged my father to bring her up to date. The police are coming, he whispered, give the kids their supper, we'll wait in the yard. Just then my brother arrived, his bicycle wheels screeching on the gravel, and wanted to know why Papa looked like he'd seen a ghost. You'll find out soon enough, my father answered, and shooed him into the cottage with us.

Clouds were piling up behind the mountain, masking the sun and promising us one of those torrential rainfalls dear to Bondrée's microclimate. I still don't know how to explain the phenomenon that occurred five or six times every summer, when the clouds, rising up from an invisible horizon, suddenly gathered over Moose Trap, and then swooped down towards the lake. The sky turned a purple grey and the trees swayed gently, catching the wind's horns, brushing the brow of the animal that would soon unleash its fury. That evening, however, the weather's unsettling light didn't make its way into the cottage. It clung to the windows, and gave the kitchen–living room–dining room a gloomy look. Usually I loved those lifeless colours that preceded a storm, as we waited for the noise, the cracking of the roof that echoed that of the sky, the salvos of water striking the windows, but this was not a normal time. Something terrible was going to descend on us along with the rain.

Quickly, my mother turned on the ceiling light, refusing to let the mauve turn to darkness, then she brought out the baloney, the mustard, the sliced bread. We had to make do with sandwiches, and she didn't want to hear any complaints. My brother and I looked at each other, calculating the risks of having her explode if we opened our mouths. Millie finally broke the silence, saying she wanted ketchup, not mustard, and my guileless brother took the opportunity to ask who was dead. A hand came down onto the sliced bread, and my mother muttered that if one of us wanted to play the show-off she'd send us to our rooms until the following day. Clearly someone was dead, otherwise Mama wouldn't have spelt out each syllable like she did every time she got panicky, because my mother panicked calmly, squashing a sandwich or a tomato, meticulously and methodically slicing up a carrot until it was totally annihilated, while her red patch widened over a pallor that only appeared when her alarm was reaching the point of hysteria.

I again thought of Zaza, too young not to have any other place to exist, and I checked Sissy's watch, which I'd wound up to ward off bad luck. At the very same time a pile of clouds broke away from the mountain, and my father pointed it out to Gilles Ménard. Facing the lake, Papa and Ménard stood around, nudged a rock with the tips of their shoes, heads lowered, turned to check out the road, and again buried the tips of their shoes in the sand. From time to time Gilles Ménard lifted an arm, which he let drop right away next to his body, then he took his head in his hands and knelt down. He told my father what he'd seen, he described the horrors baying at his heels. A corpse, perhaps, curled up in the underbrush or hanging from a beam, a second Pete Landry come to lend a hand to the first one's ghost, now so transparent that on nights with a full moon it wouldn't even be able to make a girl's hair stand on end.

I knew nothing then about this Landry except what the children had bruited about: that he was a trapper who liked birds and had tried to fly off while tying himself to a rope. But from time to time I'd visited the site of his old shack, where you could still see the foundations beneath the beams and the soot-blackened joists. In ten or twenty years you'd have to dig down to unearth the ruins of that burned-out shack, but it would still be there, witness to a man's passage through the heart of the forest. Landry's leavings would survive him, more troubling than the imprints of other men because they were linked to violence and to the impertinence of those who thought you could destroy a ghost, that you could kill what was already dead.

The first time I came across those ruins I took to my heels, certain that Landry's ghost would behead me if I loitered in the vicinity. That same night, I asked my parents about him. They replied that Pierre Landry was just a poor soul, an unhappy man, and they avoided my questions concerning his suicide, explaining that Landry had died of an illness, because suicide didn't exist among the Duchamps, the Millers, the Maheux, or the McBains. It was one of the many subjects that were out of bounds thanks to fear, fear of hell and of torment, of the shameful consequences of despair.

I waited a week before going near the shack again, keeping my distance while asking myself what would happen if I called out to Landry. Pete Landry, I whispered finally, covering my mouth with my hands, and I thought I heard something stir in the bushes, while one of the collapsed beams tilted slightly, like one of those gravestones from behind which vampires emerge. Again I took flight, tumbling head over heels, my eyes peeled for the vampire whose great black cape would soon swoop down on me to suck at my jugular. Still, I returned a couple of days later, drawn by the fascination all children have for caves swarming with creatures that never see the light of day. The place was not sinister, but Landry's shadow was abroad there still, seeking an escape from its burned-out purgatory. In time the shack's surroundings came to seem less hostile, which did not stop me from making a wide detour when I approached this part of the forest, fearing to see the debris rise up, propelled by an anger hidden under the black earth. You mustn't mock the dead. Above all, you mustn't stir up ghosts.

Disturbed by the idea that a new darkness was being linked to Landry's wanderings, I was going to ask permission to go and join my father when a police car came and parked beside the cottage. Hearing it, my brother leaped from his chair, ignoring Mama's injunctions, while she grabbed Millie and me by the collar to stop us from following him. I didn't struggle—my mother was stronger than me, just like the clouds moving in sombrely over the lake. In a few moments the rain would reach our shore and start manhandling the waves that throw boats up against the docks. I hope old Pat's not still out on the water, my mother murmured, her blue eyes rimmed by those shadows reserved for mothers only.

As Mama no longer seemed aware of our being there, I led Millie into the room we shared, and gave her permission to play with Bill, my battery-powered robot, to whom I'd given that name because he walked like Bill Cochrane, our second neighbour to the left, who had returned from I don't know what war with a stiff leg, a medal, and a beastly character, if beasts grumble all day long. Cochrane wasn't the only one in our entourage to have been in one war or another, but you always talked about it under your breath, so as not to bring back bad memories. If one of those men behaved strangely, you said that he'd done the 1939 war, he'd done Korea, he'd survived the landing, as though that explained everything, and you kept your trap shut.

While Millie was launching Bill down from the chest of drawers, I lay on my stomach on the bed near the window, which was the best place in the cottage to keep an eye on the backyard and to listen in on what was being said there. The men were talking softly and I only heard murmurs through the wind's gusts, with a word or two sticking out from time to time, words that sounded like "wound" or "tear," words stained with blood. Gilles Ménard was talking the most, waving his arms and still clutching his head, then the rain came, drumming violently against the window and onto the ground and the cottage roof. The police took shelter inside their car while Papa and Monsieur Ménard came in, looking for raincoats and flashlights. I took the opportunity to leave my room and press my nose against the big kitchen window, from where you could see almost the whole world if you put your mind to it, transforming Moose Trap into an Everest crumbling under its avalanches or Boundary Pond into an ocean crisscrossed by pirates' flags whose tatters were whipped by the offshore winds. Every tree became an entire forest, every stone a monolith as big as the Rock of Gibraltar, which my father had shown me in one of those magazines that makes you realize you don't know anything, and every stretch of beach was a desert full of rattlesnakes, sand hoppers, poisonous lizards, and other creatures right out of the scary stories in our after-supper books. Bondrée was a world unto itself, the mirror of all possible universes.

We shouldn't be too late, my father whispered, kissing my mother on the brow, right on her red circle, then Gilles Ménard followed him out to our old Ford, which made its way off through the rain. Dusk had fallen early, what with the downpour, and already the road in the headlights' beams was all gleaming mud that exposed the ruts carved out by the last deluge. Zigzagging through this mud, they took a left turn towards the crossroads leading to the highway, and their lights vanished behind the trees.

Close the curtains, Andrée, my mother sighed, in a voice so tired that you could feel the weight of everything she feared. When she used that voice you heard the future hurtling towards you with its heavy boots, and you wanted to hide six feet underground as if it wouldn't know where to find you. Her head bowed, she stood still on the carpet in the entranceway, facing the door, but all she could have seen was her own reflection in the window. Her hair and clothes were soaked, her mascara was running, and she seemed depleted of all energy. I'd only seen my mother like that when her father died, Grandpapa Fred. For weeks, after Papy's burial, she kept disappearing. Her body was still there, bent over the sink or the kitchen counter, but everything that was my mother had vanished into thin air. Her hands hung loose, our questions slid by her ears, and she had to drop her knife or her potato to remember her body.

Those absences scared me, because the unnatural grimace that froze her features belonged to someone I didn't know, and whom I wouldn't want to meet in the dark.

I closed the curtains violently to bring her out of her trance, and she instantly reappeared. In a fraction of a second she became again the strong-willed and determined woman I wanted for my mother, even if her self-assurance got under my skin more often than not. It's as dark as November, she exclaimed, then she quickly went to change and to dry her hair. From the bathroom she ordered us to put on our pyjamas, even if it was only seven-thirty, and then she brought a 7Up to my brother, who was sulking in the living room because my father had shut him out of his meeting with the police, and hadn't wanted to take him with them. To kill time, she proposed a game of Monopoly, but no one was in the mood that night to lust after Atlantic Avenue. She brought out a deck of cards for Millie, who liked building castles so she could fill them with butterflies, and she emptied the refrigerator's vegetable drawer, muttering that the men would be hungry when they got back.

While she prepared a soup that looked more like a mishmash of massacred vegetables, I borrowed one of the Bob Morane books from my brother, and settled into the La-Z-Boy. Outside the rain was still pouring down, and that's all you heard, the wind, the rain, the dry, methodical clacking of the vegetable knife on the cutting board, and the barely audible collapse of Millie's castles. I tried to concentrate on the Yellow Shadow's progress through the London night, but the tension in the house rivalled Morane's zeal in confronting the enemy. The rain obliterated Mister Ming's silhouette, and filled the room with a nameless darkness that imposed its own silence.

Huddled in his corner, my brother stared into space while chewing at his cheeks. His right foot tapped the floor with a steady rhythm that sometimes matched the cadence of the vegetable knife, whose chunk-chunk sped and slowed according to the resistance offered by celery or turnip. Even Millie was holding her breath, darting rapid glances at my mother, and not daring to demand her glass of milk. In a vain attempt to lower the tension, I declared that I was going to read on the veranda, and tried to attract my brother's attention, but he just buried himself deeper into his armchair. Mama told me to put on a sweater, and silence fell again at the same time as Millie's castle, whose Queen of Hearts, monarch of the kingdom, flew right up to my feet. Zaza Mulligan's just fallen down! exclaimed my sister. My mother turned in a flash, brandishing her knife, her forehead crimson. What did you say? Millie recoiled in her chair, pointing to the card I'd picked up, not too sure if she should answer or chew on one or two of her fingers. The Queen of Hearts is Zaza Mulligan, I explained, while Millie gnawed her right thumb, a habit of hers whenever she was afraid of being punished, guilty or not. My mother forced herself to smile, of course Millie of course, then she planted her knife in a potato and went to shut herself up in the toilet, whose confined space, it seemed, had the miraculous power of easing her anxieties.

My intuition was not wrong. Zaza Mulligan was the source of the storm that had descended on Bondrée. I put the Queen of Hearts down on the table, and went to take refuge on the veranda. Visions of wounds and gashes rolled round in my head and I prayed that Zaza had just scraped herself on branches in an alder grove, let it be so, God, let it be so, but I knew perfectly well that you don't let rip a hurricane for a few scratches.

The smell of soup was just penetrating the odour of wet earth that pervaded the veranda when beams from headlights swept across the yard from the row of birches on the left to the swing creaking in the wind. Papa was back, with or without Gilles Ménard. Ordinarily, one or two slamming doors would have followed immediately upon the engine being turned off, but my father stayed in the car, perhaps with Gilles Ménard, looking out at the dark depths from which they could not detach themselves. Finally a door shut and my father came into view at the corner of the cottage, not running, not any more, but bearing on his shoulders the very future mother had dreaded. The horror in Ménard's nerve-wracked body had caught up with him now on this rainy night, just two or three miles from a world where light still shone. No point in running when you're caught. No point in crying out when no one can hear.

Hello, my mite, he murmured, coming onto the veranda, then he picked me up in his arms and held me to his wet raincoat, smelling of fir and mould. He held me like that for a long time, and left me there, shaken by this excess of tenderness, which could only mean that the worst had happened in the woods. Someone was dead. Zaza Mulligan was dead.

The drama had taken place about a mile from the Mulligan cottage on the night of Friday the 21st to Saturday the 22nd of July, according to the medical examiner, who couldn't be more precise as to the hour of death. An investigation was launched immediately, in order to establish the exact causes of death, as well as the reason Zaza was walking in the woods at such an hour. As Boundary straddled a vague border lost in the lake's deep waters, it was hard to decide whether the investigation was the responsibility of Canada or the United States. Finally, the Maine police were put in charge of the case, the victim being American. The incident site was searched first, but the rain that had come down on Boundary Sunday night had erased all signs that might offer clues. All that remained, half-dried in the mud, were the footprints left by the police and the men who had led them to the body, Gilles Ménard and Samuel Duchamp, both still pale, both still in shock. Without any tracks or other indications, it could not be confirmed whether someone had brought Zaza, willingly or by force, deep into the woods.

The investigators had nothing solid on which to rely. There was no witness, and no call for help had been heard, unless Zaza's cries had been confused with those of the animals that crossed Boundary from north to south every night. Unless people had preferred to blame the wind and to stay warm in their beds. Hope Jamison reproached herself, saying she should have woken Ted after hearing a hoarse sound she'd too quickly taken for the yapping of a coyote. I should have seen if it was the wind, Barry Miller said to himself, or the shed door, repeated Madeleine Maheux. Guilt was already circulating its poison, the fear of having let sleep render you oblivious to Zaza's calls because it was Zaza, *that kind of girl*, who had always, as long as you could remember, been heard singing with Sissy Morgan, crying with Sissy Morgan, *run, Sissy, run!* until you'd found yourself paying no attention to the two girls, become three over the summer, Sissy, Zaza, Frenchie.

Everyone was questioned, everyone who knew how to talk, from the smallest to the biggest, but the investigation focused on the relatives and friends, the last people to have seen Zaza alive, Sissy Morgan, Frenchie Lamar, then Gilles Ménard, the man who'd discovered the body. What was Ménard doing in the woods? That was the first thing the police wanted to know, and Ménard had no answer to this question other than the most banal. He was walking, that's all, because he liked to walk, to walk beneath the trees and to see the play of light on the tangled, mossy roots. But he couldn't explain why he'd taken this direction rather than another. It was a matter of chance, a moment's whim. A detail catches your eye, an animal track, a familiar clearing, and you decide to head into the woods at that spot.

Ménard didn't know what path he would have taken had he known what he'd find that day, and the thought tormented him. Would he have raced towards Zaza, driven by the vain hope of outrunning death, or would he have left it to others to shut the young girl's uprolled eyes? Do you throw yourself towards a nightmare, towards the blade that's going to rip into your breast? Back home, the night before, while the police dealt with Zaza Mulligan, he'd only been able to doze off at dawn, haunted by the adolescent's indescribable gaze, part resignation and part stark terror, then by the long leg that slid under the sheets, the gluey sweetness of the fresh blood, jolting him awake. The blade had already seared his skin, forcing him to lie to Jocelyne, his wife, to clumsily comfort her, unable to admit that henceforth they'd be sleeping with the dead.

The investigators also questioned her, Jocelyne, a great beauty according to one of the policemen, seeing the pale freckles which attested to the harsh sun beneath which she must have run and played as a child. She confirmed that her husband often went off for hours at a time, returning, his breath rich with the odour of spruce gum, his eyes agleam with the glint of stream water or the gaze of beasts lurking in the green shade of the underbrush. She didn't know the true source of this gleaming, didn't understand how cold water could be transmuted into light in the corner of an eye, but she could describe the bitter taste of the forest, lingering in her mouth long after her husband, with luminous strokes of his tongue, had tried to impart to her with a kiss all he'd found there. But she could tell them nothing about Zaza Mulligan, other than that her ghostly body, since the previous night, walked by her husband's side, and that he'd talked to her about Zaza's torn leg, but above all about her hair, that streak of light subdued in green shadow. That's what Ménard had noticed first on leaving the path, the long red hair, not immediately grasping what the silky tangle was. He'd felt a violent blow to his chest on seeing it, like the one that hit him every time his little Marie broke away from him to cross the street. Time stopped, became just a heart beating in the void, until Marie reached the opposite sidewalk and he was able to join her, his legs wobbly, his ears buzzing: if you die, Marie, I'll go mad.

And so at the heart of the forest he thought of Marie while holding his breath, then he burst out laughing, finding himself ridiculous, stupid, fumbling in his pocket for a handkerchief to wipe away his tears, squatting down with a cramp in his stomach now, a good laughing-out-loud cramp. What he'd taken for hair was just the long red tail of a fox, dead from hunger, sickness, or old age. Fucking Ménard, he murmured, fucking Ménard, you give me a pain sometimes. When he raised his head a flash of white skin dazzled him, a few inches of white reaching out from the hair. His laughter came up short, a gunshot went to his heart, and he approached the tree at the foot of which something uncertain was lying. It's a fox, Ménard, take it easy, it's just a poor fox. But the thing was almost naked, longer than a fox, whiter as well. It had legs and polished fingernails.

Like all men his age, Ménard had seen death, but he had to lean against a tree so as not to fall. Troubled as he was by the partial nudity of the body, dressed in a simple pair of shorts and a sweater hiked up to the breasts, it took him a while to recognize Elisabeth Mulligan, even if she was the only girl in Bondrée with such a head of hair. Drained of its blood, the face now was no more than a mask, a cold porcelain object with what might have been long threads of red silk wound around it. Ménard had already seen death, yes, but he'd only seen it dressed up and powdered, stripped of any sharp memory of warm flesh, and masking the body's nearness to the earth, where humus feeds on putrescence.

An airborne bird made him jump, stay calm Ménard, and he took off his shirt to cover Zaza Mulligan. He then placed a nervous finger on her jugular, for appearance's sake, because it was clear that the adolescent was no longer breathing. The jaws of a bear trap had closed over her right leg, baring the bone, the long white tibia of a young girl with long legs, then the blood had spilled out, all of Zaza's blood. Ménard thought of the blood of Sugar Baby, so much a part of Maggie Harrison and Pierre Landry's legend, but whose death was only referred to obliquely, and never spoken of to children for fear that a little white dog might come in turn to haunt the beach, a real little dog, with real blood to mingle with the scarlet nectar of Tanager's crushed flowers. Dead as a dog, he murmured. The young girl must have fainted first, then awakened a little later, between darkness and light, and tried to clutch at the rotten leaves, her hands limp, her eyelids heavy, her breath tuned to the wind's slow drift.

At first Ménard didn't know how to react. He didn't want to abandon the remains, leave them alone in this forest where he'd suddenly learned what fear really meant, but he couldn't stay there and shout himself hoarse until his cries were lost in those of Zaza. He had to alert someone, a friend, the police, the parents. Before leaving he at least closed Zaza's eyelids, unable to bear the idea of their being wide open to light sifting through branches and entering her eyes only to find utter darkness. Perhaps he was wrong, perhaps it was better not to touch the body, but he wanted that gaze to rest in peace, wanted to expunge those clouded visions, blighted with red, which had accompanied the dying. Then he ran, breathless, to the cottage of Sam Duchamp, an honest man who'd keep him from breaking down.

Jocelyne Ménard knew nothing more but that was enough, with their cottage held hostage by a mutilated body that followed her husband everywhere, its sickening smell smothering the pungent perfume of the trees inside his mouth.

Stan Michaud, the chief inspector in charge of the investigation, had also spent the night with Zaza Mulligan, in the midst of those odours exhaled by the inhuman whiteness of cold flesh. He was watching an episode of *Bonanza* when his deputy Jim Cusack, called to the crime site to replace a sick officer, phoned him. Cusack had been an inspector on his team for three years, and he'd never seen him flinch before any horror, letting the pain roll off his cop's back without gaining a hold. But Michaud knew that Cusack's equanimity had its limits, and that one day he would crack. That day had come. As Cusack described the scene to him, Michaud saw that the façade behind which the policeman was hiding was slowly breaking down, and that this affair would be one of those that haunt you long after the dust has settled, one of the boomerang cases, as he called them, that come back at you full force just as you're having a quiet beer in your garden, and that pursue you until the first snows, if not until Christmas. In general those cases involve children or young girls, vulnerable bodies found under the crumpled metal of an automobile, or on the edge of a wheat field where a few hairs, torn away, undulate along with the yellow spikes. When he heard Cusack's faltering voice, a picture came instantly to his mind, or rather a face, that of Esther Conrad, sixteen years old, one of the boomerangs that hit him straight on every time a new one was flung his way.

The case went back ten years or so, but Esther's hand, closed around a stone shaped much like a heart, still haunted him. The hand grazed the back of his neck after the boomerangs came down, then it let the grey stone drop at his feet. For a long time Michaud thought the heart might lead him to the killer, that Esther had tightened her fist around the one object that could identify her attacker. In the pale light of the morgue, surrounded by its cold metal surfaces, he'd asked the young girl, who, Esther, *who?* But it was in Salem that he'd had to question her, in the dump where a junk dealer had found her, and he'd gone back there, ten, twenty times, with the rats scrabbling in the refuse, who, Esther, *who?* in a futile search for the initials that ought to have been carved into the heart, for the signature of the poisoned arrow that had robbed her of all she had, her life, her breath.

As Cusack was giving him the young girl's name, Elisabeth Mulligan, one that would haunt him forever after, Michaud thought about Esther's heart, now gathering dust in a box on the nondescript shelves of the State Police archives. Elisabeth Mulligan, he repeated, to commit the name to memory, then he told Cusack that he'd be in Boundary within the hour. He told his wife not to wait up for him, that he had to go to the scene of a crime, a crime or an accident, he didn't yet know. All he knew was that he was on his way to the site of a death that would sink down roots inside him.

He wasn't wrong. As soon as he set foot on the spot, lit by a few improvised flood lamps with their surreal light shining down onto Zaza Mulligan's sodden body, he received a sudden sharp blow to the throat, that of the boomerang. He stayed put until the middle of the night, talking with the pathologist, with his colleagues, with the dead, who, Elisabeth, *who?* After the body was taken away he kept wandering about the site, kneeling in the mud, studying the rusted trap, wiping the back of his neck, constantly, compulsively, there where the drops falling from the trees met Esther Conrad's hand. Back home he hesitated to join his wife, knowing there was not much chance of his getting to sleep, then he slid under the cotton sheet at last, only to find there, long and tanned, Zaza Mulligan's lopped leg. That's how sleep found him, his leg wrapped around that of a dead young girl. The nightmares came on then, the screeching of tires, the clanking of metal, the usual repertoire. He woke two hours later, as weary as if he'd slept on a pile of boards, and he went looking for Cusack, with whom he began the round of questioning.

He started with the parents, Sarah and George Mulligan, whom Cusack had tried in vain to talk to during the night. Again they were almost mute, repeating that they knew nothing, they didn't understand, blaming themselves for not having spent enough time with their daughter, then retreating again into silence, their eyes red, their hands trembling. Michaud and Cusack had no more success with Sissy Morgan, too filled with rage to be of any help in the short term. *You would have told me, bitch! You would have told me,* she kept on saying, striking the fluffy orange cushion she clutched to her stomach, her long hair flung over her face, while imploring her father to confess the truth, *it's not true, Dad, she's not gone, tell me the truth, tell me, tell me!* When he could see her eyes, Michaud said to himself that those of Zaza must have projected the same fury, that her voice must have assumed the same cadence when she was angry. The resemblance between the dead and living girls was not striking, but it must have been when the dead one was still alive. She who was weeping before him was another Zaza, a sister, a twin. Abruptly, he wanted to lift her in his arms and bear her off like a princess to a place where no trap could ever close over her long legs. He stretched out his hand in her direction, and the young girl recoiled. *Don't touch me!* A bit shamefaced, he sought support in the eyes of his colleague, then the two of them took their leave. They'd come back when Sissy Morgan had regained her calm.

Outside, the sun was already beating down. It would be a hot, stifling day. A day without end. Heat waves, like cold spells, always made the work harder. During the one you dragged your feet, hoping for wind, rain, thinking of the rotten smells aggravated by the humidity. And you were unbelieving, you stupidly told yourself that nothing so awful could happen in the bright sunlight. Summer didn't seem right for tragic endings, and you looked to the heavens for the corpse to stir a finger, to half-lift an eyelid, since it was only the muggy weather that kept it lying there. You tried to persuade yourself, despite the flies buzzing about the wound. In the second instance, it seemed that devastation was everywhere to be seen or soon would be, that the drama you were probing was just a prelude to the one to follow. A prophetic death, embracing an icy gloom, lapping up the cold and spewing it back at you in glacial exhalations.

Michaud needed a respite before visiting the wanderer who'd found the body, Ménard, Gilles Ménard, a francophone who probably wouldn't understand a single word he said. What with things unfolding so quickly, that hadn't even occurred to him. As Cusack mopped his brow, he pretended he had to piss, and asked his colleague to find someone who could act as an interpreter. While waiting, he was able to ponder the fact that despite his name he only spoke a few words of French, a shortcoming he'd once vowed to remedy, wanting to learn the language of his ancestors, a language that for him was like a whiteout, a blizzard, drifting snow. He would have liked to tell the story of the land that flowed in his veins in words native to that land, *poudreuse*, *verglas*, *nordet*, which he would have connected to tough, straight-talking verbs. His view of his origins was idyllic, clichéd even, inspired by the rough bark of bare trees, but it was amid that roughness that he felt he belonged. Then as the years passed, the desire, along with the words, succumbed to fatigue. What was the point, he said to himself, since he had no ancestor with whom to talk. What was the point, since his day-to-day life was also filled with *howling winds*, *freezing rain*, *northeasters*, *gusts*, *blasts*, *flurries*, and he had no child to whom he might pass on that heritage.

He watched Cusack knock at the door of a yellow cottage whose shutters bore cutouts of clubs and diamonds. Hansel and Gretel's house, he thought, forgetting that the gingerbread house belonged to the witch. He hadn't swallowed anything since that morning other than a cup of black coffee, and the thought of spongy bread made him salivate, even if he wasn't that fond of sweets. He was more a steak-and-potatoes kind of guy, that was how he'd been raised and that was how he'd been fed, and he wasn't the least bit curious about food off the beaten path. Dorothy, his wife, sometimes tried a new recipe, adding fruit to pork tenderloin or ham, slices of pineapple that brightened up the plate but that he pushed to the side, scraping at the meat on the sly when Dorothy had her back turned, so as to get rid of the disgusting syrup that altered the taste of the meat. He only liked food that was not gussied up, that was raw, natural, as close as possible to its original state.

Those thoughts made his stomach growl, and he wondered whether he and Cusack might be able to grab something at the campground after he'd come out of the house belonging to Gretel, whom he'd thought he'd spotted on the doorstep behind her mother's striped apron. Hope Jamison, Gretel's mother, had told Cusack that a certain Brian Larue, who lived on the other side of the lake, could act as an interpreter for them, assuming he'd agree to do it. Larue was apparently a loner, a recluse who didn't mingle with others and stayed shut up in his log house with his books, visited occasionally by a girl, his daughter, who lived with Larue's wife, who'd left him for whatever reason, perhaps the books themselves and the way they could take over some men's minds.

Go in the car and see if you can convince him, Michaud said to Cusack, I have to think. He didn't like using his higher status to slough work off on his subordinates, but the heat had plunged him into one of those foggy states that slow your movements and clog your mind, with all the hopes dashed by time and fatigue face to face with happy memories, redolent of innocence and youth. He had to deal with all that free of any distraction, to focus on the landscape, on a tree picked out from among other trees, on a stone, a bit of froth, to try to empty himself out.

While Cusack moved off towards the car, Michaud went down to the lake, sat on the sand, and located a willow tree near the shore that might ease his lassitude, while removing his shoes, too heavy for the season. The sand was white-hot, but if you buried your feet in it you soon reached a layer of coolness that soothed your entire body.

Despite the beautiful weather, he was alone near the lake. No child splashing in the water, not a single man fixing his dock or his fence. Boundary was cloaked in the kind of calm that follows on a drama, the numbness of days of mourning when everyone feels compelled to whisper, to lower the radio's volume, to keep the children inside. That silence would last a day or two at the most, and then the noise would reassert itself. Zaza Mulligan's death, like any other death, would not forever stifle the survivors' laughter. Life would resume around the still centre of this absence, and all, except for her intimates and cops like himself, who were powerless to ward off ghosts, would forget that in that space lorded over by absence, there once existed a young girl. That's the way it had to be, there was no role in this play for those who were no longer there.

As he was thinking on this, a door opened behind him and little Gretel bounced down from the gingerbread balcony. *You stay here and you be quiet*, her mother whispered, and the door closed. The silence came back for a few moments, then Michaud heard the child hopping on the gravel, and a small voice, unable to say no to life, carried into the humid air. *"Hurry Scurry had a worry / No one liked his chicken curry . . ."*

*"Stuck his finger in the pot / Chicken curry way too hot,"* Michaud continued, picking up on the little girl's rhyme, remembering that he was hungry, and, barring proof to the contrary, that he too was alive.

That night my father didn't shut his eyes. He installed himself on the veranda, telling my mother that he'd join her soon, but he was still there on the old rattan loveseat when the crows got me out of bed at dawn. The night before, he'd refused to tell us where Gilles Ménard had taken him, not knowing how to reveal the death of a child to other children. He'd preferred to put that painful task off to the next day, and to spare us, for a few hours more, the nightmares that would keep us from sleeping. But today he'd have no choice if he wanted to stop rumour from falsifying facts, and our parroting the gossips and weasel-faced men set yapping by the scent of blood under Bondrée's dulled sun.

Come here my mite, he said quietly, in that voice, a bit hoarse, that all adults have early in the morning, a voice that's done too much breathing, perhaps, or that has to get used to the light, and he motioned for me to sit down next to him. As much as I wanted to know what had set Gilles Ménard to running, I feared what my father was going to tell me. I have to make pee-pee, I lied, throwing myself into the bathroom, where I took the time to count forwards and backwards all the red squares alternating with the white ones on the wall facing the toilet. Twenty-one, I whispered, opening the door, twenty-one, twenty-one, as if that were a magic number whose repetition would alter the course of time, and stop Gilles Ménard in his tracks. By the time I rejoined my father the sun was rising behind the cottage, and I prayed, shutting my eyes, for it to be yesterday's sun, let it be so, God, let it be so, but my father had aged too much since the day before for Sissy Morgan's watch, quietly ticking away in my bedroom, to have come to a stop.

It's Zaza Mulligan, he blurted out before I could get away again, repeating my sister's words, it's Zaza, it's the Queen of Hearts. She's had an accident, she's not coming back. Sitting cross-legged on the loveseat's faded cushion, I played with my toes while waiting for the rest, but my father didn't utter the word that would have made Zaza Mulligan's fate clear if I'd been able to get it out of him. I asked if that meant that Zaza was in the hospital, and he answered no, that Zaza from now on was nowhere. Maybe in heaven, he added, but he didn't believe that any more than he believed Communists were going to invade America and turn Maine into a concentration camp. He said that because it was less complicated than to try to explain death and to explain that heaven was just a dream that allowed my mother to deal with the world's absurdity. He'd known for a long time what I'd know later, that the earth was, like us, just an accident, that the body was just dust, and that no will, divine or anything else, could bring this dust back to life somewhere in the beyond. It's down here that dust came back to life, in the midst of the world's senselessness.

I wasn't able to worm out of him the word he refused to inflict on a twelve-year-old girl, the word that would age me in one fell swoop and would fade the freckles that dotted my cheeks, but he'd said enough. Zaza Mulligan was no longer anywhere. Zaza Mulligan was dead. I went to get a raisin bun from the breadbox and walked down to the lakeshore, avoiding my father's eyes, where my image had gone watery in the few tears that had welled up there, tears of love, of those who anticipate the worst: if you die, my mite, I'll hang myself.

At that hour the beach was deserted, aside from a few ants that began to swarm around a pile of branches being grazed by the first rays of the sun. I threw a breadcrumb in their direction, and two of them grabbed hold of it, breaking it into pieces to carry it to their nest on the tips of their mandibles. I plunged my teeth into the pastry, but the bites went down the wrong way. Zaza Mulligan is nowhere, sweetie, my father had murmured, meaning Zaza didn't exist anymore, because no one, no one could be nowhere. And yet I couldn't picture to myself the sudden inexistence of Zaza, couldn't conceive of a reality where all that made up Zaza had disappeared. How could I still say Zaza if there were no more Zaza?

I tossed the rest of my breakfast to a duck passing close to shore with its little ones, quack-quack, then I walked as far as the stream mouth that separated our cottage from that of the Lamars. The previous day's rain had increased its flow, but by the end of the summer the trickle of clear water would disappear. All that would be left would be the bed carved out by its passage, the imprint of its existence. But the following spring the stream would be reborn, it would keep on reviving forever, until the forest dried out and became a desert, or a mountain appeared, turning it into a waterfall. Maybe that's what would happen with Zaza Mulligan, perhaps she'd become a mountain, forest, desert, since it wasn't impossible that a bit of Zaza flowed in this water, a bit of her dust, which would settle into its sandy depths and come back to life with the autumn rains. I didn't know where her body had been found, but she might very well have lost consciousness near the stream like princesses in fairy tales, in a long sigh causing their veils to fall, or she could have drifted there to ease her wound, like the deer, bear, and moose, leaving behind a bit of her physical self.

I watched the water flow until the sun rose over the trees, captivated by the progress of the leaves and bits of grass hastening towards the frothy banks, then I began to walk upstream, hoping to find some sign of Zaza Mulligan's presence, a jewel, another bag of chips, a Pall Mall cigarette butt, but my father, who hadn't taken his eyes off me, came running over, you're not leaving the yard today, my mite. I understood right away what that meant. I was forbidden to go off on my own as long as we didn't know why Zaza had fallen off the edge of the world into this nowhere I couldn't imagine, as long as there was no answer to all the questions raised by death when it strikes without warning. In other words, never.

A girl had disappeared, and as a result the hypothetical disappearance of all girls took the age-old foreboding of any normal parent and blew it up into an enormous tumour, a menace to all unable to conceive that their flesh and blood might not survive them, might not be pledged to eternity. The unforeseeable took centre stage, clacking its teeth, and hordes of parents, aghast, shut their eyes, murmuring that it could have been Sissy, Françoise, it could have been Andrée, Sandra, Marie or Jane Mary, names fate would doom them to incant forever, were the hypothetical to become real. Zaza had awakened this fear, and the summer would never be the same. The freedom of movement I'd enjoyed up to then had just gone up in smoke. I'd be placed under surveillance, along with everything that was too small or too weak to defend itself, everything that had to be restrained so it wouldn't die. Faced with this injustice,

I wanted to protest to my father that I'd die anyway one day, but his anxious eyes, scanning the underbrush out of which a rabbit had just bolted, didn't deserve that I torture him any further.

I went back to the beach, and saw that the quarantine was already in effect. Besides me, there was no child near the lake, and you only heard birds, and fish jumping at the surface to catch flies. Even old Pat Tanguay wasn't in the hole his boat had made for itself in Ménard Bay. Bondrée was under quarantine, but also in mourning, because a girl was dead, because we were all going to go that way. I wrote a word on the beach with my left big toe, "Zaza", and under my breath, apologized for my anger. *Sorry Zaza*, I know it's not your fault. Then I cried, burying my neck in the collar of my pyjama top so my father wouldn't see that I was afraid, me too, afraid that Zaza's end augured the end of our happy days.

Brian Larue, as the principled grandson of a Canuck, had made it a point of honour to learn his grandfather's language. He did, however, hesitate when asked to act as an interpreter between the police and Boundary's francophones. Laruc was a loner, and the idea of having to violate the intimacy of men and women set apart by a dead body was repugnant to him. He agreed to it for his father's sake, for the pride this man would have felt, raised as he was in a hybrid, bastardized language with no proper place in the world, if he'd only known that his son was working to affirm his origins, that he now mastered the two tongues spanning the confines of his childhood. He was also drawn to the task by his daughter, Emma, who would soon be as old as the victim, and would enter that long corridor where women must make haste once night has fallen. Some thought that Larue had called his daughter Emma because of his admiration for Flaubert and Madame Bovary, but that was not so. If he appreciated Flaubert, he avoided the Bovarys like the plague. It was his wife who had chosen the name, seeing there a resemblance to the verb "aimer." Larue was too dumb at the time, too much in love, to contradict her and point out that Emma put the verb in what was, in fact, the past tense, *j'aimai, tu aimas, il aima*: he loved. He regretted it now, whenever he thought of his daughter's bearing the name of a heroine whose love became just a memory.

It was almost noon when the investigators finished questioning Ménard, and he felt both drained and dirty, as if Zaza Mulligan's blood had seeped right up to his hands. He wanted nothing so much as to throw himself headfirst into the lake, but it looked like the day had just begun, because Stan Michaud, in charge of the investigation, was determined to knock on every door and to grill every last halfwit in Boundary. He seemed to be taking the affair personally, and would not give up until he knew what had impelled Zaza Mulligan to venture into the woods in the middle of the night. Larue himself was also questioned. Michaud was certainly not going to work with someone who, if there was a crime, was as much a suspect as anyone else living in Boundary. But the interview was brief, Larue being as pure as the driven snow, which allowed Michaud to explain to him in detail what he wanted from him: to translate without omitting even a comma, to note any hesitations, inconsistencies, extra words, unusual emphases, in short to slip into the skin of a cop and to pull the zipper up to his chin.

Michaud must also have a daughter, Larue thought, a little Emma resembling Zaza Mulligan and all young girls, a young Nicole or Deborah who in his mind's eye he saw mouthing her first words, *daddy*, *puppy*, every time she crossed the threshold Saturday night to go out with her friends, equally oblivious to their own beauty and to the danger it represented to them.

But Larue was wrong, Michaud's only daughters were those he questioned in dumps and damp forests, and for that very reason his grasp of the perils to which they, in their innocence, exposed themselves was all the more acute. However it may be, Larue warmed to Michaud when the man shook his hand with a joint-crushing grip, and his grey eyes bored into his own as if to assure him that he was dealing with someone he could count on, a person of honour. Larue saw in those eyes the determination of someone who never laid down his arms unless they were torn from his body, someone who faced up to life's follies but carried on all the same, head high, because to be on the move is less despairing than to stand still. The world needed men who sacrificed their lives, pitting themselves against the violence and idiocy of others.

Seeing Michaud wipe his brow with a dubious-looking handkerchief, he forgot his wish to throw himself into the lake, and followed him and his partner to the campground, where they scarfed down one or two hot dogs and a cone of fries before getting on with more interrogations. Michaud insisted on paying for Larue's fries and hot dogs and, what with the heat, offered him a Mountain Dew, and the three men ate in silence around a picnic table on which were incised almost all the names of the young people who'd spent the summer at Boundary over the last twenty years. A work of art, Larue thought, an object to be preserved in the archives of adolescence, while Cusack, the partner, squirmed around on his bench, uneasy with the silence, the flies, and Michaud's gaze transfixed on Zaza's name, carved into one of the table's rough boards. Cusack tried a few times to get a conversation going, but he soon gave up, faced with Michaud's familiar silence. Still, he griped about the humidity all through the meal, casually dipping his fries into the pool of ketchup at the bottom of his cardboard cone, hoping, in vain, that one of the others might react. But they were lost in thought, in the memories stirred up by the names carved into the table.

Michaud was concentrating on Zaza's name and on the sun that had browned the young girl's skin, while Larue, light years away, was thinking about Monica Bernstein, his first love, of her first name carved into the bark of a birch that had perhaps now given up the ghost or been ground up in the jaws of a machine that converted trees and their memories into newsprint or firewood. The picture of steel teeth chewing into bark made him think, of course, about Zaza Mulligan, whose memories had poured onto the forest's damp floor, but then he turned back to Monica, today a teacher in Bangor and the mother of three children, two girls and a boy. If Meredith, Emma's mother, had not taken Monica's place, giving him the eye between the shelves of the Stanford library, he'd never have known Emma, whose absence he couldn't envisage without thinking in terms of his life running on empty. Yet he didn't miss his non-existent children. If Emma hadn't been born, it would have been the same thing. He'd never have known that a girl called Emma might have changed his life. His tomorrows were rooted in this stroke of luck, in this pearl born of a night of love that might well have been only a night of sleep or insomnia, and this dizzying primacy of fate shook his faith in any kind of freedom. Nothing, or almost nothing, was rooted in a man's choice.

*Deep in thought?* he heard as he was pondering Emma's next visit in just a few days, and he saw Michaud on his feet next to the table, waiting for him to pull out of his reverie. He'd just sacrificed a few moments of the real world to its dark side, there where unknowns, disowned by chance, have gone to ground. He would have liked to have remained in that world for a few moments more, thinking of those many lives that had slipped through his fingers, but the worried look on Michaud's face brought him back to the here and now. *Very deep*, he answered, then all three left for the cottage of Marcel Dumas, the old bachelor who'd been woken by the laughter of Zaza, Sissy, Frenchie, when the young girls had left the campground on Friday night.

Dumas was a dry, nervous little man whose hands trembled when he reached for his Zippo to light one of the hand-rolled cigarettes he'd prepared that morning, to last him until night. Fifteen a day, no more, as his lungs were weak. Still, he smoked four in just half an hour, restless, tense, smoothing his grey hair with a shaky hand, repeating that he'd heard nothing of what the adolescents were saying. The words of drunken young girls, incomprehensible. He also hadn't noticed if anyone was following them. He'd only glanced out his window long enough to see who was responsible for the noise, long enough to glimpse the bottle Frenchie Lamar was holding out, seeing it passing from one hand to another as she swayed along. Michaud insisted, nevertheless, that he repeat his story, *ask him what time it was, Larue*, because Dumas's nervousness was not a good sign. Either he was made uneasy by the situation, like all those people who lose their composure at the very sight of a police badge, or he was hiding something. Michaud thought the latter, but Dumas stuck to his version of the facts. He'd neither seen nor heard any more than he'd told them.

*We'll be back*, grumbled Michaud, leaving Dumas's cottage, a remark Larue didn't bother translating, then they went to knock at another door, then another, and another still, where they were greeted by solemn faces, aware already that the police were doing the rounds of Bondrée, with a cadaver on their hands. The afternoon was drawing to a close when Samuel Duchamp welcomed them onto his veranda. He wasn't the one who'd found the body, but it was he who, along with Gilles Ménard, had asked his neighbour to call the police, and led Cusack to the scene of the crime.

And so he'd seen the dried blood, the torn skin, the lifeless face. No surprise that he seemed so beaten down. When the three men arrived he rose to shake Cusack's hand, as one shakes the hand of a brother-in-arms. Horror creates bonds, and a bond had been forged between Duchamp and Cusack when they knelt near Zaza Mulligan. Michaud remembered having seen this fellow the night before, keeping his distance while his team scoured the site, but he'd paid him no heed. All his attention was then focused on Zaza Mulligan, on Esther Conrad. He barely saw the restless shadows moving about under the floodlights.

Duchamp also shook the hands of Michaud and Larue, but more formally, without a meeting of eyes to acknowledge a shared ordeal, and without the suggestion of a mutual understanding, since there was as yet no connection between them. He invited them to sit down while his wife brought lemonade in a large, misted pitcher. Michaud's wife owned the same pitcher, which she'd acquired by saving up packages of Kool-Aid, and he regretted not being home, preparing the barbecue for Monday night hamburgers. As for Dorothy, Dottie, his wife, she was no doubt wondering whether she should light the charcoal briquettes or wait a while, in case Stan only arrived at nightfall. She was used to this. Since Stan had been named chief inspector at Skowhegan, fifteen years earlier, she practically lived alone. Her evenings dragged on while she waited, then a car door slammed and Stan appeared, most of the time exhausted, his face haggard from coping with a violence whose inroads he could do so little to stem. He was not made for this job, he was too sensitive, too vulnerable, and yet no one better than he knew how to ferret out villainy. When he could still stand on his own two feet she served him a whisky, a Bulleit or a Wild Turkey, raw whiskys the way he liked them, and they sat in the living room, where he buried himself in a book about nature or slumped down in front of the TV, while Dorothy devoured the new Patricia Highsmith or gave herself over to her latest pastime, drawing, yoga, puzzles, or word games. Some nights he told her about his day, how he'd had to testify at the trial of an adolescent who'd tried to strangle the bastard who was beating his mother, how he'd helped out his colleagues, surrounding a mare frightened by a brush fire. Other nights he said nothing, or almost nothing, and Dorothy understood that he'd seen what no one wanted to see, that he was wading through mire that would bury him in the end, mire on the move, the kind men are so good at manufacturing.

Unlike other police wives, Dorothy didn't complain about her situation. She worked three afternoons a week at the local library, had a few good friends, including Laura Cusack, the wife of Stan's deputy, and she was not the type to get bored. When she was not re-potting a plant or re-covering a cushion, she sank down into an armchair with a book or magazine, and didn't see the time pass. In any case, she and Stan had lived together too long for them to fill whole evenings with words. An hour or two was now ample for non-essentials, for the voicing of thoughts insistent enough that you had to express them aloud, or for when you had to face again things that went deep, fear, anxiety, and had to reframe words that refused to be daunted by the passing of time. Never mind, Stan still felt guilty, knowing she was there in the garden or the kitchen, wondering if she should peel the potatoes or if she could step into a warm bath. He'd phone her soon, when he'd finished with Duchamp.

Florence Duchamp, visibly intimidated by the presence of all these men, was on the verge of leaving them alone with her husband, but Michaud insisted she stay.

He wanted to question her as well, because anything he learned about Zaza Mulligan might be useful, a detail, a word overheard by chance. Neither Florence nor Sam Duchamp could recall, however, a single incident that ought to have put them on their guard, any strangeness, any bizarre behaviour. They didn't really know Zaza, and had always observed her from a distance. She belonged to another world, one that didn't mix with theirs. For years they'd seen her go by with Sissy Morgan, singing with Sissy Morgan, the Andrews Sisters, Florence Duchamp murmured, lowering her head, saddened at the thought that one of the sisters would sing no more, thereby silencing her shadow, unless the shadow were to cloak Bondrée in mournful melodies. Only Andrée, their daughter, had been able to get close to the adolescents. She'd even gone looking for Zaza, two days earlier, along with Sissy.

Tell her to come here, Michaud said. Two minutes later the child was showing them the matchbook and the bag of chips she'd picked up along a path, Sissy's watch, and the mother-of-pearl button she held in the palm of her hand, edged in gold and gleaming in the July sun. An object she hesitated to add to her treasure chest, fearing it would compromise the magic of her coloured feathers, would subdue the brilliance of her dusty jewels.

After closing her hand over the button, she described the earring she'd given to Sissy, a tear, a pink raindrop, then the route she'd taken, crying Zaza, Zaza Mulligan, from the McBain cottage to that of Brian Larue, the book man who was there before her now, translating each of her words in an assured voice, at ease with words, *a tear, a drop of pink rain*. She'd only ever seen him from afar, a tiny silhouette moving about in the shadow of the mountain on the other side of the lake, and she imagined him to be as grey as books. But he was blond, fair as wheat and sand together. She was also astonished that his skin was so brown and his eyes so pale. The books, contrary to what she'd supposed, had not leached out Larue's colours. Perhaps his luminosity came from them, from the word "sun" and the word "light" rising off the pages, their brightness flaring in the forests where the characters roamed.

But a cloud darkened his gaze today, a cloud that was not usually there. Zaza Mulligan, who'd forced him out of his books to face the odour of real blood. Books never hurt you, that's why he'd chosen them. Every time he drifted away from them, it was only to come face to face with the clear-cut pain in what was real, stretching all the way to this veranda, even into the eyes of this child, Andrée, who replied eagerly to the questions being asked as if she thought it still possible to save Zaza Mulligan, because children believe in resurrection, in the reversibility of death. They can't accept the finality of certain silences, and speak to the dead while hoping one day to be able to take them by the hand.

Seeing that she was watching him, he placed a hand on the child's scraped knee, just like Emma's, just like that of all the little girls still running free, to ask her why she'd picked up the bag of chips. Because those were Zaza's favourites, she replied, with "*vinaigre*." *Vinégueure*, she added proudly, then immediately regretted it when Larue burst out laughing. He at once felt guilty for his dumb reaction, out of place under the circumstances. He'd just not been able to hold it back, what with the sincerity of this *vinégueure* with its Beauce accent. Sorry, he murmured to the little one, but she'd clammed up. He'd wounded her pride, and he'd have to be more diplomatic if he wanted to beguile her again, which he hoped to do, because he'd thought right away, on seeing her, that this little girl might be a friend to Emma, who was too solitary and too closed in on herself, that she might be a summer friend of the kind that leaves behind the fondest of memories. But Andrée didn't blame Larue. She blamed herself, and was furious for being so stupid. The hell with you, Andrée Duchamp, keep your mouth shut, don't translate anything anymore, you look like a real idiot.

Seeing the uneasiness that had crept in, Michaud brought his interpreter back to the point, to the Humpty Dumpty bag, asked her to say again where exactly she'd picked it up, if it was empty or full, wet, stepped on, never mind what. Michaud also wanted to know whether the matchbook was near the bag, if she'd already seen one in Zaza's hands, and if one could presume that the two objects had hit the ground at the same time, one from the hands of Zaza, the other from those of someone unknown. If the matchbook had at least borne the address of a bar, a restaurant, or a motel, he could have perhaps traced it back to its owner, but it was an anonymous matchbook like you saw everywhere, bearing only the Canadian maple leaf.

He could probably learn nothing from them, but this cursed matchbook and the bag of chips were all Michaud had to go on for the time being. He thought to himself that without his knowing how, those objects might yet lead him somewhere, give him some sense of the route Zaza had taken Friday night after saying good night to her friends, what paths she went down when she wanted to be alone, where she took shelter, places, to be exact, where you might follow her, wait to lure her farther on into a snare-filled forest, for that's how he saw the place where Zaza Mulligan's life ended, a zone where traps converged, and from which you did not emerge unscathed. The proof was that not he, nor Ménard, nor Duchamp, nor Cusack, had emerged intact from that night where Zaza Mulligan lay dead. They'd all left a part of themselves behind, a vestige of innocence that had survived into adulthood, a vision, a dream in which the forest did not come to resemble a realm beyond the grave, but remained a world that was liveable still. There were places under a curse and this was one, its traps biding their time for decades.

One of his men, the day before, had talked to him about a certain Peter *Laundry*, a trapper who'd hanged himself deep in the bush, and whose traps could still be found today, buried under vegetation, under fallen branches, under rot, like engines of death strewn over the landscape of countries once ravaged by war. The forest had cast Landry into a state where he no longer thought like an ordinary person, and years later his hobbled mind, and the woods' malevolence, were still at work. Was Zaza Mulligan the first victim since Landry and the dog called Sugar Baby, or had there been other deaths along the way, other vanishings no one had found suspicious, not conceiving of what nature could do?

He had a bad feeling on hearing Landry's story, remembering that some men never entirely leave the places they've haunted. Their sadness outlives the beating of their hearts, and makes of them terrible spectres bent on destroying the tranquility of peaceable kingdoms. The power of these phantoms eluded him, but he had the disturbing suspicion that Zaza Mulligan's death foretold others still to come. That was why he'd insisted that the child be precise in every detail, describe every nuance, *golden or lemon yellow*, because he feared the onset of a new cycle of violence. And she had responded well. If her parents agreed, he'd perhaps come back to question her some more, as she seemed to know Boundary better than anyone. Not only its residents, but also its trees, its paths, its cul-de-sacs. For the moment he was exhausted, his shirt stuck to his back, and he wanted to go home, take a shower, and touch Dorothy's cheek, to feel that softness he'd have liked to see on the surface of his own skin.

*Enough for today*, he murmured, and he asked if he could use the phone. The Duchamps had no phone, but he could go to the McBains', the first neighbours on the right. But the prospect of having to shake other damp hands made him give up on the idea. Dorothy would understand. Dorothy always understood. But he did shake the hands of Duchamp and his wife, then that of Larue, arranging to meet him the next day. They'd work out the details of his hiring later. He then got back into his official car along with Cusack, who wanted to make conversation, unable to bear the silence despite the wind whistling past the open windows. Cusack was young, one of these days he'd learn to be quiet, once he realized that words only calm one's anxiety for a very short time. Meanwhile, Michaud pretended to listen. He grunted, knitting his brows, he nodded his head, tossed out an occasional *yes* for the sake of appearances, all the time trying to elude the boomerangs which, along the road, were threatening to hurl themselves out of the woods.

The policemen came back the next day with Brian Larue, all three exhausted, all three mopping their foreheads under the big spruce tree where my father had dragged the chairs. Jim Cusack, the youngest, was killing horseflies, half of which didn't exist, with his handkerchief. He scratched at his neck, anticipating the bite, then gave a slap to his shoulder or his knee, swearing under his breath. After a few minutes my father began to scratch too, out of empathy or a kind of infectious uneasiness I suppose, seeing the imaginary flies missed by Cusack heading his way. He suggested they go in the house, but Michaud wanted to stay outside for the breeze, if you could call that semblance of wind a breeze, since it barely stirred the trees' limp leaves.

My mother must have been watching their little game from inside the cottage, because she turned up with a bottle of lemon oil my father and Cusack used to anoint all their body parts not covered by clothing, except the top of the head, which Cusack rubbed compulsively, victim to one of those uncontrollable itches resulting from irritation, heat, fatigue, and for which there was no remedy. You have to lie down, forget you exist, and start anew the next day.

As for Michaud and Larue, they seemed immune to flies and mosquitoes. With the backs of their hands they intercepted the drops of sweat trying to slip into their eyes, dried their knuckles on their pants, and squinted at the sun filtering through the branches. The air was still and Brian Larue lit cigarette after cigarette, probably to combat the smells of lemon, spruce, and sweat all mixed together, because it didn't seem likely that someone could smoke away like that just for the pleasure of it. Every time Michaud asked me a question, he exhaled the smoke from his last puff, then translated, while knocking off the ash with a tap of his thumb from under the filter. Michaud wanted to know if I was familiar with the paths that split off from the east side of Turtle Road, Otter Trail, Weasel Trail, that of Loutre, that of Belette, and if I'd seen Zaza with a boy or a man. I'd seen Zaza kiss Mark Meyer, the campground attendant, at the start of Otter Trail, but I couldn't say anything about that in front of my father. I was afraid that if I uttered the word "kiss," he'd imagine me frenching with Réjean Lacroix or Jacques Maheux, two idiots who organized spitting contests and thought they were geniuses because they peed farther than Michael Jamison. So I said maybe, a stupid answer that was the same as an admission. Michaud, not so stupid, kept at me until I confessed that I'd seen Mark Meyer put his mouth against that of Zaza, which was the only way I could think of to say it.

The questions then came fast and furious, and I realized that they'd found Zaza not far from Otter Trail, a well-lit path where nothing bad, it seemed to me, could ever happen. I'd picked up Gertrude, my first frog, in the middle of that path, where I hid her under a nest of leaves. I went back to see her every day, and Gertrude was never in the same place, she got bigger and smaller all the time, but for me the frog I made jump along my forearm was always the same one, and her name was Gertrude, *the Otter Trail Frog*, even if she was a francophone frog, a real frog after all. I also went up Otter Trail when I wanted to plot a nasty trick, undisturbed, and to hide myself away behind a tree trunk where the ferns shielded me from people's eyes. I even remembered for a long time looking for otters, though they'd abandoned the lakeshore and the river as soon as humans moved in, just like Pete Landry, who fled into the bush on Otter Trail or Weasel Trail. Maybe Zaza had taken flight also, following Landry and the otters, for a reason that had something to do with the presence of men. We'd probably never know, Zaza no longer being there to tell us why she'd run off into the night on Otter Trail. Only the man or boy who'd urged her there, as Stan Michaud seemed to think, could tell us why Zaza never came back, but that man wouldn't talk. If he'd wanted to talk, he'd have done so already. If he stayed silent, it's because he knew that a single word on his part would bring down a barrage of blows on his head.

I turned all that over in my mind while Jim Cusack pulled at his scalp, while Brian Larue spat his life away, while my father tried to balance his chair on the spruce roots snaking over the ground, forming knots with other roots before returning to earth, and Otter Trail suddenly seemed dangerous to me, because you could die there, because you could meet there men who harboured a lethal secret. I didn't know how Zaza had died, my parents refused to tell us. Waiting to learn about it some other way, I could only use my imagination, could only reproduce scenes of horror I'd seen on television, where hands holding a shiny knife blade advanced through the darkness. Otter Trail, from now on, would be haunted by Zaza Mulligan's shadow, then by that of a faceless figure who could leap from the dew-drenched ferns at any time, ready to rip out your eyes to protect his secret. Because Zaza had strayed, nothing would ever be the same.

My chair was sinking into the ground among the twisted roots, when my father placed his hand on my shoulder. You all right, my bug? He called me that when things were serious, bug. I could have taken offence, but I knew that the bug he saw in me had nothing to do with an insect. It was a bug that wasn't really a bug, that didn't smell bad and that knew how to climb trees. Bug was just another word for mite, not really more flattering if you think about it, but it was a word full of affection, and nothing gave me more pleasure than to hear him call me that. As long as he called me bug, I knew he loved me. I told him yes, I'm all right, why tell the truth when it's got a dirty face? Michaud asked me one last question, then everyone got up, Brian Larue coughing, Michaud cracking his knuckles, Cusack starting in again to kill non-existent horseflies, and me looking at the roots over which everyone made their way without asking themselves if it hurt.

Before leaving, Brian Larue invited me to visit his daughter, Emma, who'd be arriving in Bondrée the next day. She looks like you, I'm sure she'd like to know you, then he tempted me with Emma's dog, a short-legged dachshund called Brownie that no doubt picked up all kinds of dirt in its fur and scared off other animals, squirrels and field mice. His strategy worked all the same, because if Emma Larue turned out to be the same kind of nuisance as Jane Mary Brown, I could at least fall back on the dog, given that my parents refused to adopt one, claiming that it hurt too much when they left us, and they didn't want to see us going around red-eyed for weeks. All they saw in the animal was its death, forgetting the big paws on your knees, the furry behinds that warmed your feet, the smiles from ear to ear. That's why you wanted a dog, because a dog, it's lovable. If it was as dumb as a cabbageworm, there'd be no problem.

For that matter, I asked myself why they'd bothered to make us, Bob, Millie, and me, because we were going to die too, maybe before them, like Zaza Mulligan, whose parents had shut themselves up behind closed curtains, refusing the summer, refusing the sun. Even Zaza's brothers, Jack and Ben, back from Florida the day after the body was found, were unable to tempt them out or to take them back to Portland. They wanted to stay near Zaza, near her last words, her last steps, and would only go to Portland for the burial, which had to be delayed because of the autopsy.

That's what Brian Larue told my parents when he thought I was out of earshot, that they were going to cut up Zaza's body and go right under her skin to look at her, in case the state of her heart might explain why it had stopped beating. Michaud, standing beside Larue, mumbled something about a young girl who had a kind of stone heart or crippled heart, and I didn't understand anything he said. I thought about Zaza's heart, her gaping belly, like the plastic model at the front of my classroom in school, with its yellow liver and its orange spleen, run through with diagonal grooves. I also thought of Sissy Morgan cloistered in her room. Since Zaza's death, Sissy had been invisible. No one had seen her coming down Snake Hill humming "Lucy in the Sky," no one had seen her dive off the end of the Mulligan dock, shouting *whatever, Sam!* an expression with meaning only for Sissy and Zaza and belonging only to them, *whatever, Sam!* their red and white bathing suits describing perfect arcs against the blue sky. I thought of Sissy's sadness as Laval Maheux passed by on his new bike, a sign that the quarantine was coming to an end. Children began to come outside, mothers to shout after them, *Michael, Norman, don't cross the lifeline,* and Michael and Norman cried out in their turn from this side of the buoys you weren't supposed to go past, the lifeline beyond which the swimmer lost his footing and risked being swallowed up by the calm water. Life returned. The wind carried the sounds made by the living, but Sissy's sounds were missing, and the sounds of Zaza. There were holes in the echo sent back to us by Moose Trap, in the colours of the landscape, holes that would never be filled, even if another duo were to appear, an Emma-Andrée duo, for example.

I was wary of meeting this girl, and at the same time couldn't stop myself from dreaming. I saw myself wrapped in a cloud of smoke, a Pall Mall in my hand, and a bunch of "*foc* Emmas" on the tip of my tongue, ready to materialize along with the smoke, but there was only one duo like that of Sissy Morgan and Zaza Mulligan. Zaza gone, such an entity was no longer imaginable. Franky-Frenchie Lamar was still around, but she didn't have what it took to aspire to the title of Queen Zaza. In any case, I would have bet a million dollars that her friendship with Sissy Morgan was over, Zaza not being there to hold the three of them together. Besides, Frenchie was just an appendage, a more or less viable add-on, a kind of extension that only held true because the others tolerated it. Without Zaza, no balance was possible. There would never be another duo, only a truncated Sissy, weakened by the loss, a lame half-girl who could not be made whole.

I kicked at a rock without wondering if that caused it pain, then I went back into the cottage, where my mother made me swear never again to set foot on Otter Trail. For now, she didn't have to worry. I had no intention of going for a stroll there where Zaza's voice would rise from the ground with the dew, but one day I would return, when curiosity got the better of my fear, and I'd had enough of behaving like a coward. I'd wait for the rain to wash the blood away, all of Zaza's blood, for the wind and the birds to carry off the last of her hair, and I'd go there, to the end of Otter Trail, because that's what children do who can't stop themselves diving from high on the rocks, eyes shut hard but skin all aquiver. And there, bent over the flattened ferns with their dim impress of a body as fanciful as Jim Cusack's flies, I'd murmur Zaza, Zaz, as I once whispered the name of Pete Landry near what was left of his shack. And perhaps Zaza would answer me, who knows, and would tell me softly what closed eyes see, before I'd take off, asking no more, happy to be alive, happy to be a child.

Stan Michaud and Jim Cusack spent four days in Boundary, knocking and again knocking at the same doors, questioning the same people, pulling from their tents those staying at the campground, or going to seek them out near the lake. These strangers were perfect suspects, but they all also had perfect alibis, a girlfriend who hadn't left them alone all night, a neighbour in the camp with whom they'd partied until dawn, a child who'd received a fishhook in the behind and had to be taken to see a doctor, but Michaud persevered, going over the same detail twenty times, dragging Cusack into Otter Trail and asking him to wait at the edge of the woods while he walked alone in the footsteps of Elisabeth Mulligan. At those times he kneeled where the young girl had fallen, near the hole left when the trap was removed, and he dug around the hole in case Zaza had buried there a gold heart or one of stone. The trap was now at the local police station, inside a box Michaud opened when he felt himself at a dead end, up against a wall behind which there was perhaps a light or a truth that would solve the mystery. He studied the trap as he had examined Esther Conrad's stone heart, hoping the object would speak to him, that a sudden insight would come to him while the rain drummed on the dirty windows, then he folded the box's flaps back down, leaving only the narrow gaps giving onto a deep darkness.

It was dark at the end of Otter Trail as well, but at times a ray of sun entered into the opening where the trap had been wedged. It then seemed to Michaud that Zaza was smiling, that in this light the young girl's last rush of happiness was declaring itself, defying her pain on a summer's day as flawless as youth. *How, Elisabeth? Why?* But the day remained silent. The silence was easy to explain. Elisabeth Mulligan had died for nothing, for no reason, because most young people die that way, to no proper purpose, with nothing to explain the speed with which events unfold. This death, like almost all premature deaths, was devoid of meaning. Unless you were to see death justified by the privilege granted to the living of breathing the air on earth. Those who breathed more rapidly, perhaps, or more intensely, would be condemned to an earlier death. Faced with the frequent dramas where blood was shed, Michaud found himself thinking along those lines as a matter of course, always asking questions that had no answers. Why so young? Why so beautiful? Why this one and not that one?

In the days following Esther Conrad's disappearance, he'd also pondered those senseless questions: why, why, why? He remembered that Dorothy, just as he was reflecting on the transience of beauty, had talked to him of jonquils and roses, of lilacs that you gathered most always before they were ready to die. Such was the fate of a certain kind of beauty. He didn't know what the answer was, he thought of horses you put down when their gaze goes dim behind the froth on their breath, but that act of mercy had nothing to do with flowers picked in the middle of gardens, then he went back to his first idea, that death had meaning only if the heart stopped from exhaustion, if it was the result of a conscious act, of an inadequate adaptation to life.

Zaza Mulligan, he knew, was not one of those who had lost faith in the need to survive. Her hair was too long for her not to have loved life. Besides, you didn't choose torture to put an end to your days. Barring proof to the contrary, she did not belong either to that handful of unfortunates whose fate was determined by an assassin. Despite his lingering doubts, he couldn't help concluding that Zaza had died accidentally because of the errant ways of a man called Landry, who didn't know he was becoming unhinged. That's what he'd said to her parents, and that's what he'd write in his report, accidental death, senseless death, for nothing, in the prime of life, since no concrete evidence contradicted that thesis, and the medical examiner had detected no anomaly during his autopsy other than a slight heart murmur, which perhaps explained the young girl's red cheeks when she insisted that her heart beat more strongly. Still, he'd hold on to the trap in case the object were to break its silence, and he'd keep his eyes open, you never knew where killers might resurface, or where a chance occurrence might offer a glimpse of a premeditated act, the hand decanting poison or propelling an innocent victim to the bottom of a ravine.

After telling George and Sarah Mulligan that his investigation was over and that they'd see him no more, he went to pay one more visit to Brian Larue, whom he regretted not being able to add to his team, not only because Larue made it possible for him to negotiate the ins and outs of a language he felt too old to go back to, but because he had the impression that he was one of those men with whom you could discuss anything without their doing an instant pirouette to bury their heads in the sand. If he'd known Larue better, he'd have talked to him about the solitude of those who consent to lay hands on the skin of the dead, cold and increasingly viscous, with the odour of decay they trail behind them, an odour whose origin they can't communicate to those close to them without obliging them to touch the viscid skin in their turn. Larue would have understood, since his hand, over recent days, had brushed against Zaza Mulligan's body several times. What was the point, however, of reminding a man that he too shared a contagion? Once at Larue's, he pretended he'd just come to thank him one last time, but Larue saw his bowed shoulders, his eyes ringed in shadow, and he invited Michaud for a drink. You don't refuse your house to a man in need of rest.

Michaud wasn't used to drinking so early in the day, but he accepted a cold beer, which he savoured in the shade of the porch, slumped in an armchair where he would have soon fallen asleep had he been alone. Beside him Larue also drank, turning his bottle around in his hands, its label, wet with condensation, shredding into thin strips that stuck to his fingers. From time to time one of them made a remark about the heat or the stubbornness of old Pat Tanguay, who must have decided to fry himself in his boat with his fish, but neither seemed ready to broach the subject that connected them, Zaza Mulligan. They were both lost in thought, in the contemplation of clouds or the observation of the young girls below them, playing on the beach. Even if Michaud didn't know Larue's daughter, he soon guessed, seeing little Andrée Duchamp jumping off the end of the dock, that the child running behind her was Emma. As for the dog pacing the dock and barking, that was surely Brownie, the dachshund Larue had mentioned.

For about twenty minutes the girls took turns diving, splashing Brownie and creating little rainbows over the lake's calm surface, then they sat down on the dock, their beach towels over their heads to protect themselves from the sun and to contain in the damp cloth's shadow the secrets children invent. They talked heatedly, agitating their thin arms outside the shelter of their towels, and Michaud thought to himself that you could already see, in the refinement of the muscles, that those would soon be women's arms. Their wrists would be adorned with gold or showy bracelets whose jingling would create that music proper to women who talk with their hands and who with broad gestures trace out words they want to be heard more than others. Michaud had always been fascinated by those noisy creatures, not afraid to laugh out loud in the middle of the street, clacking their heels on the sidewalks. But they frightened him too. He preferred discreet women, like Dorothy, whose femininity was less strident. He was just wondering what category Emma and Andrée would fall into when Larue offered him another beer, which he willingly accepted even if he shouldn't have, even if the heat amplified the effect of the alcohol. He felt good on this porch. Larue's empathetic silence was calming, after a week during which everyone wanted to be heard on the subject of Zaza Mulligan's death, weighing him down with absurd opinions and gossip so petty that it verged on the obscene.

Coming back with the beer, ice-cold O'Keefes bought on the Canadian side of the border, Larue pointed to the clouds gathering in the south, foretelling a storm. Michaud voiced his concern about forest fires, talking about the one that had razed part of Maine in October 1947, the worst fire the state had ever known, destroying almost half of Mount Desert Island, burning houses on Millionaires' Row in Bar Harbour, and consuming in all more than seventeen thousand acres of land. *"The year Maine burned."* Michaud sighed, citing one of the big headlines of the time, then he went silent again. The girls, still wearing their towels, were now sitting in the boat pulled up on shore, facing the lake.

If the light had been lower you could have taken them for frail ghosts, but it was too bright, the colours too vivid for one to associate those silhouettes with any kind of spectre.

Michaud would have liked to include that tableau in an album dedicated to immortality, two little girls and a dog in the summer light, he would have liked to photograph the scene so as to keep it on hand for trying times, to be able to oppose it to the pictures faded to grey that burdened his mind, but he knew that was hopeless. His head was full of scenes imbued with innocence, schoolgirls playing marbles, a moose swimming across a lake at dusk, a child petting a cat, all of which melted away, faced with the vulgarity of other images. In any case, those pictures only described a passing moment of what was real. They omitted the schoolgirls' boredom, the death of the cat, and that of the moose that reached shore only to be greeted by a detonation it would hardly have a chance to hear, and to be thrown onto its back, wondering why it had fallen. The girls sitting near the lake would vanish too at the end of the summer. Jewels would encircle their wrists, and the dog would be forgotten on the doorstep.

In normal times alcohol prevented him from lapsing into those spiralling trains of thought where the dark side of things, at each bend in the road, encroached on the light, but today his thoughts were spinning right down to the heart of the spiral, a progress that seemed to gather speed as the alcohol took effect. It must have been his fatigue, and the memory, still fresh, of Zaza Mulligan. Still, he burst out laughing when old Tanguay, in the middle of the lake, started cursing the flies, proof that the ridiculous has an immediate impact, whatever the circumstances, and he shifted his attention to the children, in case they'd be able to level out his spiral.

As for Larue, he was watching them too, congratulating himself on his good judgment in inviting Andrée Duchamp to visit Emma. Emma had baulked when he'd told her the news, arguing that it was up to her to choose her friends. But it took no more than ten minutes for the two girls to forge what would become a friendship. Inseparable, that's how he saw them already, two little girls in each other's image, like Sissy Morgan and Zaza Mulligan, two children who would suffer equally from their parting, but nothing would make him want to spare them that unhappiness. It was the price of childhood friendships, and that price was never too high. Michaud must have guessed what he was thinking, because he suddenly started talking about the sweetness of certain ages, with little silhouettes slowly unthreading in the half-light, then he rose, telling Larue to keep a close eye on the children. *Don't let them grow old too fast*, he added, shaking Larue's hand, and Larue wanted just then to ask him if he too had a daughter, as he had supposed, but he held back. He and Michaud would probably never see each other again, other than on a commercial street in Portland or Bangor where they would greet each other in passing. Why, then, trivialize the existence of his daughter, if there was one, with a perfunctory question? They stood in silence until Michaud pointed to the dark mass advancing on Bondrée, composed and threatening. It was time for him to leave.

Larue watched him go off, his shoulders as stooped as when he arrived, then he heard his car's engine start up at the same time as the first lightning zigzagged over the opposite shore of the lake. Several people, right after the lightning, saw the car go by with its flashing light turned off, crossing their fingers that they would never again see it in the neighbourhood. When it disappeared beyond the turnoff leading to the highway, a few women sighed, and the storm broke.

At the Ménards', the Lacroixs', the McBains', the men pulled their barbecues under the awnings. The smell of grilled meat mingled with that of the rain, and the voices of nervous mothers vied with the rumbling of the storm, *Michael, Marnie, don't you go near the lake.* Life went on, but along with those who thought that the storm would wash away the last remnants of the drama, there were some who couldn't help thinking that it had all begun just like that, with the rain. They watched the sky, praying that the lightning wouldn't strike their children.

# AFTER ZAZA

No thoughts went through Zaza Mulligan's mind when she cried out. She was now pure terror, an endless cry whose meaning and origin were unknown to her. Then the hand pressing down on her shoulder, hot and humid, closed over her screaming mouth. Zaza tasted its sweat and its salt, and a strong odour of wood, and the insults she tried to hurl at her assailant turned into gurglings, arg, argul, gargul, more horrifying than the forest whose trees leaned down, whose trees waltzed to the rhythm of her gurgling and the man's commands, *shut up you little bitch, shut up, shut up*, words uttered through tears and detonations, words spat in the face of a heedless God, *shut up, Jim, please, shut up . . .*

Even if they hardly knew her, most of the people spending the summer near Boundary Pond attended Zaza's funeral out of a sense of propriety, out of compassion for George and Sarah Mulligan, or because of the guilt gnawing away at them already, the sense that their distress had been inadequate to the event, because it was Zaza, because she'd been asking for it. All, from the most cynical to the most kindly, wore mourning, even old Pat Tanguay, who'd exchanged his filthy upper garment for a clean shirt. No one had expected to see him there, because he'd spent recent summers fulminating against the Mulligans' outboard, even threatening George to put it out of commission with a shotgun, but Pat remembered the hilarity of the little girls, their explosions of joy that sometimes echoed as far as the mountain, and that had more than once stopped him from throwing himself into the depths of that black hole widening around his boat when it felt like the agony in his joints was just the prelude to an absence of all pain. At those times he was tempted to finish everything off right then and there before the curtain fell, until one of the girls cried out *whatever, Sam!* and the swell stirred up by their laughter dispersed the black circle surrounding his little boat, into which he collapsed, feeling like an old fool. He at least owed that to Zaza Mulligan, a clean shirt and a few genuflections.

The church was already full to bursting when Stan Michaud dipped his fingers into the font, in case the water, reputed to be miraculous, might ease the headache he'd had on waking, a migraine accompanied by sharp flashes, like those that afflicted him two or three times a year when he felt as if he'd missed something crucial in a case, a detail trying to find a way through the charged synapses in his brain. Before finally falling asleep the night before, he'd gone over the Zaza Mulligan case while thinking about the tie and suit he'd have to wear the next day, the sadness he'd have to face, tormented by the persistent feeling that he'd not asked the right questions, and that some son of a bitch was mocking his ineptitude by hammering on his skull. To his mind, the Elisabeth Mulligan affair, like that of Esther Conrad, was one of those unresolved cases closed only because they'd reached dead ends.

After taking a look at the crowd he sat in one of the church's last pews, where cops usually sit to have a better overall view and to distance themselves as much as possible from the mourning family, which doesn't want to be reminded that the deceased died a violent death. Several people whom he'd questioned in Boundary had already taken their seats in the church, most of them in the back, not daring to mix with the close relatives. He recognized Gilles Ménard, the McBains, Samuel Duchamp, his wife and their three children, as well as the campground attendant, Mark Meyer, looking cramped in a suit that he mustn't have worn for a long time. Michaud didn't like his looks, and he would have loved to grill him some more, but Meyer had an airtight alibi. The night Zaza disappeared he'd left the campground around ten o'clock with his father, who'd taken him to West Forks, the village where he lived, for his weekend off. Despite his innocence, the young man seemed nervous, and kept glancing from left to right as if he knew he was being watched, and someone indeed was watching him, Bob Lamar, the father of Françoise, called Franky-Frenchie, sitting a bit farther off behind the Morgans. It was clear that Lamar couldn't abide Meyer, and you could understand his aversion to him. Meyer was an insignificant little Don Juan who owed his charm to his suntan and his white teeth. Michaud didn't know why Lamar was staring at the young man, but he would have sworn that he'd got too chummy with his daughter. He had the look of a father who sensed the stench of carrion behind the courtesies of a suitor.

The priest was just coming into the chancel to the accompaniment of booming organ music when Michaud finally caught sight of Sissy Morgan, flanked by her parents, as still as a statue. When the priest asked the congregation to rise, she didn't move, didn't cross herself along with the others, and her shoulders began to convulse when Zaza's name was read out from the pulpit. Tears closer to cries than sobs rose up beneath the nave, obscuring the priest's voice, and triggering the lamentations of Sarah Mulligan, Frenchie Lamar, and Stella McBain. The sniffling and moans of one were succeeded by those of others, spreading throughout the church, and heightening the discomfort always associated with that sort of ceremony.

Michaud, for his part, didn't weep. He hadn't for years. His pain manifested itself differently, it ate him up inside, generating sleepless nights that left his eyes red, but as dry as those of criminals. It's that dryness that drew him close to them, and enabled him to glimpse what people see who don't shed tears. Every time he had to lean over a lifeless body he went deep into himself to where the springs had run dry, and positioned himself behind that matte screen from where a killer coldly contemplates others' fears. He'd taken that indifference on himself while looking down on Esther Conrad's remains, an indifference to cruelty that heeds no entreaties, and that gave him a strong sense of the detachment involved in a murderous act. Esther had had no chance. He'd had the same feeling next to Zaza Mulligan. The screen had come down over the forest, and for an instant he'd glimpsed the hatred behind a hand that kills. Zaza Mulligan had not died as the result of an accident, he'd thought, looking at the body. And he hadn't changed his mind. Someone had stood there, as near as could be to a child who was going to die, with dry hands and eyes, someone who was perhaps present in this congregation. Instinctively, he sought out those who were not weeping, mostly men, but that proved nothing, since many of them had no real connection to the deceased. But Michaud had learned at his own cost that there was no better shelter for the guilty than the light of day, there where evil may easily dissemble itself among the innocent. So he kept his eyes open, just in case. He noted the calculated gestures, the blank stares, the hands that didn't tremble enough.

During communion, he spotted Pat Tanguay in a side aisle, as stooped, as vulnerable as on the lake. Was it the setting? Was it the circumstance? He instantly felt immense compassion for the old fisherman, whose bent fingers drummed out on the prie-dieu the melody taken up by the organ, a requiem that shook the whole church. As the organist attacked the last chords, a searing pain flashed through Michaud's skull, like a drought-fed fire igniting, and he let himself drop back onto the bench. Pat Tanguay no longer existed, nor his hands crippled by arthritis, nor Sissy Morgan's anguish. When the fire abated at last, the coffin was on its way down the centre aisle on the black-clad shoulders of Jack and Ben, the first bearers, the brothers.

He lowered his head, but not soon enough to dodge the eyes of Sarah Mulligan, the mother, reddened by the constant flow of salt and water.

The procession seemed to him to last forever, and he cursed his migraine, which had jolted him out of time as it kept pace with the mournful music, and which had prevented him from making an early exit. He would have preferred to monitor the procession from a distance, so as not to discomfit anyone with his policeman's eye, but the harm was done. Sarah Mulligan had been hurt, and there was nothing he could do about it. As soon as he'd mustered the strength, he put on his dark glasses and slipped outside. The day was warm and the sky cloudless, but no one heeded the brightness rebounding from the hearse's gleaming chrome. Gloom had filed out of the church along with the coffin, and hung suspended there under the blue sky.

Normally, Stan Michaud would have gone to the cemetery, it was his job to be there, to observe, to bow his head before the tearful prayers, to endure the sidelong glances, but this chore was beyond him. Glint from the chrome lanced right through him, splintered into needles that stabbed him beneath his eyelids. There was no point in going to the cemetery, all he'd see would be a jumble of luminous forms bent over a trench that was just as luminous. There would be no police officer today standing in the shade of one of the Evergreen Cemetery's trees to watch Zaza Mulligan's coffin being lowered into the ground in a shower of sparks.

Before going back to his car, he shot one more glance at the crowd, in case he might spot Brian Larue. In vain. The book man was back in his den.

Zaza was already slipping away. Zaza's beauty was fading along with the thousands of images from those boundless yesterdays lingering in death's wake, the piano lessons, the pillow fights, grey feathers fluttering about faces lit up with radiant laughter. *Where are you, Zaz? Where were you? Why?*

Standing near the grave over which the coffin hung suspended, somehow weightless despite its bulk, Sissy Morgan turned over in her mind her idiot memories embellished with non-existent flowers, ridiculous suns, and dreams both vain and stupid. Numb with tears, she was adrift at the heart of those murky thoughts that had filled her head ever since her father entered her room, pale as a ghost, to inform her of Zaza's death: *don't say it, Dad! Please don't...* but the dreaded words issued from Vic Morgan's mouth like a swarm of lifeless flies that filled the air and came swooping down on her. The ground opened up and the whiteness of death, already there in the earth's clefts, blanketed with its light everything that was once alive. Sissy Morgan's thoughts took on the consistency of glass and began to retreat from the inaudible words flitting about the room, spilling like so many obscenities from the ashen lips of Vic Morgan, the father who couldn't shield her from the suffering every life must know. *Dead, Zaza. Dead, indeed.*

A week had passed since then, in the course of which Zaza's belly had been cut open along with her heart, her head, but the thought of it was still receding far down the narrow endless corridor opening into Sissy Morgan's mind. *Make it go away, Dad*, she'd murmured, letting fall to her feet the flower that had been placed in her hands. A lily, perhaps. Then the dull sound of shovelfuls of earth on metal cued them to leave. A few birds flew over in the blue sky. On the ground, the sun turned the shadows black.

Dorothy was making jam when Stan came in. The sweet smell of raspberries filled the house along with the end-of-afternoon sun, and lent it a festive air. It reminded Michaud of his childhood, the still-steaming puddings he devoured in huge quantities before going back outside into the August light, the warmest of all for him, immensely mild and rich. As far back as he could remember August had been his favourite month, a month of yellow plenitude, when the heat did not scorch. His most vivid memory, in fact, went back to a late August day, a memory beautiful as a mirage. He'd found himself alone in the middle of a field near a heavy-branched apple tree, surrounded by golden hay, and that image represented all that was perfect and true. Nothing could be excised from that moment, or added to it. Everything was there: solitude, silence, the smell of hay and apples, the day's veiled hue, together with a sense of freedom, not the freedom of movement he enjoyed, nor the sense of endless space in the prospect across the field, but a freedom embodied in his perfect fusion with time, his serene understanding of that place, his awareness of a moment that nothing, no misfortune and no impediment, could ever take away from him. If one were to ask him who he was and what was his ideal, he'd have no choice but to describe that scene, which, fleeting as it was, represented all the beauty that could exist in the world. It was not happiness, but fullness, that was the only word that came to his mind, and it seemed to him that the quintessence of his entire self had been contained in those few moments.

He'd known other moments that came close to that one, under autumn trees, near a lake ablaze with the odorous light of Thanksgiving, but none imbued with that purity and humble splendour. Curiously, it was always a smell that brought back memories for him, along with a feeling of happy solitude occasioned by the perfume of fruits or lilacs. If he were to bring all those memories together, his past would be reduced to a few minutes only, beyond which he seemed not to have existed at all.

What are you thinking about? Dorothy asked him as she took the saucepan out of the oven and saw him standing still in the doorway. He hesitated, not knowing how to express the joy he felt in inhaling the sugary air, while experiencing an acute spell of vertigo at the idea that his life was being compressed, the more it ran on.

Of my mother's puddings, he replied, preferring to focus on what was left of his past and to avoid the return of his migraine, which had become a nebulous headache during the few hours he'd spent sleeping in his car parked on a small road on the way out of Portland after Zaza Mulligan's funeral. Their smell made me happy, he added, going to Dorothy to plant a kiss on the back of her neck, which also smelled sweet, honey slightly tinged with the scent of beeswax. *You smell of childhood too*, and that was so. Dorothy gave off childhood aromas that calmed him, odours that had survived the inevitable loss of innocence.

Dorothy mocked him, refusing to believe that something of her youth still clung to her skin, and she served him a glass of Wild Turkey, choosing for herself a kir, a cocktail she'd recently come across in a magazine and that she saved for quiet days like this one, when Stan was able to relax without a conclave of ghosts hovering over them. Without asking for his assent she led him into the garden, beneath the arbour they'd built twenty-five years earlier, when they were young, when every nail they hammered in spoke to them of the future of the wood, of the aging to which they would bear witness.

We're going to have to trim the ivy, she said, clinking glasses with Stan. They'd have to cut back the climbing roses, those Nancy Haywards on the fence, that were starting to spread across the lawn. She could have asked Stan how his day had gone, but she didn't want to summon the shadows that would rush in if she made any reference to young Elisabeth Mulligan's funeral, which Stan had attended with an eye to tracking down a murderer who perhaps existed just in his head or in his minimal trust in humankind, his inability to believe that violence could at times be accidental. In Stan Michaud's mind, no stone rolled to the bottom of a hill without some man having set it in motion.

Michaud had no wish to talk about the day either. He wanted to forget it, and to discuss roses, the ivy, the dahlias and phlox, while allowing the warmth of the bourbon to spread through his chest and slowly numb him. *Enjoy your drink?* he asked Dorothy, not able to fathom the vogue among women for mixed drinks with at times two or three bands of dubious colours superimposed on one another. *Delicious*, she replied, reminding him that she liked change, liked treating herself to drinks and dishes that went with the season. In three days July would give way to the month of August, the month of berries, and the cassis liqueur made her feel as though the ripening of the blackberry bushes was not far off.

Did you know that this drink was named after a French priest? And she went on to talk about Félix Kir, a man who had fought on the field of battle, and who was as devoted to his fellows as much as he was to God, whose existence he affirmed with a somewhat dubious sense of humour, "*you don't see my ass but you know it's there,*" she continued, seeing clearly that Stan was bit by bit withdrawing into himself, indifferent to Canon Kir's straight talk. What had she said to lose him that way? It must have been her allusion to war. She tried to make up for it by reminding Stan that they ought to pay a visit to his sister over the weekend, but it was too late, the shadows were back. While feigning an interest in her words, it was with them that Stan was conversing, with the shades that had come in under the arbour by whatever route, perhaps via the muddy trenches that Félix Kir had known.

She wasn't entirely wrong. Stan Michaud was at that moment walking through other trenches, this time laid out by a man who had rejected the war. He was following in the footsteps of Peter Landry in the depths of a forest bearing his name, strewn with traps that for him represented yet another product of warfare. Zaza Mulligan, barring proof to the contrary, was one of the thousands of victims of a conflict that had thrust Landry deep into Boundary's woods. Without that war, Zaza Mulligan would still be alive.

Overpowered by the smell of jam, he'd for a while forgotten the young girl, allowing the sweetness of August memories to wash over the garden, but the stench of death proved stronger in the long run. It now enveloped Dorothy, who seemed to have given up trying to free him from the trenches of Peter's Woods. *Sorry*, he murmured, then summoned his memories, called on them with all his strength, for him, for Dorothy, the apple tree, the field of yellow grass, whose perfection he tried to describe to her despite the inadequacy of words to translate what sifts through the skin to inspire a human being. *The colours of childhood*, he added, *the shades of August*, revealing for the first time to the woman with whom he shared his life that memory of a lasting paradise.

They spent the evening surrounded by those colours, those odours mingling with that of the jam, steaks he grilled over charcoal, braised beans lightly impregnated with the taste from the coals, a taste of endless summer. Stan made up his mind to bury Zaza Mulligan for a few hours, to plant an apple tree over her grave in a yellow hayfield. He'd dig her up the next day, he knew it, or the day after, and would apply himself to other affairs while waiting for her to wake and deliver him a blow on the back of the neck, because she was the stuff of which boomerangs were made. Meanwhile he'd try to live, to breathe normally. He'd trim the vine, would along with his colleagues form a ring around frightened mares, he'd gain his heaven by passing through hell, since unbelievers like himself had no other destiny at hand but that of the damned.

You had to scour the woods and clean up this forest that had become a danger to children. The day after Zaza Mulligan's funeral, Saturday 29 July, a group of cottage owners gathered at the house of Victor Morgan, Sissy's father: Samuel Duchamp and Gilles Ménard, the men who'd led the police to Zaza Mulligan's body; Bob Lamar, Frenchie's father; Ted Jamison, a neighbour; Ed McBain, Morgan's best friend; and Gary Miller, a carpenter used to heavy work, along with his son Scott, a strapping seventeen-year-old a head taller than his father, who seemed determined to prove that he was as tough as anyone.

It was Vic Morgan, given the state of his daughter, in the throes of a revolt that left him feeling helpless, who'd decided to act. No other child would suffer the fate of Elisabeth Mulligan in the Boundary woods, no other young girl would lose her sister because of reckless risk-taking. After the funeral, as people went back to their cars with their heads down, he'd taken Bob Lamar aside and urged him to recruit Ménard and Duchamp. After what they'd witnessed, those men would be the first to want to rid the forest of its traps. For his part, he committed himself to bringing onside two or three volunteers.

On the morning of the 29th, Vic Morgan prepared

sandwiches, coffee, fruit juice, and waited for the others to arrive while Charlotte did her nails, repeating that this business would only get more people hurt, supposing there still were more traps in Peter's Woods. As far as she was concerned, Zaza had been the victim of a deplorable accident that had no chance of recurring. The proof was that no one before Zaza had been caught in any traps. If the forest had been full of them, other walkers, that Djill Menarde for instance, would long ago have left behind one of their limbs for the coyotes.

Charlotte was probably right. In these instances Charlotte's coldness was always right, but Vic Morgan's mind would only be at rest once every inch of Peter's Woods had been ransacked. He felt responsible for Zaza Mulligan's death, responsible for not having been there, for never having been there when the girls decided to get drunk, to show their legs to all and sundry, to throw their lives to the winds. But he couldn't share this feeling with Charlotte, who only noticed their daughter when she threw a tantrum, and who only remained with them because she would have been unable to live in a household where she couldn't oppose her indifference to the futile agitation of others. Charlotte was like that, her features were locked in an acrimony that only receded during the make-believe of social soirées, and there was no point in trying to change that. Too much reality would kill her.

When the men began to arrive, she went to her room. Vic had everyone sit around the big kitchen table to outline his plan. Bob Lamar, who knew some French thanks to his wife, did some rough translation when necessary, but the plan was clear. They would separate into groups of two, and each team would go through a sector with a fine-tooth comb, then they'd start in again the next day, hoping that new arrivals would join them in the meantime. Morgan had drawn up a map and numbered each of the sectors, starting at the lake and leading into the forest, beyond the various paths used by the children and adolescents. It was a large territory that a handful of men could never cover in one weekend, but all seemed determined to go the limit, to search every bush, to look under every pile of dead branches, every suspicious mound of earth. Their children's safety was at stake. If need be, they'd devote their next off-days to the task, until they were certain that Boundary was free of the traps set by Pete Landry, whom some began to call a bastard, a damn irresponsible moron, adding that Landry had sold his soul to the forest, and it had quite simply swallowed him up.

Sam Duchamp quite naturally teamed up with Gilles Ménard, as if Zaza Mulligan had created a bond, obliging them to stalk this evil side by side. They'd drawn sector three, the one with Juneau Hill, which Ménard knew well from having often explored it towards the end of the many summers he'd spent at Bondrée, when he got the urge to gorge himself on blueberries. He went there early in the morning, before the heat of the day, and in less than two hours filled a five-pound pot, eager for all that nature had to offer, every kind of aroma or food. He'd show Duchamp the spot, because there were enough berries for three or four pickers and as many bears. Before taking off, the men armed themselves with sticks to stab the ground, and agreed to meet at five o'clock at the campground, where they would plan for the next day.

Ménard and Duchamp searched all morning, talking little and stopping only to piss or to clean off their boots. They chewed on Morgan's sandwiches, thickly buttered, as they walked, made hungry by their climb and by their fear of missing a trap. At noon they stopped near the clearing, where several blueberry bushes were weighed down with the still-white fruits, and ate their own sandwiches while talking about the summer's passing, their wives, their children, unable to utter the word "trap," but thinking only of that, a jaw whose rust was covered in blood and pieces of skin. They were back on the job within twenty minutes, jabbing at the ground. Shortly after five o'clock they turned around without reaching the end of their sector, where they'd found only buckshot shells from the previous autumn.

At the appointed hour all the men were back at the campground, dirty, sweat-stained, their arms and necks covered in scratches and insect bites. Morgan offered a round of soft drinks and they took stock of the day around two picnic tables they'd pulled together, one of which was engraved with all the names of the young people who'd brought life to Boundary. No one had found a trap in his sector except Scott Miller, Gary's son, who'd found a rabbit trap that couldn't have dated from Landry's time. They were getting ready to share out the territory for the next day when they saw other men arriving, who'd heard about the search in the course of the day. At six-thirty, almost all the Boundary men were pacing the campground, even old Pat Tanguay, even Bill Cochrane, with his evil humour and his wooden leg. Jack and Ben Mulligan also joined the group, wanting to avenge their sister's death, to remove all trace of Peter Landry from this cursed forest.

Vic Morgan was moved by this massive arrival of men, fathers, brothers, and sons who refused to accept the shedding of blood, and he had to pull himself together. He bent his head and cleared his throat before speaking, something he had to do, since it had been decided that he was to be in charge of all the operations. By seven o'clock all the sectors had been mapped out and distributed among the teams come together over a glass of Coke or ginger ale. Each knew what was to be done the following day.

The second search day was hot, exhausting, and from the first to the thirteenth sector laid out by Morgan and Ménard the day before, you heard men snorting and swearing, men bursting out laughing, and sticks striking the earth or turning it over while the ferns rustled and the birds went silent, frightened by this invasion of animals grunting and slicing at the ground.

At the end of the afternoon those animals emerged from the woods, smelly and dirty, a thrush began to sing, and the campground was again overrun. With the consent of Conrad Plamondon, the owner, a few women had spread plastic cloths over the tables, where they'd set up cold drinks, little cakes made by Stella McBain, the pastry queen, sandwiches, macaroni and potato salads, stuffed eggs, waiting for the men's return the way you await that of soldiers. When, two by two, they came through the campground gate, the women rushed up, seeking news.

Almost all the sectors had been gone over, except those covering Moose Trap and its cliffs. As the majority of the men went back to work in the city during the week, the most fearless and athletic among them would head up there the following Saturday. While swallowing a sandwich or a little stuffed roll, they gave an account of the day. The hunt had not been good, which was in itself reassuring news, a sign that the past was not eternal and couldn't indefinitely cause harm to the present. Only Valère Grégoire and Henri Lacroix's team brought back a trophy, a bear trap similar to the one that had torn into Zaza Mulligan's leg. The contraption was instantly transferred to the back of

Grégoire's pickup, and he took responsibility for getting rid of it. Someone suggested that the police should be notified, but what could the police do with an old trap, since young Mulligan had died accidentally? Once this dismal object was out of sight, things became more relaxed, and they could all do justice to the meal prepared by the women in the kitchens of Hope Jamison and Jocelyne Ménard, where a mood of happy confusion had reigned all afternoon between the steaming dishes, the children slamming doors and wanting to taste, the gossip surrounding TV and film stars. One by one the plates and platters were emptied, the pitchers of fruit juice, the coolers filled with bottles submerged in ice water that cooled hot hands and damp brows. They discussed the baseball season and the performance of the Boston Red Sox while munching on sticks of celery. They talked about politics, gardening, woodcutting, forgetting little by little the drama at the source of this little gathering that was much like a village fair.

After the meal, the campground resembled a battlefield. The grass was flattened, paper plates littered the ground, along with plastic glasses and paper napkins the women gathered up before heading home on the arms of their husbands, their sons, their brothers. In all the Boundary cottages that night, that of the Lacroix, the Cochranes, the Jamisons, the Duchamps and the Maheux, they basked in the satisfaction of a job well done, treating themselves to a much-deserved beer. Even Florence Duchamp, who only drank at Christmas and New Year's, allowed herself a glass of Labatt 50 that reddened her cheeks and flushed the little circle, her third eye she said, laughing, that marred her otherwise white brow. Afterwards, all lights were turned off. Boundary and its children were able to sleep in peace.

Chauves-Souris Falls pours down on the west side of Moose Trap between Brian Larue's cottage and that of the Tanguays, where several streams converge to form Spider River, given that name by the woodcutters because of the way the water spreads wide as it flows down the mountain, more like a witch's messy head of hair than a spider once the leaves are down and you can see the channels carved out by the thaw. Despite all the prohibitions still being imposed on us, not to stray far from the cottages, not to take Otter Trail, nor Weasel Trail, not to scratch our noses after five o'clock, my parents agreed that I could spend the weekend at Emma's, after drawing up a list of dictates as long as the Green Giant's arms put end to end. Saturday night Emma led me to the falls, telling her father we were going to play in his cabin behind the cottage, while I scrunched the list sticking out of my pocket into a ball and swallowed it whole.

In bright daylight there was nothing threatening about the place, the water swirled to the foot of the falls and surged between the rocks of Spider River in a commotion that resembled a sustained round of applause. The sun set the wet stones to sparkling, and you could sometimes spot a fish working its way through the labyrinth. It was a place where life accelerated past the static trees, making you want to run, to leap from stone to stone, to plunge headfirst into the cascade of clear water. After nightfall, however, the ambience changed. There was no more applause, just gusts of wind at the very heart of the falls. In the black coulee opened up by the river there drifted eddies of foam, the only bright zones on moonless nights, looking like drool from the maw of a prehistoric animal. Among the trees lining the shore, you no longer wanted to run. You held your breath to pick out the forest's tangle of sounds, lost to the wind, captive to clamour.

About a hundred feet from shore, two recently fallen trees formed a shelter invisible from the path. That's where Emma led me, into this burrow where you had to bend double, your nose to your shoes, if you didn't want to scrape your head on the rough trunks. We would have been more comfortable in the open air, side by side on a log, but Emma saw spies everywhere. So we invented a new lotus position, the upside-down lotus, so as to be able to emerge with all our limbs intact, and we talked about the men who'd searched the mountain all day, armed with sticks and lances to scare off an animal with no name, a dead animal but one still roaring. Emma and I watched them entering the forest, wondering if they'd capture the animal and its babies, then we saw them come out towards the end of the afternoon, tired and dripping with sweat, as the barbecues were being lit. My father was with them, wearing an old hat like that of Pat Tanguay. I ran towards him with Emma, and stopped short when I saw that there was dried blood on his hands and clothes and on the hands of Gilles Ménard, whose pale face was back, the mask that he'd never lose altogether, with the folds at the corners of his eyes and mouth.

Emma's father, who'd been part of the search the previous Sunday, went to meet them to see what their hunt had turned up. My father immediately took him aside, probably to tell him where the blood came from, then he said goodbye to me, enjoy yourself mite, as if nothing was up. Before I had time to reply he turned his back with lightning speed, sent flying a few bits of gravel at his feet, and in a flash was out of sight behind Valère Grégoire's pickup, as filthy as his headwear. Brian Larue, who'd had a clear view of my father's evasive manoeuvre, took us into the cottage, Emma and me, repeating that there was nothing to worry about, that the blood was not blood, just mud from the red earth of the Moose Trap ravines, a clay that stained everything it touched, skin, hair, stream water. Might as well take us for a couple of twits.

Under the fallen trees at the Chauves-Souris Falls, Emma, half her hair twisted around a root, asked me if I'd seen Zaza Mulligan's blood, if I'd noticed traces of it on Gilles Ménard's shirt the night he'd arrived at our place all in a panic. We didn't for a minute believe Emma's father's explanations, which my father himself would have given us had they been true. The two men had conspired to keep us in the dark. All the adults had been lying to us for two weeks, just feeding us information from a tiny eyedropper good only for dim-witted Lilliputians, whenever we said something that made them afraid we were inventing any old thing. They wanted to protect us, but only succeeded in stoking the fears of some and the curiosity of others, who made up their own stories, their own versions of the facts. Emma and I, we belonged to the second category, those who dreamed up anything at all, preferring to rack our brains rather than to wait around like idiots for our parents to decide to talk to us. Huddled under the trees with Brownie, our eyes as wide as quarters, we were alert for sounds, for furtive movements in the high branches, conjuring outlandish stories in which Moose Trap in its turn conspired against men. In those stories, Pete Landry wasn't dead. He emerged at night from the flames licking at his shack, his arms in the air, lava flowing from his scorched lips, and kept on setting traps that were no longer meant for animals, but for young women called Tanager, Tanager of Bondrée, Zaza of Boundary. That's what our fathers were looking for in the forest, Tanager's traps.

After raising the possibility that the blood staining my father's hands was perhaps that of a young girl who'd lost consciousness in the jaws of a trap, we curled up to one another, not difficult to do given our cramped quarters, and observed the river in silence. In front of our shelter bats skimmed the black water, more restless than butterflies, sowing death so as not to die. For several minutes we watched the coming and going of the little animals that had lent their name to the falls, wondering if Brownie's growling was meant for the bats or some demon associated with the flight of those mammals found so often in horror stories. Emma didn't dare admit that she was afraid, me even less, but when Brownie darted out of the shelter for no apparent reason, we decided to go back before Emma's father discovered that we weren't in the cabin. Two hypocrites not wanting to admit that their teeth were starting to knock against their palates.

In the path winding towards the lake, following the twists and turns of the river, the bats stayed with us along with the roar of the waterfall, like a north wind moving us on in the midst of a storm but only showing itself in a nebulous billowing of the waves, captive to waters that would be torn to shreds when the falls could no longer contain its rage.

The night was clouded over and we could barely see two feet in front of us, forced to grope our way while the bats, better prepared than two girls for navigating in the dead of night, flitted about without encountering any obstacle. Where the path bordered a bog, one of Emma's running shoes got stuck in the mud and she had to go down on her knees to extricate it. Listen, she whispered, listen, I think someone's following us. Set on edge by his mistress's nervousness, or by what inspired it, Brownie emitted a weak yap and began growling again in the direction of the darkness that had closed in behind us. It's all in your head, I replied to reassure myself, but there really were sounds above the path that could as well have come from the tread of a man as of an animal. Put on your shoe, we're getting out of here, I whispered in my turn, then there was a loud crack, too loud to have been caused by the flight of a hare or a raccoon. Brownie, who was also scared stiff, then started to bark wildly, a sign that we were right to be afraid. *Run, Emma, run!* And we ran, tripping over roots, stones, mounds of earth, until we finally saw the gleam of the lake. *Run, Emma, faster!* Brownie on our heels, we burst into the cottage, where Brian Larue was preparing two glasses of Quik to take to us in Emma's cabin. He asked us where we'd come from like that, and Emma said nowhere, we'd just been running for the fun of it, and we'd drink our Quik in her room.

We quickly changed into our pyjamas, hid our dirty clothes under the bed, and five minutes later, seated cross-legged on the quilt embroidered by Emma, we swallowed our Quik while checking the noises outside, louder now as the wind had risen. It was Pete Landry, Emma finally blurted out, and I agreed, even if I was no longer sure that this story of the living dead held any water. For an hour or two we tried to imagine the creature that had pursued us, describing its gaze, its mouth and its black teeth, going over our progress from the falls to the bog, looking for clues, noises to which we'd paid no attention, then fatigue got the better of our fears, and the wind, in Emma's room, finally died down.

I've often thought back on that night, wondering if someone really was watching us from afar, a man, a stalker of Tanager, but I'll never know, no more than I'll know if the pictures that come back to me are the same as those seen by the bats or if they belong only to childhood fears. All the same, when from my window I see darkness fall, I tell myself that the very existence of those pictures, and the very persistence in my memory of that cracking of dry wood, attest to something real that nothing will ever be able to refute.

When Gilles Ménard spotted the fox, a low grunt came out of his throat, a growl that had him stepping backwards, frightened by the hollow sound he'd not been able to repress, itself triggered by fear, elemental and instinctive, a reflex shutting down thought and commanding you to flee. Unable to take one step more, he lifted his left arm to tell Sam Duchamp to stop, and pointed to the animal.

A fox, said Duchamp, then he went to get closer, but Ménard stopped him, seeing only the animal's redness, the hair on the moss, the thread of blood following the lie of the land. No, it's not a fox, he whispered in a dead voice. It's not a damn fox, Sam, look, he implored, placing himself in front of Duchamp to be sure he was real, and above all to keep him away from the animal that was just another ruse of Peter's Woods, a mad deception born of the play of shadow and light. When they'd go close they'd see the skin, the legs, the bare belly. They'd see the watch circling the thin arm, and would know that the fox was only a mirage. Go call the police, he added, but Duchamp didn't move. Gently, he eased Ménard to the side and approached the animal, a fox of that year, almost cut in two by the trap's jaws.

The death was still recent, the blood still fresh, the last gasps almost palpable. No need for the police, Duchamp muttered, going back to Ménard, who'd given him a fright a few moments ago when he came out with that groan, a sound he'd never heard, a kind of rasp that idiots might make, and he was scaring him almost as much now, totally motionless, his gaze frozen, fixed on the red tail.

Wake up, Gilles, it's just a fox.

It's only a fox, mimicked Ménard, only a poor fox, then his shoulders were wracked with trembling, his eyes filled with tears and he burst out laughing, goddamn Ménard, sometimes you give me a pain, and his laugh went manic, became a series of yelps and bleats he couldn't stop, goddamn Ménard, goddamn idiot, and Duchamp started laughing too, happy to see Ménard coming down to earth, laughing like crazy, his stomach cramped and his nose running, goddamn Ménard, goddamn idiot. Then their laughter stopped bit by bit and Ménard went to vomit behind a tree.

When he came back, his face had gone numb again, but at least he could talk. Have to take care of it, he said, pointing to the animal with his chin, have to bring back the trap. He walked up to the fox with Duchamp, who was still sniffling, unwilling to wipe his nose on his sleeve. Kneeling next to the fox, they each took hold of one end of the trap, reproaching themselves for being dumb, not having brought along gloves, and they managed to pry it open, sweat on their brows, preferring not to look at the wound from which viscera were spilling, but Ménard saw all the same, he saw the torn skin, Sugar Baby's entrails, he saw the tibia of a young girl with long legs and the nails painted pink near a pink satin ribbon, a modish colour that you didn't find deep in the woods. He saw Zaza Mulligan running along the shore, he saw life and death, birds gliding, mutilated birds, he saw his little Marie in a field of pale grass, a dog sprightly as a cloud following her close.

We can't leave it there either, he mumbled. And so the two of them dug a hole in the soft earth, a hole the size of a fox, and they left with the trap, silent, looking for other traps.

Back at their meeting place, Ménard entrusted the trap to Valère Grégoire so he could dispose of it, and thought of Marie, his tiny Marie seeing the blood on his hands that he hadn't washed, then the look of Andrée Duchamp, Sam's daughter, who came to meet her father with little Emma Larue and stopped cold on seeing the blood. Instinctively, he stuffed his hands into his pockets and moved off, as if it were possible to hide blood that had burned itself into someone's eyes. After the two children had left, he went down to the lake, took off his shoes, and walked in until the water covered him entirely. Marie would not see that blood, never. Marie would never stop running.

A bit later the men separated, shaken by the thought of an animal sacrificed to no purpose, but animated by a feeling that binds you to your fellows in a time of misfortune. Zaza Mulligan's death had changed Boundary's landscape, leading people who barely talked to one another to stand together, to slap each other on the back and offer encouragement, *fucking Morgan*, goddamn Lacroix, trading languages and curses, exchanging recipes for Rice Krispies squares. Nothing would be the same from now on. You'd wave from one porch to another, you'd honk while passing Duchamp making his turn around the lake on his bicycle, go Duchamp, you can do it, you'd borrow screwdrivers and cups of sugar, and the children, come the night, would no longer whisper the name of Tanager, Tanager of Bondrée, in flight before the hissing of the waves.

Kneeling next to Zaza Mulligan's unconscious body, the man took his head in his hands to silence the sound of shells bursting inside his skull, to cover the screams of the girl, another whore, another Maggie Harrison, screams blending with those of his barracks mate, Jim Latimer, the best poker player in the 1st Infantry Division of Uncle Sam's army. *Shut up!*

Then he spat on the young girl's face, *take that, you little bitch*, before renaming her Marie and lifting her in his arms, *sweet girl, sweet Marie, sweet Tanager of Boundary*, to carry her to the trap he'd unearthed for her from out of the spongy forest soil.

And light, so light in the man's arms, Zaza Mulligan saw the sky through her lashes, the sky between the branches, and the stars on high spread their wings, unsealing her smile at the same time: the sky between her lips. Just before losing consciousness again, feeling the cold iron on her right leg, she thought of Sissy and described to her the firmament above, the birds dancing. *A bunch... a flight... Sissy, a cloud of flickering birds*, a scattering of birds and luminous winds. A flight of silent owls. Then her voice was but a breath. *I saw... Sissy... a flight of flickering doves*. And death eclipsed the night.

# SISSY

## DAY 1

The last time anyone saw Sissy Morgan, she was going down Snake Hill kicking her feet in front of her, looking haggard, her hair dishevelled, her red eyes dry at last. Summer's colours had been back for some days, its sounds and smells, along with children's laughter, for how to stop a summer season from blossoming under the sun? People still thought about Zaza, but thought of her as a forewarning, as with all senseless deaths that awaken us to the perilous privilege of being alive. Only those close to the young girl were still blind to the summer, which was, however, very much there, its greens and blues blending together in the light.

Then one evening people saw Vic Morgan circling the lake shouting out his daughter's name. His hair was wild, his shirt open, there was saliva at the corners of his lips. He was then heard knocking at the Mulligans' door, at that of the McBains, the Lamars, the Millers, an anxious parent talking fast, in a halting and panicky voice. Sissy had left the house that morning and had still not returned, even though she'd eaten nothing, not even drunk the café au lait he'd prepared for her. Before Zaza Mulligan's death Morgan would not have run like that, but now he knew death ran faster than he did, and he was afraid the whore had caught up with Sissy and her red eyes to throw her from a cliff, under a car, off the end of a dock. He saw Sissy's body thrown up by the waves, he saw his daughter sinking, stones tied to her feet, stones tumbling onto the back of her neck, and he felt himself propelled along with her into a rush of white water bearing away his sanity with all the rest.

Before Zaza Mulligan's death, one would also have tried to reassure Morgan, saying his daughter would soon return, that she was the sort of girl to disappear at the drop of a hat, you know, *that kind of girl.* That night, however, they listened to Morgan in silence. A few people even went to see him, saying they'd have a look around and question their neighbours. At nine-thirty, as Sissy was still missing, the men pulled on their jackets, embraced their wives, whose eyes were fixed on the dark lake, and soon you could see the beams from their flashlights coming together, wavering among the birch and aspen leaves, then moving off into the woods as they cried Sissy's name, Sissy Morgan.

Florence Duchamp toyed with the belt of her dressing gown while watching her husband Sam depart, Stella McBain insisted that Ed wear his windbreaker, *the nights are getting cold*, Marie Lacroix emptied out her kitchen drawers, turned the room upside down looking for Henri's flashlight batteries, and they all waited, what else could they do, as they stared out at the black water.

Around two o'clock, Stella McBain heard hurried steps coming towards the cottage. Ed burst in with Ben Mulligan on his heels, and he picked up the telephone without paying any attention to Stella, who was riddling him with questions in a shrill voice she couldn't recognize as hers, *What's happening, Edward? For God's sake, what's happening?* Then the word "again" resounded in the cottage, and Stella McBain collapsed into the rocking chair, which in its turn creaked out *again, again, again* . . .

Before sunrise, this Sunday 13 August, it was almost bright in Boundary, because all the lights, from Ménard Bay and along the shore to where Moose Trap came down, lit up one by one. There were also lamps outside that shifted about lazily, came together, moved apart. A swarm of artificial suns. And there were flashing lights, sweeping red across stunned faces.

Stan Michaud was not watching *Bonanza* when the telephone rang. He was dreaming that he was falling, plunged into an endless descent, like James Stewart in the Alfred Hitchcock film he'd seen with Dorothy in Portland during one of those weekends he still allowed himself a few years ago, far from the house, between motel sheets smelling of bleach, then Dorothy's perfume, then his own musky odour of which he was a bit ashamed, but into which Dorothy, sighing, buried her face, at the same time easing his embarrassment. The ringing crept into his dream like distant music, a mallet rapidly descending the bars of a xylophone. It invaded his world and he came down to earth. It was an abrupt drop, making him feel like he was falling outside himself, then he opened his eyes and picked up the phone on the bedside table, where it sat shuddering, while Dorothy moaned softly by his side. How could she sleep when that ringing could have awakened the dead?

Caught up in his dream, he had trouble grasping what the agitated voice on the other end of the line was telling him, that of Anton Westlake, the youngest of his colleagues, who for that reason drew the night shift more often than not. After a few moments he understood that Westlake was talking about Boundary, Boundary Pond, where another accident had taken place. *Again, chief,* added Westlake, waiting for his superior's reaction, but Michaud remained silent. He knew, he'd always known that one day he'd get a phone call from Cusack or Westlake announcing the boomerang's return. Wake Cusack, Michaud finally ordered, I'll be by to pick him up in ten minutes. And send an ambulance and a doctor to the site.

Beside him, Dorothy's moans had mutated into a gentle snoring, like the complaints of a dreaming dog, an animal that runs in its sleep, fleeing an evil shadow or struggling against its materialization. Almost every night, Dottie changed into a dog in flight. When he feared that those groans, more insistent, were inciting the dream animal to sink its teeth into itself, he gently nudged Dorothy, caressed her shoulder, and the snoring stopped even as the cadence of her breathing remained erratic.

He'd wake her before leaving, to calm the troubled animal in her breast, and above all so she wouldn't be anxious on seeing his side of the big bed empty.

Seven minutes after two, he murmured, lighting his bedside lamp, it's going to be a long day, then he pulled on his pants and shirt, grabbed the jacket with his ID, and gently shook Dorothy's shoulder. What time is it? she mumbled. It's time for me to turn in my badge, thought Michaud, and to let younger people dirty their hands and bring home to their houses the smell of rot that clings to the soles of your shoes. *Late,* he replied, but was it late or early? You never knew, in the middle of the night, if you should refer to the day before or the day to come.

If he'd had the choice, he'd have preferred that the previous day could have lingered on, a quiet evening spent reading, gazing at the stars, finishing a crossword puzzle. So he said "late," though he really meant early, very early on the morning of a day that would have no end. Go back to sleep, he added, before planting a kiss on Dorothy's brow, and heading to the bathroom. His eyes were puffy and his beard was starting to blacken his cheeks, but he had no time to shave. He plunged his face into cold water, rinsed out his mouth, and that was it, he was ready to leave.

A light dew covered the grass, the car, the flowers, the whole world. He hoped, selfishly, that Laura, Cusack's wife, would have made coffee for them, as she sometimes did. He shivered as he inserted the key in the ignition, and drove off. He saw no lights in house windows on the way to Cusack's, except in those of widow Maxwell, who had suffered from insomnia ever since the death of her husband, Horace Maxwell, fallen from a scaffolding when he went to pick up a stupid nail: *what have you done, honey?* Picturing Maxwell's plunge, he remembered his dream, that sensation of tumbling into a void where there was no sense of air pressure or wind brought on by his movement. He'd read an article, not long ago, about children's dreams, in which the body was propelled towards the tops of trees or swept up on a swing, higher, higher still, *push me Mom*, then was launched into a soundless sky where mothers' arms no longer existed. Was that what Zaza Mulligan experienced when she fell in the forest, that solitude where there was no sustaining arm on which to lean?

Since he'd hung up the phone, he'd tried not to think of Zaza, nor of the drama that had just taken place in Boundary. Since Westlake had not given him any details, other than that someone was dead and that the police had to act quickly, he preferred to wait, hoping that the victim was an elderly man or woman, someone who'd had time to look backwards many times before seeing the end draw near.

Parking at Cusack's he honked his horn, a short little toot just to announce that he'd arrived. He might at the very least give his man the time to take a piss. Laura, Cusack's wife, half-opened the door to tell him that Jim wouldn't be long, then he appeared, his shoulders hunched, with a thermos and plastic cups, just as Michaud had hoped. Thank Laura, he said, accepting the cup Cusack held out to him, and he took the time to swallow a few mouthfuls before putting the car in gear.

A dirty business, mumbled Cusack, but the roar of the motor covered his voice. He didn't know any more than Michaud what awaited them, what kind of death they were going to find. But he couldn't stop Zaza Mulligan's body from creeping into his thoughts, with her matted hair and her long legs. He'd never confessed to Michaud that, since he'd followed Gilles Ménard and Sam Duchamp into the forest, his nights were filled with nightmares in which it wasn't Zaza stretched out on the carpet of moss, but his wife, Laura, murmuring *sorry, Jim*, through her closed lips as she sank into the ground repeating *sorry, sorry, sorry*, until her whole body was swallowed up except for a long lock of red hair. Except Laura didn't have red hair, and that lock of hair frightened him even more than the burying of the body, he didn't know why, as if Laura were becoming Zaza, as if Laura didn't exist. He would have liked to tell Michaud about his nightmares, but he couldn't find the words, didn't know how to talk, never could express what was tormenting him, ever since, when he was little, he'd heard goblins gnawing away in his closet.

Women weren't so complicated. They sat in front of a tea or coffee and talked about their dreams and disappointments without ever having the feeling that they were exposing or betraying that part of themselves that they could only communicate clumsily. They didn't have that pride that blew relatively banal things way out of proportion. And they knew how to laugh. He remembered going by his house to pick up a file one afternoon when Dorothy was visiting Laura. The two women, Laurie and Dottie, were sitting at the kitchen table, laughing with tears running down their cheeks. He'd asked what was so funny, and Laura had held out in front of her a glass of pink alcohol, sputtering it's Canon Kir, Canon *My Ass*, and the laughter burst forth even louder, for nothing, for a stupid joke, because they'd simply had to let themselves go. He envied the two women's friendship that transcended their difference in age, the youth of Dottie when she was with Laura, the seriousness of Laura when Dottie couldn't hide the deep lines in her face. He'd never experienced such complicity with his chief, nor with any man, and wondered how it was getting old, if you got ugly when you had no one to whom you could confess your fear of dying or of not being able to get it up, if you had no one to whom you could vent the spleen that locks up your jaws if everything stays inside.

*Some more coffee, chief?* And Michaud, also lost in thought, held out his cup. They'd barely left Cusack's house, and he had the feeling they'd never get to Boundary. What with nothing around, he'd turned on the siren and the flashing lights to give himself the illusion of going faster, as it was impossible to accelerate on those hilly, winding roads. He'd probably wake some people in a few isolated houses, but what was one or two hours less sleep as long as you were alive.

Coming out of Rockwood, they saw two deer crossing the road, their eyes widened by the bright headlights. Michaud had to swerve to avoid them, and in so doing he spilled his coffee. The car's tires dug into the gravel on the shoulder, a few branches brushed across the windshield, and he gave a hard jerk to the steering wheel to get the car back on track. Unnerved by the speed with which it all happened, he stopped the car to mop his brow and pull himself together. Behind them, the deer had made it back into the forest, they wouldn't be joining the dead animals you often saw lying in the ditch. *Sorry*, mumbled Michaud, his heart beating wildly in his chest, because he'd perhaps come close to his death himself, his and that of his partner, who was not now thinking about death, but about the fact that people around him were always excusing themselves, *sorry*, while their only fault was to be mortal. Michaud had manoeuvred well, he didn't have to feel guilty. Still, they'd come close to flying into the woods and having their bodies end up between white sheets, surrounded by the smells of medicine and sickness.

Cusack replied to Michaud's faint *sorry* by assuring him that he'd done fine, a real pro, and then they went silent. What could you add that wasn't irrelevant, under the circumstances? Still, Michaud was surprised by Cusack's recent reticence. Not long ago he'd have felt impelled to make a joke, to tell a story about deer and squealing tires, but he'd confined himself to reassuring Michaud and handing him a rag from the glove compartment so he could wipe his shirt. Zaza Mulligan had found the chink in Cusack's armour, and had used it to pass through the breach leading to his heart. All the police go there sooner or later, all the bright ones, but Michaud couldn't help feeling a certain compassion for his deputy, who'd just lost his virginity, in a sense, along with his protective shell, and didn't yet know that beneath that old skin another shell would grow, harder to penetrate, it had to happen, because if you were in mourning for your virginity you either changed jobs or you stuck the barrel of your gun down your throat.

They were just about to get back on the road when the ambulance Westlake had called passed them. Michaud took off immediately and followed the other vehicle, whose tail lights at times vanished around a curve, swallowed up by the night, to reappear when the road straightened through the forest. Michaud kept his eyes on those lights while thinking of his childhood, the lights on the tractors in the fields when you had to cut the hay before the rain, of his first patrols along the border, with the smugglers' lights blinking weakly between the trees, swallowed up by darkness, as had been the tractors over the hill, the throbbing of whose engines was itself muted. He thought of the laughable way in which those lights only deepened the night's mystery, amplifying man's puniness at the heart of that darkness. And he also felt small, lost on this road and hurtling towards the abyss, at the wheel of a vehicle wailing away that a disaster had just befallen some among us, though countless dramas occurred in the forest to which no attention was drawn, no flashing lights and no sirens.

Just before Boundary, the ambulance driver stopped at an intersection, not knowing whether to go left or right, allowing Michaud to wrench himself away from his thoughts. Abruptly, he changed lanes and passed the ambulance, signalling to the driver that he would lead the way, as Michaud knew where he was going, he knew it only too well, he was going where no one wanted to go, to one of those places where only men stupid enough to be cops headed in the middle of the night, while others slept and dreamed they were falling or sleeping with Elizabeth Taylor or Sophia Loren. He drove for two or three miles along a secondary road, then he put on his flashers for the benefit of the ambulance and turned onto Boundary Road after he had switched off his siren, which could neither speed up nor slow down the flow of time. Now all he had to do was let himself be guided by the glow down below, where the flashlights described a shifting shape, breathing to the pulse of a wounded animal.

Gary Miller came to meet them, waving his light to show them where to park farther down. Miller looked like someone who'd lost his dog, his eyes sombre and his jaw set, ready to strike out at anyone who uttered the dog's name. *It's over there,* he told the police, directing his light towards the undergrowth, then without a word he guided them through the branches, the dead trees, the young firs choking off each other's air. Behind them, the ambulance workers, with their stretchers, cursed the branches under their breath, while the doctor accompanying them, the same one who had pronounced Zaza Mulligan dead, wondered what he was doing again in this unhappy wood. After about ten minutes they came out into a clearing where other men were gathered, most at the edge of the trees, on the periphery, and one last one on his knees in the centre of the clearing, Vic Morgan, holding in his arms a limp body he was rocking in time with his prayers, *open your eyes, Sissy darling, tell me something,* prayers that rose up like a song of love in the cool darkness.

No one dared to go near, no one dared to interrupt that song to go and place his hand on Morgan's shoulder and tell him that his daughter would never again open her eyes. All were motionless, even Ed McBain, Morgan's closest friend, waiting for a sign from him, waiting for dawn, a bit of real light in the clearing. *Stay here,* Michaud ordered Cusack, the doctor, and the ambulance workers, and he crossed the invisible barrier separating Morgan from the other men, because that was what was expected of a chief inspector, that he wade into the mud, where no one wants to go. That's why he was paid, so he could serve as confessor, go-between, or advance guard, that he turn himself into a kamikaze when the situation required an imbecile to throw himself from a bridge to help another imbecile. He was called in extremis as soon as there was a bit of blood and broken glass, then he was scorned if he dared to stop you for speeding, so as to prevent more glass shards from glistening on the wet road. That was his role, to endure the contempt and walk through the mud, so he told those around him not to move, *stay here*, and he went to kneel in front of Morgan.

Seeing Sissy, whose head was resting in the hollow of Vic Morgan's arms, Michaud almost fell backwards, and had to repress the question that was pushing him away: *what the hell?* Sissy Morgan, whom he'd seen whole a few days earlier, had no hair. Someone had sliced away her long mane and her skull was now covered with only a few scattered tufts, like the bald heads of ancient dolls. But Sissy's wholeness had not just been violated by an absence of hair. Below her left knee her long leg had disappeared, severed by the trap, torn away by the dry clack of rusted metal.

Michaud's first feeling was not one of compassion, but of anger. Who could be so demented as to attack an innocent child in that way? For a moment he just wanted to drive from this damn clearing all the men planted there like stakes a sledgehammer had pounded into the soft ground, not daring to talk, not daring to smoke, and to leave Morgan with his daughter, to leave him alone, goddammit, leave him bloody well alone, since nothing would be able to bring back that child, but then he grabbed hold of himself. If they left Morgan with Sissy, they'd find him totally insane in a few hours. He'd already aged ten years, maybe more, how to know when time hurls itself into the void, and he seemed already blind. His scorched gaze swept across the night without seeing it, searing away in turn the shapes, the shadows, the men who were no longer there. He didn't see Michaud either, considering him an object whose presence was as insignificant as a speck of dust on his shoulder, and he kept on singing, *Sissy my darling, Sissy my love.* Michaud let him rock his child for a bit longer, while trying to master the rage tautening his nerves under his skin, then he bent over him. *She's dead*, he managed to murmur, in defiance of the damn lump turning somersaults deep in his throat. He wanted to take the young girl from Morgan's arms, but Morgan came out with a hoarse noise, a kind of bark, and he tightened his grip around Sissy, crushing her limp arms, crushing her breast, a dog refusing to let go of its bone.

Fighting his desire to leave the man in peace, Michaud repeated *she's dead*, signalling to Ed McBain, who was holding himself ready to intervene, to grab hold of Morgan while he pulled his daughter out of his arms. A dirty job, a cop's job. *She's dead, Vic*, McBain murmured in his turn, *she's dead*, because there was nothing else to say, *dead, for Christ's sake*, then he seized Morgan's shoulders, who crumpled, letting slip from his knees Sissy's limp body, which rolled onto the ground, *dead, Sissy, indeed,* her tufts of hair pointing at the starry sky and her neck curiously bent.

While Michaud gently turned over Sissy's remains, *who, Sissy, why?*, ashamed of having lifted up her father's arms, McBain helped Morgan to stand and led him off, *come on, Vic, come on*, his eyes brimming with tears and his voice thick. Vic Morgan, now, didn't resist. He held Sissy in his blinded eyes, his arms still tensed beneath the weight of the absent body. The doctor then came over, leaving his thermos with its coffee at the foot of a tree, lamps were brought in, and the inspection of the body, the site, was able to begin, with

Cusack bombarding the scene with flashes from his camera, a Polaroid that had cost a fortune and had made a big hole in Michaud's budget.

Sissy Morgan, it appeared, had succumbed to the same kind of wound as Zaza Mulligan. The same in life, the same in death, with the difference that this time the trap had severed the left leg, whose lower section lay a few steps from the corpse. A man who came up to position his light at the side, along the perimeter marked out by Cusack, fought back a strangled cry when he saw the end of the leg and the foot, a high-pitched sigh that caught in his throat, and he went to vomit far from Sissy, splattering his shoes and his pants. Along with the vomit, out came a groan, like that of Vic Morgan. Everyone there lowered their heads, unable to groan in their turn, to expel the breath on which they were choking.

As for Michaud, he was trying to deflect the paths of boomerangs that were zeroing in from every direction, coming together to form an instrument whose blades slashed into his raw flesh. He'd known they'd return, he'd known that instinctively, as soon as he'd had to give up watching the end of *Bonanza* three weeks earlier. And with them there returned the young girls, Esther Conrad, Zaza Mulligan, their faces superimposed on that of Sissy Morgan, all three pallid, all three victims of the rage beauty can inspire, because there was no doubt in Michaud's mind that Sissy had been murdered, from which he deduced that Zaza Mulligan had suffered the same fate, dragged by force onto a path she didn't want to take. The horror before his eyes could not have resulted from a banal coincidence.

That was what the medical examiner thought as well, as did all the men gathered under the cold sky, that the past couldn't strike twice with the same precision. Zaza

Mulligan, just like Sissy Morgan, had not stepped on her own into the trap between whose jaws she'd spilled her blood. Sometimes you needed a second death to explain the cause of the first, Michaud thought to himself, looking upon the pale face of Sissy Morgan, now identical to Zaza's, two sisters, two silenced twins. You needed that mirror image, that concurrence of motives, that perfect overlapping of two distant events so as to understand, too late, that the first prefigured the one that would explain it. Sissy Morgan's end shone a terrible clarity on that of Zaza Mulligan, which all the men present would have preferred not to see: Pete Landry's traps came out of the earth, but it was not a dead man who had disinterred them. A killer roamed Boundary's woods.

The anguish, the tension, were palpable in the silences and the sniffling, but you also sensed the slow ascension of rage. They were seeking a motive, a reason for this carnage beyond the two girls' provocative beauty, Zaza's navel, the cut of Sissy's white shorts. Those illicit thoughts had to be cast out in the light of these killings, and now a loathing set in, the desire to strike down and pummel to death, the men's feeling of impotence magnifying their anger exponentially.

Michaud saw this dark energy as an electric current connecting the men, fathers, brothers, fearful in the knowledge that there was a monster on the loose who could act again. He knew that sooner or later a meltdown would come, and people would start suspecting a neighbour, a son, a brother, if the killer was not caught soon. The tension abroad in the clearing was nothing compared to the undercurrent of suspicion that would run through Boundary from one end to the other as of the next night, and he feared the worst, the projection of shame onto an object without face or body. If he wanted to sort out this affair before people went at each others' throats, he needed calm, he had to deal with Sissy, *who, Sissy, why?*

While the medical examiner raised up the dead girl's hand with a delicacy he must have reserved only for women whose acquiescence was now complete, Michaud asked Cusack to send someone for reinforcements. They'd need them for a meticulous search of the site, because Michaud wanted every square inch of this cursed clearing and all the paths leading up to it to be gone over with a fine-tooth comb, even if the men had to sleep in the open and survive on spruce sap for the next ten days. His rage was seething inside his chest, and he'd sworn, as soon as he saw the heart-breaking and macabre tableau formed by Vic Morgan and his daughter, that no such tableau would ever again take on life before his eyes.

As Cusack gave orders to Scott Miller, who went to summon the reinforcements and bring them back, Michaud left the body to thank the exhausted men for their help, and asked them to go home, explaining that the affair was now in the hands of the police, and their presence would only cover the tracks, of which there were already too many, would tramp possible clues into the ground, in short, sow confusion in an operation that he wanted to be as precise as clockwork. He did, however, omit the last remark, while asking them to remain in Boundary with their families until he gave them permission to leave. There were some protests, a few men wanting to help in the investigation, others having only one thought in their heads, to pull their wives and children out of their beds as soon as they got back, throw them into their car along with the dog, the cat, the canary, the youngest's collection of duck feathers, the eldest's record player, and break camp before dawn. Several voices were raised at the same time, forgetting the respect due to the dead, and Michaud could make out nothing in this jumble of languages out of which curses emerged from two worlds where resentment was articulated by mocking an array of sacred entities, finding common cause, ultimately, in blaspheming the figure of Christ.

Bob Lamar, who was part of the group that had found Sissy, and who was acting as interpreter, fortunately came to his aid, wiping his red eyes fiercely with his hand, and confusing the names of Frenchie, his daughter, and Sissy, the deceased. Despite the anguish eating away at him, Lamar supported Michaud, and he was able to persuade the men to go home to sleep, knowing that none of them would in fact sleep that night, and perhaps not the next night either, because Zaza Mulligan's long legs would from now on be curled around the severed leg of Sissy Morgan, fouling their sheets with a thick liquid to which would be glued some strands of knifed-off hair. Only Ed McBain stayed behind to watch over Vic Morgan, who refused to leave Sissy, and to prevent him from decapitating himself with the trap that had killed his daughter, his only child.

After the others left, a strange calm descended on the clearing. At the edge of the woods, Ed McBain waited beside Vic Morgan's slumped body, the stretcher-bearers withdrew to the opposite side, waiting for a sign from the medical examiner or Michaud to carry the body away, and Cusack swept the ground with his flashlight, seeking a bit of truth among the dozens of footprints pressed into the wet grass. At the centre of it all were the medical examiner and Sissy, the face of one caught in a halo of white light, the other lit three-quarters. An unreal scene in a world too hard-edged. Michaud came near and saw the medical examiner's lips moving, as if he was reciting a prayer. But he wasn't praying, he never prayed, certain that the body he was cutting up had never possessed any other soul than the one delusively generated by the mechanics of the heart and brain. On the contrary, he was reciting a poem, a pagan prayer exalting the power of death, and mourning the tenuousness of the beauty there before it. *"How with this rage shall beauty hold a plea / Whose action is no stronger than a flower?"*

Shakespeare, he told Michaud, when he saw that he was being observed, then he added that there was no more he could do here, he had to take the body to the morgue where his instruments awaited him. Michaud replied that he could soon leave, but that he first needed a few minutes with the young girl before the stretcher-bearers intervened. He wanted to gather his thoughts in her presence, to try to make her talk. The medical examiner didn't react, he knew the dead talked. So he left Michaud with Sissy, who would reveal secrets to him as well when he came to examine her internal organs. He withdrew to smoke, repeating a few lines from a poem that had come back to him when he had once again noted the fragility of a man's bones: *"Since brass, nor stone, nor earth... can vanquish death."*

As for Michaud, he performed the same ritual as not long before. He knelt next to Sissy and asked her who, how, why? suddenly ashamed to be presenting himself before her in a coffee-stained shirt. On the young girl's face some tears had flowed, whose sinuous path you could see in the thin film of dust covering her cheeks. As according to the medical examiner the trap's bite had resulted in an immediate loss of consciousness, the tears must have preceded the wound, and the dust as well. And so they were caused by the aggressor, by the fear he'd provoked, along with, perhaps, useless supplications, useless imprecations, "son of a bitch!" He could well imagine Sissy Morgan calling the murderer everything under the sun, flinging her fury in his face, a meagre consolation because murderers listen to nothing, not insults and not prayers. Their will is impervious, their intentions firm. *Who?* he repeated, looking for marks on her skin, scratches, a stone heart in a closed hand, then he saw a letter, an M or a W traced in the dirt covering the blood on her elbow. He called Cusack immediately to ask him if he saw the same thing. A bird, like children draw, replied Cusack, unable to detect an initial in the blurred mark. But Michaud held to his guns, it was a letter scrawled by Sissy, that would perhaps reveal the identity of the murderer, William, Walter, Mark, or Michael. Cusack didn't dare contradict him, the chief needed clues, messages to grab onto. He knew the story of young Esther Conrad's stone heart, which some had used to mock Michaud. He'll end up seeing the Virgin Mary appear beside a corpse, one of his colleagues joked one day. Cusack defended Michaud, whose fervent desire to see some sign on the skin of the dead was not at all laughable. The chief inspector was looking for monsters, and thought he could find traces of them in his victims' final silence. In the present instance, Cusack distinguished neither an M or a W on Sissy Morgan's arm. He thought of a crooked line left by a branch or a stone, but who could say whether Michaud might be right, whether the murderer's name wasn't Warren or Mitch? Take a few photos, Michaud told him, and the Polaroid's flash sizzled once more in the night, after which Michaud thanked Sissy, *thanks for the letter, Sissy*, and signalled to the stretcher-bearers that they could do their work.

One could already see a glow rising up behind the trees, a yellow glow confirming that summer was not over, when the black-wrapped body left the clearing, followed by Ed McBain and Victor Morgan, who was not only blind but deaf, deaf and mute. Shortly afterwards the reinforcements arrived, the ground was divided into four sectors, the birds awoke, the sun rose, but neither Michaud nor Cusack felt the warmth. They were thinking of the severed leg sitting in a black sheet near to Sissy, they were thinking of shorn hair, they were thinking of Morgan and the killer, who was perhaps even now stalking a third prey.

On the dark veranda, my mother stared at the lake while toying nervously with the belt of her dressing gown. Five minutes earlier, my father had passed by to exchange his sandals for his hiking boots, had filled his flask with cold water, and had left with Bob to join the men gathered at the foot of Côte Croche. After Zaza Mulligan's death, my brother declared that he was a man, and no one could stop him from doing what men do. So he got himself a flashlight and joined the first group, which you could see from my bedroom window, five or six nervous men to whom more would soon be added, because there was a new drama now, Sissy Morgan had disappeared. Her father had arrived at suppertime, his hair as wet as if he'd been running under a fine rain, it was all stuck to his temples. He talked with my father, then he said to me, *look, Aundrey, look everywhere*, his hoarse voice all shaky. He also asked Bob, my mother, the neighbours, and all of Bondrée, *look, please, look for Sissy.*

My mother let me skip dessert and go searching with Sandra Miller, who'd burst into our yard at the same time as her father and Scott, her giant of a brother. I rushed outside pursued by the insistent tick-tock of Sissy's watch, and her voice, troubling as that of her father's when faced with the mysterious designs of God, begging me to find her friend.

*Look, Aundrey, look everywhere.* Sandra might well have been older and wiser than me, don't stray an inch from Sandra, my mother said, in a fit of heartfelt, crazy love, but she was still a hundred times more of a pain in the neck, maybe because she was almost as old as Sissy and Zaza, the age when you disappear on a dark night. Whatever the case may be, I had to jostle her a bit to drag her towards the hypothetical nowhere of Sissy, *come on, Sandra,* we haven't all night. Once away, we looked everywhere we could, everywhere we were allowed to go. All I found though was Bobine, the doll my sister had lost at the beginning of summer, which had crawled, it seemed, under the pile of boards stacked up behind the Ménards' cottage. It was pretty messed up, but still in a state where it could live the life of a doll.

At nightfall, after the clattering of dishes, after the bathing suits had been taken down from the lines stretched between two trees and replaced by wet dishtowels, no one had yet found anything, not Sissy nor any trace of Sissy. The sun had just set behind Moose Trap when the men decided to head into the woods, when my father came by to change his shoes, when the women started to watch the lake while playing with their belts.

Had Sissy Morgan gone to join Zaza Mulligan? Everyone was wondering the same thing without saying it out loud, the women especially, who feared seeing her appear on the shore, washed up by the foamy waves. No one thought she could have been dragged against her will into the darkness of the forest, because they didn't yet know that Pete Landry's traps were heaving up out of the earth to move about stealthily at ground level. They imagined the worst, a young girl throwing herself off the end of a dock, but not another trap, not another Zaza. It was only when the men began emerging from the woods, Ed McBain out of breath,

Ben Mulligan rubbing at his puffed eyes, and Gary Miller looking scary, that they saw that it was pointless keeping their eyes on the lake. Sissy Morgan would not be coming back out of the waves.

Seeing Ed McBain running, my mother let out one of her mouse squeaks and pulled the sides of her dressing gown over her chest, over her mother's belly, repeating, no, my God, no, no, no… three useless words, because they'd never been any use, because they came always after the fact, when God could no longer intervene. An utterly worthless negation, which cancelled itself out, but persisted in calling on God. No, no, my God, no… Hearing my mother utter those words, I knew that something irrevocable had happened. Sissy Morgan had disappeared. Sissy Morgan was dead or gravely ill.

On the pale wooden chest of drawers where I'd put it down when I came in, Sissy's watch was still tick-tocking, a sign that the earth was still turning in time with the second hand and the hours and the pace of days they counted out, but I had the feeling that everything had stopped dead, that my mother in her old dressing gown would never leave the veranda, that Millie would not wake up, that my father would not come back, talking man to man with Bob. No, I murmured in my turn, seizing hold of the watch, then Millie stirred in her sleep, setting our universe in motion again at the heart of a world my mother was trying to deny. Risking a rebuff I went to join her on the veranda, but contrary to what I feared she held me tight against her and, together, we went out to see the light beams slashing through the darkness, more and more numerous as the rumour spread that it was too late now to search for young Sissy Morgan.

Instead of going home the men came together, walking towards each other with their heads bowed, but without talking, shaken, unable to express what they felt, with a kind of incredulity that numbed their limbs, the same that drove the women to call on God. Sometimes you saw one who was in a hurry, who didn't yet know and was rushing to join the group. Someone drew him aside to give him the news, as if he didn't want to subject the others again to the ugliness of certain words, and shoulders slumped once more as the man's head went no, one word, one only, that was of no use, either, to him.

Mama and I looked for Bob and my father among all the men. But they were with those who hadn't come out of the woods, those still searching or who had to stay behind at the site of the tragedy that was keeping the others from going home. Seeing that I was shivering, Mama went in to look for a wool blanket to put over my shoulders, and we moved down and sat on the swing, one facing the other, in the light breeze sweeping across the road, waiting there for my father and my brother. Mama could have gone to question the men shuffling through the low-lying mist. Suzanne Lamar, Frenchie's mother, had run to meet them a bit earlier only to leave in tears, her pink slippers clacking on their heels, but my mother wasn't yet ready to cry. She preferred not to know right away the details of Sissy Morgan's disappearance. As long as she'd not yet heard the words making the rounds from one group to another, hope, however unreasonable, was still possible.

Are you cold, my mite? she asked me after Ted Jamison, one of those who didn't yet know, went by on the road at a run. We can go in if you like, but she didn't really want to leave the swing, and neither did I. It was the first time she'd let me stay up with her beyond my usual bedtime, the first time she hadn't treated me entirely like a child. I wanted to make the most of this privilege, even if I understood nothing about what was going on, and felt undeserving of this confidence that made me want to cry. The end-of-the-world sentiment running through Bondrée involved me too, and my mother didn't try to protect me from it, something for which I was grateful, despite my fear. She wanted me near her, a mother and daughter waiting anxiously for the return of a husband and son, a father and brother, who would come back exhausted from one of those expeditions that are the lot of men.

It was three forty-seven by Sissy Morgan's watch when a police car, followed by an ambulance, passed behind the cottage, dispersing the fine mist through which everyone was trudging. Shortly afterwards, an expensive car parked in the McBains' driveway. After a few long moments, Charlotte Morgan got down, wearing a kind of floating pyjama that made her look like a ghost. Stella McBain came right out to throw herself into her arms, but Charlotte Morgan's arms stayed hanging by her side, limp, the arms of a ghost, as Stella wept and moaned *poor girl, poor little thing.* But next to her, Charlotte Morgan's ghost didn't weep. It looked at the night, it looked at the lake, transfixed by a reality slipping away beneath her feet, all wreathed in mist, then Stella McBain led Mrs Morgan inside, the door closed, and the moans drifted out through the open windows, *poor girl, so young.*

My mother was ill at ease, aware that we had just witnessed a scene whose intimacy was not meant for our eyes. In the middle of her forehead the little red circle grew bigger, and she began to twist her belt out of embarrassment, but above all because of Stella McBain's words, *poor girl, poor little thing,* that said more than she wanted to hear. Come my mite, it's time to go in, she said, taking me by the hand, and we walked through the dew, a mother and her daughter in the middle of the night. Back inside, no longer able to play with her cursed belt and with nothing to do, she brought out bread, paté, Cracker Barrel cheese and mustard, they're going to be hungry. Then she spread Cheez Whiz for me onto a pile of soda biscuits and we went to sit at the table, she in front of a cup of tea drowned in milk, me in front of my pile of crackers, which I swallowed while keeping my eyes on the window over the sink, hoping to see my father's head or Bob's, while my mother gathered into little piles the crumbs fallen on the table, crushed them with her thumb, and started all over again, creating little mounds of fine powder where the crumbs had turned back to flour. That procedure got on my nerves, but at least it made me think about the fact that we belonged to the small number of privileged people who could play casually with their leftover food, as if fields of corn, alfalfa, wheat, and I don't know what grew on trees, and the trees grew right into the desert. In front of those little piles of flour I told myself that if you could gather together all the crumbs fallen from my mouth in a year—fifty-two boxes, times about a hundred biscuits, times more or less twelve crumbs per biscuit—you could harvest a good bag of soda biscuit flour. Result: two Chinese babies would be less hungry. That made for a super good reason for rich people to learn to multiply rather than add.

The pile of flour was starting to collapse, and yellow light was profiling the top of Moose Trap, when the screen door to the veranda slammed. My mother and I leaped from our chairs as if they'd been hooked to the door's hinges by a rubber band, our hearts leaped as well, our two hearts together, and my mother spontaneously took me in her arms on seeing Bob's face, the face of a boy who wanted to be a man. It was day, but the night was not about to end.

When he saw Sissy Morgan on top of Snake Hill, the man saw Jim Latimer all over again, the best poker player in the 1st Division Infantry of Uncle Sam's army, reeling on his rubbery legs, looking for his torn-off arm, then he thought of Pete Landry, hanging at the end of a rope. With her shorts that were too big for her, and her air of not knowing if she should turn left or right, or if it would be best to stop and languish where she was, Sissy Morgan resembled Landry, Sissy resembled Jimmy, a puppet brutally robbed of one of its limbs, a doll whose fatuous pain made you want to beat it to death to make it shut up. It was clear to him at that moment that Sissy Morgan was soon going to die, like Latimer and like Landry, like the puppet and the doll, like Zaza and Sugar Baby. *Such was life. Such was fucking life.* He brought together his thumb and index finger to form a circle through which he targeted Sissy. Pow! And the girl's body, with its disarticulated limbs, collapsed in a red, sun-doused flash.

# DAY 2

Knowing he wouldn't sleep, with all the caffeine he'd absorbed during the night, Mordecai Steiner, after making a detour to pick up his car, followed the ambulance to the morgue where he asked the stretcher-bearers to lift the body onto a metal table, then he closed the door and pulled on his gloves. He wanted to finish with this business as quickly as possible, to make the young girl talk before the alterations in her body muddied what it had to say, and to head home as soon as he'd shut everything up in one of those mental compartments he only unsealed for professional purposes, to utter words like "asphyxia," "rupture of the aorta," "serous drainage," chill words that enabled him to do his job without being entrapped by beauty, youth, or some sentiment that would transform his scalpels, in his eyes, into instruments of butchery. Because Steiner was not a butcher, no more than any other medical examiner he knew. His work was one of inquiry, a vocation he exercised according to the rules of the métier, conscious that he was exploring a terrain where there was perhaps buried a quantum of truth that might shed some light on the nature of man.

Before proceeding with the autopsy he closed his eyes, as he always did, calling up some lines from *Macbeth* that consigned all spectres to the realm of non-being. *"Thy bones are marrowless, thy blood is cold . . ."* That was his ritual, his way of reminding himself that a cadaver was nothing but residue, matter, only matter, from which he could at times derive clues that would explain a death, if not its meaning. He found a grandeur in Macbeth's dread, which helped him to maintain a distance between himself and the body before cutting into its flesh. *"Thy blood is cold,"* then he opened his eyes and relieved Sissy Morgan of her blood-soaked clothes.

The intact leg was covered in blood, the thighs as well, contrasting with the milky whiteness of her chest. Mordecai Steiner was used to those horrific tableaux with clashing colours that reminded him of Francis Bacon's grisly canvases, depicting the susceptibility of flesh to the mind's savagery and the imminent decay of every living thing. What he did fear, however, was that the bodies of young girls would disclose to him wounds pointing to the violation of an entire being through the defilement of intimate parts nature should have made fiercely impregnable, and he thought of the *vagina dentata* that once haunted the minds of men.

With delicate gestures he first washed the stained limbs, *"thy blood is cold,"* indifferent to Sissy Morgan's past beauty, since cold flesh cannot be an object of desire. He then examined those hollows where he could judge whether an erect penis had tried to turn Sissy Morgan into a disposable object, or whether the young girl, by some marvel of the death throes, had caused damage to her aggressor. He gave a long sigh of relief, close to the joy of one who has found his or her child unhurt after a fall, when he found that no man, ever, had penetrated Sissy Morgan's body. *Thank God,* he murmured, just like all those unbelievers raised in a faith, then he cut into the young girl's chest.

Two hours later he was ready to write a preliminary report in which the words "mutilation," "laceration," "splinter" figured, cold words that sealed up the wall he'd erected between the man in the autopsy room and the one he'd again become when he removed his gloves and his white coat spattered with organic matter. His report would also contain words like "fetishism," "knife," "hunt," because he'd been able to determine that Sissy Morgan's hair had been sliced off with a hunting knife, like those with which you carve up carcasses. Along with the trap, the knife pointed to Boundary's murderer being a hunter, someone whose power resided in capture, and then in the spoils he stripped from his prey: meat, antlers, fur, and in this case, hair, the perfect emblem for femininity, trophy for a sick soul.

He sent a copy of the report to Stan Michaud, whom he'd so often seen murmuring into the ears of the dead that he wondered if there wasn't a channel through which Michaud communicated with the departing spirit via the cooling blood. Michaud performed no miracles, but Steiner hoped deep inside that Elisabeth Mulligan and Sissy Morgan had in secret whispered to him some despairing words, some accusatory utterance that would enable him to seize by the collar the scumbag who'd butchered them, to then serve him up to their devastated fathers. He imagined the tortures appropriate to such a monster, then he calmed himself, conscious that most monsters had not chosen what they'd become, and he finished his report, in which he mentioned the dural haematoma he'd detected in the anterior part of the parietal lobe, an ante-mortem wound caused by a blunt object: a stone, a piece of wood, or a length of pipe.

He couldn't be certain, but all indications were that Sissy Morgan had been knocked out before being dragged to the trap that would be fatal to her. So much violence disturbed him, and he hoped that the young girl wasn't conscious when the trap closed on her leg, though the dried tears on her grey cheeks seemed to indicate that she was. He tried to reconstitute the sequence of aggressions in his notebook, the cutting of the hair, the blow that was struck, the trap, then he turned off the fluorescent light buzzing overhead, and rolled the body into the cold room. He couldn't do any more for the moment, other than advise Michaud that his murderer was also a dangerous maniac, which Michaud surely already knew, but Steiner wanted to tell him so in his own words, clinical words that would bear no contradiction. And so he phoned the Skowhegan police station, where a certain Anton Westlake promised to pass the message on to Michaud, still back at the scene of the crime. And he made his way home.

It was around noon when Michaud called him back from Boundary. He was exhausted, you could hear that in his raspy voice, but he seemed for the most part anxious, uneasy at the thought of not being able to act quickly enough to forestall the discovery of a third victim. He's going to do it again, he murmured when Steiner spoke to him about the murder's brutality, and he thought immediately of Françoise Lamar, who was the next logical victim. He'd sent one of his agents to the Lamars' that very morning to keep an eye on the young girl and the cottage, but he was no less worried. He knew from experience that those lunatics were not content with a single attack once they'd savoured the power a body's violation accorded them, and along with it the defilement of a person's wholeness. That was what he feared, that the violence would go on. At first he'd entertained the possibility that the killer's hatred was directed only at Zaza Mulligan and Sissy Morgan, teasers, schemers who, as had been intimated to him, disturbed Boundary's moral order, but the humiliation and pain inflicted on Sissy Morgan changed the equation. The hatred was growing, and the killer was still hungry.

*Knocked out*, he told Cusack as he put down the telephone at the McBains', whose luxurious cottage would in some sense become their headquarters, the control room for information going in and out of Boundary. *Knocked out*, he repeated, explaining that the young girl had been struck on the head, probably while she was trying to get away. Struck from behind, by a coward, a loser. They had to look for the object he'd used, but since the wound hadn't bled, you might as well try to find a Bedouin at the North Pole. Shaken by the examiner's voice describing the killer's apparent modus operandi, Michaud sank into a chair and contemplated the reflections making the McBains' dining-room table gleam, an oak table that was surely worth a fortune, and that he and his colleagues were going to soil with their fingerprints and coffee stains.

When the McBains suggested he set up headquarters in their home rather than stay in the cramped space of his car, cursing a radio that only worked part of the time, Michaud accepted at once. Along with Cusack he followed Ed McBain inside, and the two of them sat at the oak table, around which they were able to work out their action plan while emptying the coffee pot Stella McBain had brought them. Let's start over, he grumbled, pushing to the side a few sheets of paper blackened with hasty writing, which were sitting next to the coffee pot and a plate of buns that neither he nor Cusack had touched.

Yet they'd eaten nothing since their meals the night before, shepherd's pie for Cusack, pork chops for Michaud, served with a sauce of seasonal berries that he'd pushed around the edge of his plate, trying to avoid the disapproving gaze of Dorothy, who'd run to the grocery store a bit earlier after having cut the recipe out of some magazine vaunting the salutary effects of colour on one's mood and digestion. No matter how often he insisted that it was neutral tones that made him both more regular and easier to live with, Dottie was determined to refine his tastes. He should have been famished, but the very sight of pastries set out in a circle on a tray ornamented with wildflowers made him queasy. It was the same for Cusack. His shepherd's pie still weighed on his stomach, and inklings of corn rose into his throat, a residue he repressed with coffee well laced with sugar and cream. That's the way the two men functioned, they ran on caffeine and adrenaline, and they'd probably not be able to swallow anything solid until the day was done.

They were dealing with a hunter, Steiner had claimed, and Michaud agreed. But he had to use this information with caution, because if he mentioned a hunter, Pete Landry's story would be resurrected, hysteria would run rampant, and he'd lose all control of the situation. What counted now was to forestall the death of a third girl. He could count on Steiner not to let anything get out. Michaud had known the medical examiner for years, ever since the Esther Conrad affair and even before. He knew he wouldn't be betrayed by the man who recited Shakespeare to the dead, who went down with them to that realm of shadows where their soft voices could be heard. Michaud, for his part, begged them to come forth just for a moment to tell him about the implacability of those dry eyes that refused their supplications, to speak to him about the purpose of a life when there was no point running or dreaming and when the humblest dream could be snuffed out by the blow from a scythe in the midday sun.

Stella McBain, a bit let down that they hadn't tried her buns, first-prize winners at the Farmington fair the year before, had just brought them a second pot of coffee when they decided to go over to the Morgans'. They had to start there, with the parents, those closest to the girl, even if it was doubtful that they'd be able get anything from them other than cries, insults, exhortations, as if they had the power to go back in time and resurrect their daughter.

It was Vic Morgan who came to the door, his beard long, his hair dirty, and with a gesture ushered them into the living room, where Ed McBain was serving a scotch, certainly not her first, to Charlotte, the mother, dressed in white satin pyjamas whose top was stained. Alcohol, thought Michaud, observing that Charlotte Morgan could barely sit straight in her chair. Instinctively, he pulled the tail of his jacket over his coffee-stained shirt, embarrassed by the image Charlotte Morgan was projecting, and not wanting to be associated with it. In future he would bring along a change of shirt and would not wander around in his jacket when the temperature was over eighty degrees. McBain offered him and Cusack a glass as well, but both refused, then he left them with Morgan. I'll wait outside, he said from the door, and he left.

The faithful friend, Michaud thought to himself, who'll never fail you, remembering that his sole true friend had gone to meet his maker a few years earlier: Nick Perry, the greatest consumer of French fries in all of Maine, dead of a heart attack at the age of fifty. Since Nick's death, he had only Dorothy. No old comrade to confide in. It sometimes happened that he'd have a drink with his colleagues, take part in a baseball tournament or a fishing excursion, but he didn't feel close to any of the partiers who filled his glass or yelled at him to move his ass so he'd get to second base before the ball was heaved in by the opposite team's outfielder. *Run, Stan! Move your fucking fat ass!* Nick Perry was the only man in whose company he could sob, to whom he could confess that he sometimes felt like cutting his own throat or emptying his gun's magazine into the gut of the travelling salesman who'd just run over a young boy with his outsized car, the only man in whose presence he could burp, fart, or vomit, without the other moving away and holding his nose. From now on, there'd be no more Nick. Only colleagues called Jim, Anton, or Dave, honest cops, guys he respected, but with whom he'd never take off for two or three days into the woods, as he'd done several times with Perry, toting their gear in backpacks and sleeping under the stars while telling sexist jokes and then, abruptly, talking about their lives, their dreams. Vic Morgan was lucky to be able to count on an Ed McBain.

Although they were sitting opposite each other, Vic and Charlotte Morgan's eyes didn't meet. Morgan seemed to have passed his blindness on to his wife, who hadn't noticed the stain on her blouse, unusual for a woman whose appearance constituted her identity, and her vacant gaze remained fixed on a cut-glass candy dish whose green and orange veins were intertwined. Uncomfortable, the two policemen sat down on the loveseat, each squeezed into a corner so their knees wouldn't touch, then Michaud pulled out his notebook so that he would seem to be in control, before expressing his sympathies and starting the interrogation.

*That little bitch*, the mother blurted out when Michaud asked her if she knew where Sissy was going when she left the cottage the day before, *that little bitch, never told me anything*, then she went silent again, her eyes on the candy dish.

Michaud was shocked by the mother's words. You don't call your daughter a little bitch, living or dead. Facing the pursed lips of Charlotte Morgan, who was fighting off a rush of tears, he saw all the same that she could love from a distance only, one that would shield her from being overwhelmed by any tenderness. There was a softness beneath the apparent bitterness, just as there had been in Sissy's words to Zaza Mulligan, *you would have told me, bitch!* The mother and daughter had only their anger with which to face death, and they took refuge in a hatred with no true object, so as to avoid falling into that pit where tears will take you. If they couldn't talk to each other, it was because they were too much alike. Michaud wouldn't bank on Charlotte Morgan's chances of eluding a life-threatening bitterness. Without that double who was her daughter, that mirror in which she could recognize herself without hating herself too much, she'd become more desiccated than ever and would nurse that aridity by dousing it with alcohol. He didn't envy the woman's fate.

As for Victor Morgan, he didn't react any more to his wife's *little bitch* than to the questions put to him by Michaud, who calmly rephrased them, trying to penetrate the fog surrounding the man. Morgan remained lost in his thoughts, his brow furrowed as though he was searching for a word, a misplaced idea, sometimes venturing a sad smile, doubtless linked to a memory, then he uttered a few words for himself alone, evoking a little pink dress, a few birthday candles, looking at the policemen as if they were strange characters who had just turned up in his living room. They were about to leave when he at last mumbled *the trap, shouldn't have been there.* The trap shouldn't have been there, he repeated, but Michaud, it was clear, didn't know what he was trying to say. Morgan then talked about the search organized on the two preceding weekends, the combing of the woods, men thrashing the ground with their sticks, the flies sucking their blood, the traps thrown into the back of Valère Grégoire's truck. *The trap shouldn't have been there.* As Morgan went on with his story, Michaud felt his face going red, flushed with the heat that comes from exasperation and that brings fire to your eyes. Why, dammit, hadn't the men clustered together the night before mentioned that they'd already gone through that bloody clearing with a fine-tooth comb?

This information was crucial, and not one of the idiots staring at him with their mouths hanging open had thought it would be a good idea to provide him with it. As if the police were too dumb to add two and two. He let loose with a "Jesus Christ" while looking for a handkerchief to mop his brow, then he asked Morgan who, *for God's sake*, had searched the clearing. Morgan didn't remember, didn't remember anything anymore, repeating every ten seconds that the trap shouldn't have been there. Seeing that it was hopeless to persist, Michaud put away his notebook, but not his handkerchief, which he clutched in his fist, thinking that he was going to have to turn himself inside out to question people who would only give him half the truth, convinced as they were that some details were none of the police's business and ought to be passed over for the good of one and all.

As he was leading Cusack outside, Charlotte Morgan headed, reeling, towards the bar, and offered him a drink, *one for the road, Detective*, but he didn't hear her, he was thinking about the trap, deliberately buried in the high grass covering the clearing. He thought of the man who'd brought it there. He thought of the anxious faces that had hidden the truth from him. *Come on,* we're going to Valère Grégoire's, he told Cusack, to see what he did with those damned traps, and he left the Morgans in the good hands of Ed McBain, the faithful friend who would never betray them.

Seeing the police car park in front of his house, Brian Larue shut his book and went to greet Cusack, who was walking, head lowered, towards the cottage. Like almost all of Boundary's able-bodied men, Larue had taken part in the search for Vic Morgan's daughter the day before, but he'd gone home before the police arrived, not wanting to stand around in the humid night along with twenty or so devastated men who would soon be glaring at each other, wondering if their neighbour, the one with a strange tic who spent his time scratching his left ear, might be the bastard who was setting traps for their children.

He was waiting for someone to come and ask him to take on the role of interpreter again, and he was ready, ready to transpose the fear and the lies into words that differed in their sounds, yet shared the same sense of incredulity. He wanted to contribute to the arrest of whoever it was who, in a few days, had transformed Boundary into an accursed place where no one could scan the landscape without thinking of the violence stored in the memory of those streams that flowed out of the forest. Thanks to that man the lakeshore would soon be abandoned, like every paradise after the encroachment of evil, and would go back to being wild, reasserting its natural state as Pierre Landry had known it, Landry the trapper who was said to be the source of this sickness infecting Boundary, whereas Boundary had lost its idyllic status as soon as men, in Landry's wake, began putting down roots there. Evil couldn't spring from one individual alone. It always arrived in numbers and then more numbers, in the accretion of hatreds that came with numbers, with too many destinies cheek by jowl jockeying fiercely for fulfillment.

He shook Cusack's hand, a tired hand, and joined him in the police car. *It'll be a long day*, murmured Cusack, then they drove in silence from Larue's to the Grégoire cottage, behind which Michaud awaited them, sitting on a stump and staring at his feet, you would have thought, though in fact he was observing ants, a colony that had built its nest next to the stump. Dozens of insects were busying themselves around the small sandy hill, following trajectories whose logic escaped him, some transporting minuscule bits of debris, food, or material that would contribute to the community's survival, others going he knew not where. There were those who compared the bustling of those creatures to that of humans, but this did not hold water. The ants' agitation had a meaning, while the frenetic activity of men had no goal other than to limit their awareness of their own mortality. When Cusack's car came near, Michaud stood, taking care not to crush any ants, there was too much death in the air for him to remain indifferent to the life of any creature, any innocent and inoffensive beastie, and he went to greet his partner.

Seeing Larue get out of the car, he felt a weight being lifted off his shoulders. With Cusack, he was locked into a cop's way of seeing things, whereas Larue came from another world, that of books, which reflect reality with a different sort of acuity, taking a small sample of the real and weighing it against a whole that existed only in the sum of its parts. That was what he ought to be doing too, looking on Boundary as the microcosm of a humanity that never changed. In theory, he should have followed the rules and hired an interpreter, but he wanted only Larue for this investigation, whatever the consequences if the higher-ups objected.

*Sorry to take more of your time*, Michaud apologized, but Larue knew it wasn't the chief inspector's fault that time had come to a stop for everyone, given the twin dramas. In fact, the prospect of working with him somewhat lightened his burden. He'd learned that with Michaud, no interrogation was going to turn into a farce or a power game where billy clubs were brought out. Ignoring the apology, he followed Michaud and Cusack into the Grégoires' cottage. It was filled with the aroma of cabbage soup, which reminded him of his mother's, which he'd forced himself to eat despite its smell. As for Michaud, he thought of Dorothy's cabbage rolls, another recipe from a magazine, and wondered if she was at the cemetery at that moment, as on most every Sunday. Dottie only went to Mass from time to time, but she continued to visit her parents, Mary Forbes, 1889–1962, and Franklin Attenborough, 1887–1957, whose gravestone she adorned with flowers from her garden as soon as the crocuses and daffodils came up. In winter she brushed off the stone with her naked hands, so their names would be legible facing the wind, and she talked to them of her life, on her knees in the fallen and falling snow. He'd phoned her at about six o'clock, when she usually got up, to tell her that he didn't know when he'd be home, or if he'd be early enough for Sunday night's blood-red steaks, though to refer to them as such struck him as being in bad taste under the circumstances. He'd call her later, after he'd questioned some of the witnesses, and had some idea of what lay before him.

Valère Grégoire apologized for the smell of soup. Berthe, his wife, didn't want to lose the cabbage they'd bought at the Farmington market the week before. Then he suggested they talk in the yard, but Michaud preferred to stay inside, where he could find out a lot more about the occupants of a place than on a square of lawn. The cottage was clean, modestly furnished, and it gave off an obvious warmth, that of simple people who enjoyed life. On a small table there was a collection of rocks picked up by their children, Denise, Gilles, and Estelle, said Berthe Grégoire, while putting away a pile of comics where Superman adventures were mixed in with a magazine called *Spirou*, which Michaud in his head pronounced Spyrow, probably spy stories.

Before beginning his questioning, Michaud asked Berthe Grégoire if he and his colleagues could interview her husband alone for a few minutes, then he regretted his clumsiness, seeing her flush, but she said no, no problem at all, smoothing her cotton dress with her tanned hands. Her dress well flattened, she called the children, Denise, Gilles, Estelle, who were spying on them from behind the curtain dividing their room from the living area, three little "spyrows" who followed her outside.

Michaud accepted the coffee that Grégoire offered him, the same instant coffee he drank every day, which didn't have the richness of Stella McBain's percolator coffee, but allowed him to bond with Grégoire, who also hadn't shaved, and wore the same soiled clothes as the night before. Another person who'd spent the night pondering, and whose hands trembled from fatigue, from too much caffeine, from the after-effects of the shock, or the fear of being found in the wrong.

Michaud asked him first about the scouring of the woods over the weekends of 29 July and 5 August, *the search*, he said, *the combing*. Grégoire told him about how the men had gathered around Vic Morgan, whose idea it was, to ransack the forest and avoid another tragedy. At that point in his story he shook his head in sympathy with Morgan, whose initiative had not succeeded in saving his daughter. Under other circumstances he would have spoken of the irony of fate, but there was nothing ironic about the death of a child. He couldn't remember who was in charge of the sector where Sissy Morgan was found, but he would swear, his hand in the fire, that the trap had been brought there after the search. No one, not even an idiot, could have passed it by without seeing it. Unless he did so on purpose, Michaud thought. But he kept silent on that, while taking advantage of Grégoire's bringing up the subject of the trap that had diabolically appeared in the clearing, to ask him what he'd done with those that been entrusted to him.

Under his beard Grégoire went red, knowing right away what Michaud was suggesting. He pounded his fist on the table, swearing that he'd dismantled the damned traps piece by piece before taking them to the dump. He could lead them to the vacant lot where he'd thrown them if they wanted proof, and he slammed the table again with the back of his hand. You tie yourself in knots to do the right thing, then you're being accused, *câlisse*, he burst out, looking at Larue to translate, because he wanted him to translate everything, including his *câlisse*. Cusack tried to calm things down by explaining that no one was accusing him of anything, but Grégoire was beside himself. It took his wife, alerted by the tone of his voice, for him to pull himself together. Don't get upset, Valère, they're just doing their job.

Standing on the doormat, Berthe Grégoire again smoothed her dress, and again left, excusing herself, like so many women who never feel they're where they belong and would apologize for existing if they were asked. As for Valère Grégoire, his jaw was still clenched. He'd gone silent, but his anger was there in his noisy breathing, the anger of a man who had to hold back the violence that erupted in him, bitter and resentful, every time someone thwarted him or questioned his integrity. This Grégoire was not easy to figure out. Michaud would have wagered that he was eaten away by a frustration he could only master by seizing an axe to go and split a pile of logs, or by careening his pickup truck along deserted gravel roads. He'd seen too many crooks get on their high horses to believe that Grégoire's indignation was proof of his honesty.

All right, he sighed, Agent Cusack here will go with you to pick up the traps, we'll need them for the inquest. In fact, he didn't know what he'd do with the dismantled traps, but he wanted to confirm that they were where they were supposed to be, and to see whether Grégoire would overturn the table before leaving the cottage. One last question, he said, as Grégoire rose without smashing everything to pieces, where were you Saturday afternoon? A long silence followed, and Grégoire muttered, in the woods, I was chopping wood up on the hill.

Alone?

Alone, Larue translated, then Grégoire left with Cusack.

The campground fries were greasy, and Michaud shoved away his cone with a belch. He'd thought that eating something would do him good, but the soggy potatoes were indigestible. He could have gone knocking on the door of the McBains', and Stella would surely have prepared one of her own dishes that had won a prize at the Schenectady fair in 1963, but he didn't want to abuse those people's hospitality. He'd be going there soon with Cusack, to a meeting that had been set up with the men in charge of inspecting the clearing and the road along with their team. For the time being, he needed a rest in the open air. He'd spent all day walking from one cottage that stank of cabbage to another reeking of tobacco, and he felt a wave of nausea mounting in him, identical to those of sleepless nights and empty stomachs. Tomorrow he'd bring his own food, pork or roast beef sandwiches, depending on what was in the refrigerator, and he'd limit his consumption of caffeine. Meanwhile, all he could do for his nausea was to quietly inhale the August air that was saturated with ancient odours.

Cusack had also pushed away his fries, but he'd swallowed his hot dog as if he was afraid someone was going to take it from him, only to regret it, as along with the reflux of corn, there was now that of mustard and sausage. He'd just returned from the dump where Grégoire had tossed the dismantled traps, and he was starving. He'd tried to make Grégoire talk, but he'd apparently told them all he had to say. The trap pieces were sitting in the trunk of his car, and he was wondering what on earth Michaud could do with them. I don't know, be sure that no asshole gets to them before we do, he'd answered when Cusack asked the question, then he'd closed up the trunk and followed his partner to the campground canteen, the front of which was adorned with an enormous potato, proclaiming *Bienvenue chez monsieur Patate, Welcome at Mr Potato*. Michaud was giving him the rundown on his latest visit with Marcel Dumas, next door to the campground, but, too busy digesting his hot dog, he heard only snatches of it.

Not realizing he was talking to empty air, Michaud said he wasn't sure about Dumas, he was too nervous, a rodent looking for a way out of a sealed room. He too had no alibi for Saturday afternoon, which he had supposedly spent in his cottage with his stamp collection, for which he had just received a series of twenty-five-cent South American specimens from the 1950s. Since he lived alone, no one could back up what he said, because he hadn't budged from his table until he'd heard voices calling the young Sissy Morgan. He hadn't joined in the search due to his sciatica, but he'd seen all the coming and going and could say exactly who had passed in front of his house, who had veered off towards the campground, who had taken the ascent towards Juneau Hill. From the moment he'd arrived in Bondrée, he'd made it his business to know everybody. A snoop, Michaud added, one who might give us some information, but a snoop all the same, a loudmouth with no lady friend, and what is more, like most psychopaths, fussing over a collection of stamps or press clippings.

*Like me*, Larue quipped, bursting out laughing, and Michaud realized that not for a moment had he thought of asking him what he'd been doing the night before. To his mind, he couldn't be more of a potential suspect than Cusack or himself. He guffawed too, just not being able to imagine him as a killer. *Like you*, he put in, then confessed that indeed he had to ask him some questions, to exonerate him before going on with the investigation. *Go on*, replied Larue, even if he didn't have a stronger alibi than Dumas or Grégoire. Emma had been in town with her mother, and he'd spent the afternoon at home. Unlike Dumas, on the other hand, he'd worked outside a good part of the day, repainting the walls of his tool shed, his neighbours had certainly seen him, strollers, people in boats passing on the lake. Up on his ladder, he'd heard Vic Morgan shouting. A bit later, he'd seen the men gathering, and he'd joined them. Simple as that. After assembling, those who'd answered Morgan's call left in groups of two or three, each taking its own way. He himself had gone with Ted Jamison along a woodcutters' road, which they'd followed until it stopped abruptly in front of a pile of fallen trunks. They kept crying out Sissy Morgan's name, Jamison louder than himself, with a voice that could make the spruce trees shake, then they retraced their steps, only to learn that Sissy Morgan had been found dead near a bear trap.

He couldn't tell them any more, other than to talk about the men's nervousness, the way some clenched their fists or spat at their feet, the wound that had opened up Jack Mulligan's knee as he was tumbling down a Moose Trap trail, a deep cut onto which Hope Jamison, who'd been sought out as a nurse, had poured a half-bottle of peroxide before wrapping it in a bandage on which a red circle had instantly appeared. He could describe the Bondrée lights, lit up all night as if for a nocturnal festival, a New Year's Eve, women standing at their windows, but Michaud had seen all that, Cusack too, an unnerving night whose artificial illumination had carved dark arcs into people's faces.

Remembering the night, the three men bowed their heads, then Michaud turned the discussion towards the first combing of the woods, wanting to know if Larue had participated in the trap hunt that had been kept from him either by omission or stupidity. The first weekend, yes, replied Larue, the Sunday, along with Gary Miller, with whom he'd shared a stew prepared by his wife, while talking hunting and small game. Larue had a gun in his cottage, an old Remington 30-06 inherited from his father, which he never used except for shooting at tin cans, but he was a good audience, and he'd listened to Miller talk about the smell of the woods and partridges, the cool rain dripping from the trees, which sharpened his predator's instinct as well as his love of life, of the ruddy sunlight sparkling in the frozen trees. He'd strode with him through what they'd called Sector 7, between Weasel Trail and the woodcutters' road he'd taken the day before, finding nothing, after which they'd gone back towards the campground, where the women were waiting behind tables covered with salads and stuffed eggs. For his part, he'd only downed a few morsels of sandwich while watching the children play on the periphery, then he'd left the party, for it really was a party, a gathering of proud men, happy to have pulled together, between whom the women in summer dresses wound their way, giving off their lavender or violet perfume in the midst of bodies stinking with sweat. The following Sunday he'd not joined the Moose Trap search because Emma was with him, Emma and Andrée, Sam Duchamp's daughter. But he'd seen the men emerge from the tangled trails of Moose

Trap, one with a set of moose antlers, a rare find, another limping or cursing the flies, and Sam Duchamp with blood on his hands, the blood of a red fox that had been done in by the slamming shut of a bear trap like the one that had closed on Zaza Mulligan's long leg.

*What the hell!* Michaud cried, hearing Larue mention the trap. He immediately ordered Cusack to send one of their men to the lab in Portland with those damned traps to gather all the damned prints that were on them, even if they had to go back as far as Pete Landry. That's what those traps are going to do for us, Cusack, they're going to flush out the bastard who's hiding in the berry bushes. Priority number one, and get to it!

Michaud was fuming, because there again, he couldn't understand why no one had mentioned the dead fox. The answer was clear all the same, because no one knew, a week earlier, that there was a killer abroad among them. They'd only realized it the day before, when they discovered Sissy Morgan. As soon as Michaud had digested the information, he told Cusack, who was already jumping into his car, to join him at the Duchamps'. He skimmed his cone of fries into a half-full garbage can and led Larue along the dirt road circling the lake. He'd check his alibi later. He needed someone there, right away, to help him untangle this crazy story.

Unlike the night in the course of which we learned of Zaza Mulligan's death, my parents had not tried to hide the truth from me when Bob and my father returned in the early morning looking like characters out of a horror film. In less than a day, Bob had turned into a man with the world on his shoulders, and I had become a girl keeping watch with her mother, too big now for people to put her off with tales of goblins and talking dormice. Someone had died. Sissy Morgan was dead and her death was not natural. A killer was on the loose in the shadow of our cottages, one that had made a zombie out of Bob, and etched into my father's face lines that hadn't been there before, outward signs of a kind of stupor, as if he'd received a blow from a baseball bat on the back of his head. And that's exactly what had happened in the clearing, where a dozen men, along with him, had been blindsided by a mysterious weapon. Ever since he'd been knocked senseless with no warning, my father had been trying to add up figures that made no sense, Zaza plus Sissy, and he was left dumbstruck before an equation he couldn't solve, before faulty data afloat in a spongy mass, while he juggled words that might lend some order to what was real. After what they'd seen in the clearing, my father's eyes, as well as those of my brother, had been stunned into incredulity: those things didn't happen where we lived. And yet the proof was there, in the lined faces, in the horror that spawned that incredulity, in the body lying on the forest floor. There was a killer among us.

After having removed their flannel shirts, my father and brother sat at the table, my mother made coffee, and one of them, probably my father, said dead, murdered. My mother brought her hands to her mouth, I felt my body go numb as if I was passing out without passing out, and my brother grimaced like a man whose acne hadn't had a chance to dry. All had been said: dead, murdered.

A few minutes later, Millie got up, trailing Bobine behind her by one of her dirty little arms. Ever since I'd found her again Millie had not let her go, refusing to surrender her to my mother so she could sew back the buttons that had once been her eyes but that were now hanging down beside her nose. The doll was in pretty bad shape, and I found it hard to believe it was due just to its exposure to the weather. Some kids must have found it, Yvon Tanguay or Michael Jamison, and pulled it apart before tossing it under a pile of boards. As soon as I had a minute I'd go and worm the truth out of those little snotnosed morons, too chicken to take on anyone their own size, and I'd smash up their faces just like they did to Bobine. In the meantime I forced myself back among the living, for Millie, and for Bobine, back home at last.

The rest of the day men came knocking at our door, women who couldn't bear to stay silent, Jocelyne Ménard, worried about Gilles, her husband, I've never seen him so pale, sipping her tea while darting glances around her, hoping perhaps to find a cure for her husband's despondency in the rays of sun beaming into the kitchen. He found two bodies, Florence, three if you count the fox. Berthe Grégoire, for her part, was afraid her Valère would just explode. The police had come early in the morning for the traps, those that Valère had taken apart, and Valère had lost his cool. He's not himself, with everything that's going on. He's keeping his eyes on everybody all the time.

For their part, the men were talking low in the yard, like at a funeral parlour out of respect for the dead, wondering what they could do, and when the police would let them take their families far away from Bondrée. As for Millie, too little to know what was happening, but big enough to see that things weren't going well, she wandered from one group to another with her doll blinded in both eyes, saying to her don't cry my pretty Bobine, everything will be all right.

At four o'clock, while my mother washed the cups, Stan Michaud arrived with Monsieur Larue, who had a postcard for me from Emma showing King Kong at the top of the Empire State Building. Emma wrote me that she'd be in Bondrée the next day at noon, and that she had a surprise for me. I can't tell you any more, there are spies. *See you tomorrow. Em.* I put the card into the top drawer of my chest of drawers, out of Millie's reach, under my pyjamas. I'd never in my life received a postcard, and I was as excited as if someone had offered me a three-speed bicycle with a banana seat. I was suddenly important. A bilingual girl who lived all year long in the United States, who spoke French from France without taking herself for the centre of the universe, and who tripped on King Kong, had a surprise for me that had nothing to do with my parents, nor hers, nor my brother, nor my sister, nor Jane Mary Brown, nor the police.

My enthusiasm went down a few notches when I heard my father talking about the dead fox Jocelyne Ménard had mentioned earlier, and I came back to earth. A girl had lost her life the night before, Sissy Morgan, and now they were talking about an animal covered in the red mud of the Moose Trap trails. In the middle of the mountain, my father went on, recently dead, its blood almost warm. So that's where the blood came from that made Gilles Ménard stuff his hands in his pockets after the Moose Trap search. That's where the clay came from, invented by Brian Larue to shut our mouths, Emma's and mine, from hundreds of foxes whose blood had soaked into the mountain's earth ever since it first existed. Then there was the question of a hole dug with bare hands, perhaps a prayer, the resurrection, near the lake, of a name Ménard kept repeating, Sugar, Sugar Baby, and I heard the scraping of chairs, the knocking together of cups my mother was putting back in the cupboard, the door creaking. Stan Michaud and Brian Larue went off to the McBains'. From my bedroom window I saw Michaud and Larue shake my father's hand and cross the cedar hedge, behind which other policemen were waiting. Stella McBain opened the door to them, and silence fell again over the cottage, while in my turn I addressed a prayer to the god of foxes.

It was four-thirty, and the sky was cloudless, the lake transparent and slick, making you want to dive in headfirst, but no one, not even Pat Tanguay, was disturbing the calm water. Bondrée had just entered a new ice age.

Four policemen were sitting around the McBains' oak table, Stan Michaud and Jim Cusack, Dave Leroy, in charge of the searches, and Luke Stanfield, who'd gone up and down Turtle Road with two colleagues looking for clues and gleaning a few offhanded comments along the way, in a context more informal than what you could expect in an official interrogation. A strong smell of sweat and tobacco filled the dining room, which Stella McBain would later disperse with a lilac-scented spray—a weary and fretful odour that went with the gluey marks on the table, where the men's damp hands were in repose.

No one touched the plate of chips in front of them except Luke Stanfield, who swallowed fistfuls, and swept the crumbs away with the back of his hand, saying he'd talked to two boys, Michael Jamison and Silas Brown, according to his notebook, who claimed to have seen Sissy Morgan the day before, arguing with Françoise Lamar and Mark Meyer, the campground attendant. One of his men had gone over to the Lamars', but Frenchie had denied it, saying she hadn't seen Sissy or Meyer for several days. Conclusion: either the boys were lying, or Frenchie Lamar was having them on. Michaud leaned towards the second hypothesis. What reason would the boys have to invent this quarrel? He'd visit the

Lamars once the meeting was over, and get things straight. Meanwhile he phoned the sheriff of Somerset County, in Madison, to have him send someone to Meyer's home to grill him. Make him cough up the truth, he roared. He hung up so violently that he almost ripped the phone off the wall; the instrument chimed out in the suddenly silent room. *Son of a bitch*, he grumbled under his breath, then he ordered Leroy to hand over his report before he mummified right there on his chair. He didn't usually harass his men, but he finally had something to get his teeth into, and he didn't want to see it frittered away in talk. The clearing, Leroy, what did you find?

Overall, Leroy had found nothing conclusive, cigarette butts, dozens of footprints, and some detritus that told them nothing for the time being. He had to compare the marks made by the soles, measure the prints, and determine which corresponded to those of the men who'd tramped over the scene of the crime, trying to find one or two that didn't match their shoes, assuming that one of those same pairs of footwear was not in fact that of the killer. He had to see who smoked and who didn't, who'd pissed in the bush, who'd dropped a KitKat wrapper onto the forest floor, and who'd stuck his gum onto the trunk of a tree. He had to undertake analyses, comparisons, interrogations, a real puzzle that he couldn't put together for several days, supposing, again, that he had all the pieces to hand. He could, however, affirm that the young Morgan had arrived in the clearing from the east side and that she still had her head of hair at that point, because they'd found a strand of it caught on a branch, a dozen feet from a trail overrun with vegetation, which had once been a path. It remained to be confirmed that this was truly Sissy Morgan's hair, but he was ninety-eight per cent sure. Long hair, honey blond, as his wife usually called it, a bit tritely, when she wanted to describe that warm, almost sugary colour. This meant that the ritual took place in the clearing and that the murderer had probably waited for Sissy to die before cutting off her hair. Like with an animal, thought Michaud, confirming his feelings and those of Steiner. The assassin was no innocent, where traps were concerned. He really was a hunter. Michaud took the opportunity to ask Leroy if he'd got any clues from the trap. Not yet. He first had to send it to the lab to check out the fingerprints, to know if it could have belonged to Pete Landry, or if the killer had his own supply. Days, Leroy went on, all those analyses will take days, and may teach them nothing. Too much tramping back and forth had corrupted the crime scene.

Leroy was right, the clues brought together in the clearing could all lead them to dead ends with the investigation hitting a wall while the killer was laughing in their faces. *Bastard!* Still, he instructed Leroy to save every cigarette butt and to examine them all with a microscope if necessary. Also check the shoes, unshoe the whole male population of Boundary Pond *till you find Cinderella's fucking brother*, after which he told Leroy and Stanfield that Sissy Morgan had been struck on the head, meaning they'd need another search to find the object with which she'd been hit.

First find me the hunting knife the killer used to cut off her hair. Don't be afraid to empty every bloody drawer of every bloody cottage, to look under every mattress, check every garbage can, take down every suspicious wall, and go up every damned brook on your knees, if you have to. Then find the object the kid was struck with. Do what you can, Leroy, get me everything that could knock out a girl or a horse and measure the height of the branch where that hair was caught. I want to know whether Sissy Morgan went into the clearing on her own two feet, or if she was carried.

He knew he was giving Leroy and Stanfield a virtually impossible task, but he had confidence in his men. They'd sniffed around enough crime scenes to have a sense of smell as highly developed as a pack of German Shepherds. If something smelled fishy, they'd catch onto it. For himself, he was interested in the men, those waiting anxiously for the next hunting season, he'd pay attention to the inflections in their voices, watch their trembling, nicotine-stained fingers, hoping that someone would lose his nerve, that two lies would contradict each other, throwing off some fragments of truth into the smoke-filled room. He asked if anyone had anything to add, and, given the shaking heads, he closed down the meeting, not without ordering Stanfield to clean up the crumbs from his potato chips. Stella McBain was not their maid.

Larue was waiting for them on the McBains' dock, his pant legs rolled up and his feet in the water. He'd finished off the little plate of buns that Stella McBain had brought him, to her great pleasure, and she'd immediately made him a lemonade, leaving him to lose himself in contemplating the lake, the eddies his feet made at the end of the dock, trying not to think about death, just studying the reflections in the eddies, thinking about nothing, immersing himself in the soothing blue hues of sky and water. He was just about to drop off when he heard steps echoing on the wood of the dock, pulling him out of the imageless world in which he was floating, somewhere between sky and earth, a blissful world composed of luminous shades, tranquil and mute. It took him a few seconds to get his bearings, the lake, the mountain, Michaud and Cusack, their tortured lawmen's faces, and he said farewell to sleep.

On the way to the Lamars' cottage, Michaud told him that he wanted him to be there for Frenchie's interrogation, even if she spoke English just as well as French. He wanted three pairs of eyes trained on her to read between the lines, three pairs of ears catching and dissecting her every word. Someone had lied, maybe Franky-Frenchie, maybe two kids looking for attention, but he wanted to get it clear in his own mind. On arriving, they greeted the agent who'd been posted at the Lamars', a certain Frank or Hank Milton, who looked bored to death. Seated at a table in the garden, he was playing solitaire with a deck of cards he'd borrowed from the Lamars, and seemed delighted to finally have some company. No, nothing much had happened since morning, no, he'd seen nothing suspicious. The girl was still inside with her mother, but the father had gone shopping in town. Hang on a bit, I'll have you relieved, promised Michaud, and he knocked at the door.

A woman who was a bit pudgy, pleasant, wearing blue eyeshadow, appeared and Michaud assumed she was Suzanne, the mother. She had them sit down in the living room, and called Frenchie, Françoise, who arrived dragging her feet. Frenchie was a pretty girl, her hair almost as long as that of Sissy Morgan and Zaza Mulligan. But there was something unfinished about her, a lack of sparkle that made her seem almost ordinary next to the other two. Michaud couldn't say what was responsible for that, perhaps some mental idleness. It seemed to him that Françoise Lamar would always fall just short of being beautiful, something she tried to compensate for with makeup that was too extreme, and provocative clothes. She was wearing ultra-short shorts, a tank top that was too tight, but Michaud was especially shocked by her bare feet, which accentuated the unseemliness of her dress. He would have preferred her to be properly attired, but he wasn't going to tell her to put on shoes. He'd take Frenchie Lamar as she was, a pretty girl who showed off her legs and her perfectly slim feet.

Before asking any questions, he extended his sympathies to Frenchie, *sorry for your loss,* and asked Suzanne Lamar to wait in the next room. He wanted Frenchie to be alone and to be able to talk freely. The mother didn't seem offended, she had to prepare supper. Michaud still waited for the noise of pots and pans to reach him from the kitchen before getting started. *What were you doing with Mark Meyer yesterday, Franneswoise?* The question unnerved the adolescent, who hadn't foreseen such a direct attack. She tried not to let anything show, and replied with a kind of smile that she hadn't seen Mark Meyer for several days, *haven't seen Mark since last week.* She tried to hide her nervousness, but behind the mask Michaud detected a kind of terror, probably due to what had happened to her friends, to the fate awaiting her as well if they didn't catch the murderer quickly, but also to the fear of saying too much or too little and getting herself in trouble just when everything was crumbling around her, Sissy, Zaza, a carefree existence, and joy. He had to hunt down this fear, at the risk of upsetting the young girl even more, because it was clear that she was lying through her teeth.

For twenty minutes he compared her version of the facts with that of the young kids, asked her about Sissy, Zaza, Mark Meyer, sometimes letting Cusack talk, sitting at the back of the room, a target for Frenchie's eyes, because he was an attractive man or because he seemed less threatening. Doubtless a bit of both. Michaud didn't know what made Cusack so charming, he didn't understand anything about women's tastes, but they all found him good-looking, starting with Dottie, whom he didn't understand either. Whatever the case, Cusack's sex appeal made some questionings easier, and he wasn't going to deny himself that. Little by little he let him take over, and Frenchie became less tense. She stretched out her legs, placing her tanned feet well in the foreground, suddenly relaxed, then Cusack caught her off guard and she tripped herself up by mentioning the boys. Her face suddenly went red, and she instantly pulled in her legs. Her fear resurfaced, exposed by the truth. Without realizing it, Frenchie Lamar had just admitted that Michael Jamison and Silas Brown, two little pests, two brats, had nothing better to do than to spy on girls, to wait for them when they'd unhook their bathing suits to tan their backs, and had indeed spotted her with Mark Meyer and Sissy Morgan. She chewed on her lips, and Michaud, seeing that she was about to say something else, made a sign to Cusack to wait before asking any more questions. *It wasn't yesterday*, she at last blurted out, *it was the day before, Friday, Friday morning. Don't tell Dad*, she implored, glancing towards the door, as if her father was going to open it from one moment to the next and come in to give her a pair of slaps. *He's not here*, Michaud replied softly, *you can talk, we won't tell.*

In short, it appeared that Frenchie Lamar had been seeing Mark Meyer without her parents knowing, and that they'd kill her if they found out. *Don't tell Dad!* Meyer was the reason for the argument with Sissy, who'd claimed that Frenchie had gone behind Zaza's back, Zaza who was dead, by showing herself off in that way with Meyer. But the boys were wrong, that row had taken place two days earlier, Frenchie insisted, Friday, *Friday morning.* Mark wasn't in Boundary the day before, he was at West Forks with his parents, they just had to confirm it, then she burst into tears. Through her sobbing, there emerged the names of Sissy, Zaza, Sis, Zaz, and Michaud regretted having been so hard on her. This child was just a victim, an innocent kid who'd taken a shine to an imbecile. He tried to console her, promising he'd lay his hand on the man who'd attacked her friends, *I'll catch him, Franneswoise, I swear.* Unable to stop a new rush of tears racking Frenchie Lamar, he called her mother and apologized, and then they left, Michaud, Cusack, Larue, three men troubled by the sadness of a wounded girl.

The day was almost done when they left the Lamars' cottage. Behind the mountain you could still make out a thin pink band, which the night would swallow up in a few seconds. Near the cottage, young Hank or Frank Milton was pacing back and forth among the trees' dark silhouettes. If the killer was loose in the neighbourhood, he'd only have to approach quietly to strike him on the back of the neck with a stone or a piece of wood, just as he'd done with Sissy Morgan, but the murderer wouldn't come by here. He'd wait for his next victim to wander off, out of sight of others, and he'd make his move. The vision of an arm being raised in the night went through Michaud's mind as he informed Milton that within an hour he'd be sending one or two men over to spell him off. As the thin pink band disappeared, he said *enough, enough for today*, the magical and liberating formula that Cusack and Larue had been waiting for.

Michaud insisted that he would drive Larue home, but he wanted to walk. *I need some fresh air*, he murmured, then he disappeared into the darkness of Turtle Road. Michaud and Cusack watched him move off, then they got into their car. A few seconds later the two men left Boundary, Cusack at the wheel, Michaud's head spinning, wondering what role Meyer had played in this story, always present without being there, in the middle of a trio of young girls who had set their caps for him, for lack of anything better. From what he could understand, he'd gone out two or three times with Sissy, the same with Elisabeth Mulligan, which is what had turned Sissy against Frenchie even if she herself had sent Meyer packing, after *Zaza*, before *Zaza*, it didn't matter. He'd never understand women's infatuations.

He was thinking about Dottie when Cusack braked in front of his house after a ride that seemed to him to have lasted only a few minutes. He must have slept without realizing it, perhaps snored and drooled onto his shirt, but he wasn't up to apologizing. He wished Cusack good night, and went in to join his wife.

All the police had left Bondrée for the night, one team after another, everyone had gone home, except for the agents posted at the Lamars, our first neighbours on the left, to replace the one who'd been on guard in front of the cottage all day. My parents thought I was in my room, but I'd sneaked out to observe them. There was one man on each side, and they came together from time to time to exchange a few words in low voices, then again went their own way. There wasn't much to see, the bigger one was drinking Coke, the other was munching Cracker Jack, and from time to time opened the driver's door of his car to take out a thermos or a cigarette and to check the radio, letting me see his face under the overhead light, red hair with a moustache, nothing interesting there either. I got tired of that and went down near the lake on my tiptoes.

My back propped against the rock my brother and I had named the prehistoric rock, back when we played together and our three years' difference didn't matter, I searched desperately for the Great Bear, so as not to think about what was happening to us, but the sky began to cloud over, meaning there'd be rain the next day. You could see only a few stars here and there, wavering behind the veil of fog stretching from east to west over our heads. If the world had not clouded over just like the sky on this August night, a few campfires would have been burning around the lake, at the Millers', the Ménards', from where you'd have heard jokes and campfire songs, the crackling of sparks. A normal, high summer lakeshore evening. You'd also have heard, in the background, Zaza Mulligan's record player, Sissy Morgan's jokes where she was diving off the end of the dock, the night bathers knifing into the smooth water. Lucy in the Sky's summer would be unfolding to the smell of marshmallows, Coppertone lotion, and warmed sand, and no one would dream that a summer could be cut short at its very peak. But there we were, two girls dead, killed, murdered, and maybe more to come, that's what the night was telling us, bereft of Sissy Morgan's joyful cries.

Unable to admire the Great Bear, I concentrated on a star hugging the top of the mountain, to which I addressed a prayer, for Sissy, for Zaza, whom I missed like you can miss the mess left behind by exuberant cousins at the end of a vacation. I'd never again be anyone's *littoldolle*, the bratty kid showing off her spiders and snakes to the two American girls who laughed out loud and said *foc*. The two girls would never come down Côte Croche singing "Are You Lonesome Tonight?" at the tops of their lungs. Never again, said my prayer, and the star over the mountain bit by bit went watery, went soft and damp as it slid behind the clouds. *Foc*, Sissy, I murmured, *foc*, Zaza, then I wiped away tears while the image of the two girls, my ideals, went to black along with the star. Another fire going out, but one that would forever shed light on my childhood.

I was looking for a leaf or a scrap of paper to blow my nose with when I spotted a silhouette on the beach coming towards me. The murderer… Bondrée's killer. It could only be him, the assassin, the maniac, coming out of the night and stalking his next victim. I crawled behind the rock and prayed he wouldn't see me, *please*, mon Dieu, *please*, and I was the ostrich, the tortoise, the pigeon frozen in place, my chin pulled into my neck as far as it would go. I could have cried out and the police would have come running, but I would have alerted my parents at the same time, who would have tied me to my bed with a lock and chain the next day. I'd change my mind if the killer got too close. Meanwhile, I poked my head out a quarter of an inch to grab a stick, a big piece of a branch I could bang him with on his knees, but the stick was shaking in my hands like Wile E. Coyote's body when he gets hit with an anvil full in his face, meanwhile I kept saying over and over again in my head *please, God, please*, then I heard a voice, Bob's voice, whispering my name.

*Fuck*, Bob, I whispered back, letting fall my stick, both relieved to see my brother and totally stunned by the "fuck" that came out so spontaneously, the first real "fuck" of my life, not counterfeit, not copied. If I wasn't so scared of making a noise, I would have thrown myself around Bob's neck, not just because Bob was Bob and not the killer, but because Sissy and Zaza, from high up on their humid star, had just kind of given me a pat on the back. *Fuck*, les filles! *Fuck, girls!*

What are you doing there? my brother asked, then he started bawling me out under his breath. You're out of your mind going out alone in the middle of the night. What were you thinking of? You know there's a killer roaming around, and blahblahblah, and blahblahblah, but I was so happy it was Bob and only Bob that he could have chewed me out all night and I wouldn't have talked back. Of course, the nearest cop heard us, the second cop heard the first one call his name, Carver! And they came towards us with their flashlights held out in front of them. Fortunately my brother Bob had just become a man, so he was able to explain to them, it's my little sister, I'm keeping an eye on her, and blahblahblah. I nearly burst out laughing when I saw him shaking the policemen's hands, but I bit my cheek, Bob had just saved my skin, Bob had seen death, he deserved a bit of respect.

Once Carver and his partner had returned to their posts, Bob came to sit down beside me, his back to the prehistoric rock, like he used to. We were a bit more cramped, Bob had grown, me too, but not the rock, and we had to pull apart a bit so our shoulders wouldn't touch. We stayed like that for a few moments in silence, then Bob asked me if I remembered the day we'd painted rust marks onto Papa's car with an old can of yellow paint we'd taken from the shed. I hadn't forgotten that day, no more than I'd forgotten the anger of my father, who'd gone around for six months in a blue and yellow automobile, until he was able to pay for a new paint job. But I remembered especially the solidarity that held us together then, Bob and me, all for one and one for all, and I was sure Bob was thinking the same thing. That was why he'd brought up that blunder, because we were together again, arm in arm, beside our rock.

Then we talked about Picard the grouch, who preferred throwing out the apples from his orchard rather than giving us some, the birth of Millie, the squirrel called Gobeil who'd almost swallowed one of my fingers along with his peanut, a bunch of old memories a brother and sister have, somewhere there among those images that hold a life together and make blood ties what they are. All this time, though, I had only one idea in my head, to ask Bob about what he'd seen in the clearing. I was waiting for just the right moment, but he was the one who broached the subject. His voice suddenly got serious, and he talked to me about the trap, the pale shape in the midst of the tall grass, about Victor Morgan, so beside himself that at first it took three pairs of arms to bring him under control, before he collapsed next to Sissy. That's why you mustn't go out alone, Dédée.

It had been a long time since Bob had talked to me like that, a long time since he'd called me Dédée, and I would have started to sob if someone else hadn't got there first.

Bob was telling me how the father of Jane Mary and Silas Brown had brought up all over his rubber boots, when a cry tore into the night, a shriek from the dead that spat out my name, Andrée, Dédée, my mite. My mother had just realized I wasn't in my bed, and she'd thought the worst, what any normal mother would have imagined, finding her daughter's bed empty in the middle of summer when the werewolves had decided to go back into action and limber up their claws. Hearing her shout, Carver and his buddy rushed back at top speed, lights went on in cottage windows, the McBains', the Grégoires', doors were flung open, and my brother and I went running up to the cottage, it's all right, mom, we're here.

The slap I received was as spontaneous as my *fuck* a bit earlier, but I hardly felt the burn because I'd just found my brother again, who'd disappeared for the last few years behind his hoarse voice and his long monkey arms, which had grown along with his beard.

The letter M, he repeated, the letter V, the letter W... sitting under a reading lamp, Stan Michaud studied the Polaroids taken by Cusack in the clearing. It was the first moment he'd had since the day before to look at the photos in peace, with nothing to distract him. When he'd got home, Dorothy was waiting. She'd kept some macaroni for him, which she reheated while he poured himself a bourbon and filled her in on the broad lines of the affair. Sissy Morgan, he said, abandoned in the forest, a terrible sight, a tragic beauty, he didn't know which of the images was the most compelling.

Despite the fact that his story was full of gaps, gaping holes where words refused to venture, Dorothy let him talk without interrupting, hearing the pain in his voice, his impotence in the face of an evil too cunning to be grasped. She listened to his rage as he described the edge the killer had, always outpacing everyone else by a few lengths, his determination to catch him, even if I have to take giant steps, Dottie, like in those tales where the hero dons some kind of seven league boots, because he'd sworn to Sissy Morgan in the clearing, to Esther Conrad in the stench of the Salem dump, to Frenchie Lamar while handing her a handkerchief, *I'll find him, I swear. You will*, replied Dorothy, her hand on his shoulder, then she threw out the macaroni he'd barely touched, and wished him good night. She knew she had to leave him alone, and there was no point in insisting that he come to bed. He'd go up when his second or third bourbon had got the better of his fatigue and blurred the faces of Elisabeth Mulligan and Sissy Morgan, poor girls he preferred not to think about, dead sleeping beauties.

Dottie could understand that Stan was distraught, who wouldn't have been for less than that, but his tenacity puzzled her. He seemed almost to believe that to arrest the murderer would bring the young girls back to life, and that they would at last be able to answer the question he'd been asking forever: why? Why was evil more powerful than the police, more powerful than God, stronger than beauty or the unalloyed joy of the innocent? Why? His behaviour did not hide a desire for vengeance or even a need to have justice prevail, as Stan believed no more in justice than in honesty. He took upon himself the guilt of criminals, and he wanted the dead to know that he was there, sleeping beside them, that someone cared about their last breath, about the truth it contained, the only truth, finally, worth attending to. If he could hear that breath, its burden of truth, he could perhaps tap into a silence within himself, and catch a glimpse of the killer.

While she was getting ready for bed and thinking of those strange sins her husband accused himself of, neither venial nor mortal, sins of conscience, like long snakes whose venom induced insomnia, Michaud brought out the photos, hoping to find there a detail everyone had missed, but this post-mortem orderliness told him nothing new. There was only that letter, under the wound at the elbow, which Cusack saw as a bird in flight. Maybe he was right, the letter might only be a smudge of dirt shaped like a bird, like a premonitory sign representing the soul's ascension, but deep inside he wanted to believe that Sissy Morgan, in a last attempt at vengeance, had traced one of the killer's initials on her brown skin. For several minutes he turned the photo every which way, unable to see anything but Mark Meyer's double initials, even though there was also an M in Mulligan and Morgan, in Ménard, in Maheux, in McBain, in mother... His judgment was skewed, but there was nothing he could do, he couldn't get over Meyer's young, thuggish face, *une face à fesser dedans*—good for smacking?—like he heard Bob Lamar say, an expression you couldn't translate literally. *A clown face,* he concluded, because he didn't like the duplicity of clowns' faces, and Meyer was certainly a clown, a lecherous buffoon. He'd check out his alibis again the next day and would question the dolt himself, after which he'd maybe be able to get him out of his mind.

Dottie had been in bed for a long time when he finally put his photos away in an envelope and went up, exhausted, to slip into the sheets with their scents of a mature woman and warm fruit. Three miles away, Cusack, for his part was staring at the ceiling of his room, his stomach weighed down by the four cutlets he'd put away under the uneasy gaze of Laura, who'd never seen him eat with such indifferent, robotic avidity. And she'd never known him to be so silent. Normally, he told her about his day when he came home, happy to have nabbed some lowlife or to have stopped some kid from getting into trouble, but since the start of this affair, she could only draw out of him a few details here and there. *Too sad, baby, too dark*, he replied, *don't wanna talk about it*. Everything she knew about the investigation, or almost, she'd got from Dorothy. A second girl, Dottie had told her that morning, after Stan's phone call, killed in the forest, like in novels, like in films. It was the young girls that obsessed Jim, to the point where she almost felt jealous of them, of two dead girls to whom she apologized for her foolishness, staring at the wind stirring the curtains.

And yet it was her face that Cusack saw everywhere, in the underbrush and in the graves, in the reflections cast by the curtains. Aware that Laura wasn't sleeping, he searched for words that might reassure her, but how to reassure a woman whose death obsessed you? He gazed up at the unlit ceiling light, telling himself that he too had to sleep, that at this rate he wouldn't make it. His four cutlets were burning his stomach as much as his anxieties were choking off his air, and he couldn't shut his eyes without a procession of supplicant women rising through the aqueous red veil behind his eyelids. Weary of the struggle, he got up and went down to sit in the yard, from where he watched the sky clouding over, while miles from there, Brian Larue, stretched out on a chaise longue he'd set up near the lake, was also gazing at the clouds. He heard the weak stirring of the waves, and he prayed to the heavens that he might sleep, but too many images were warring inside his head, Stella McBain busying herself so as not to collapse, Valère Grégoire pounding the table with his fist, Sam Duchamp describing the death of a fox, his little Emma who'd be arriving the next day, and whom he'd have to entrust to the Duchamps while he went around the lake with Michaud, one cottage after another, until nightfall once more. He wasn't made for this police work that forced you to invade the homes of people who only wanted to be eating peacefully, sleeping peacefully, living quietly. He was ashamed of dirtying their floors with his big boots, though he knew that it wasn't really him walking in on the people, but the killer, the killer and his dirty boots.

It was two o'clock when he finally dozed off to the sound of the waves, at about the same time that Stan Michaud began to snore, and just a little after Jim Cusack dragged himself to the couch in his living room, where he buried his head in a pile of cushions that smelled of summer's dust. A gruelling day lay in wait for the three men, the third day of the investigation, which would begin under an overcast sky and would end with the rumbling of a storm.

Sissy Morgan was wandering aimlessly, her mind still enclosed in a glassy surround that made the whole world look unreal. *Where were you, Zaz? What have you done?* Even the wind was no longer the wind, it couldn't dry her damp skin. She went down Snake Hill like a zombie, *are you lonesome tonight*, and turned towards Weasel Trail, where she sat on a pile of rocks, not tired, not thirsty, just weary, and not knowing any more if she should walk to the ends of the earth or stay there, on the pile of rocks, until her arms came loose from her trunk.

The sun was still high when Sissy heard steps cracking the branches, a fox or a hare, a fox or a man. She was getting ready to leave, not wanting to see a hare or anyone, when she spotted a man, or rather his shirt, a patch of white among the leaves. Another busybody who wanted to warn her off, tell her not to go alone into the woods. *Fuck you!* She left the path, following the windings of a half-dried stream, Peter's or Weaver's Brook, it didn't matter, then climbed a hill, Snake Hill, Shit Hill, Whatever Hill, scraping her knees but not wanting to stop, because the steps were following her. At the top of the hill she asked who was there, *who's there? Leave me alone!* Faced with silence, she picked up a stone and threw it down in the direction of the steps, in the direction of the patch of white moving through the trees, *leave me alone, you pain in the ass!*

Her anger was stronger than her fear, and for the first time since her friend's death Sissy Morgan felt the blood rushing back into her limbs and her heart beating in her temples. *You won't frighten me, you bastard!* She grabbed another stone, bigger than the first, and took shelter behind a tree. Down below it was supper time, *Michael, Marnie, suppertime*, down below it was sunny, and Sissy missed the days when she ran with Zaza, answering that call, *Zaza, Sissy, suppertime*, scampering down the hill to go and stuff herself with hamburgers on the Mulligans' deck, relish and mustard with fries.

She was gauging her chances of running back down at full speed without breaking her neck, *run, Sissy, run*, when a hand closed on her shoulder. Ready to bite and to kill, she leaped to her feet, her stone at arm's length, but she held herself back. *You?* Then Sissy saw the stone, the white stone she'd thrown before, in the hand ready to bite, in the hand of the man who was ready to kill.

*Why? Why . . .*

After some vain appeals, some curses, some insults, *stupid idiot, loser, goddamn fucking son of a bitch*, Sissy Morgan began to back off. She'd barely had time to turn around when the stone came down on the back of her skull, blacking out the unreal world where her thoughts had their dwelling place.

# DAY 3

When Stan Michaud and Jim Cusack parked in the Boundary campground access road on Monday 14 August to question the campers, it was not yet raining, but all of nature was suffused with that inert perfume that heralded a storm. This was cheering to Michaud, as were all restful scents; they were a balm for anxiety, for the mindless disquiet of gusty days. The peace radiating from the trees would help him to start the day without thinking only of the travails to come, that's what he was saying to himself when he saw two reporters coming his way, one with a notebook, the other with a camera. *Son of a bitch*, he swore, turning towards Cusack, but the camera's flash was already popping. *Chief Inspector Stanley Michaud arriving at the scene of the crime*, or some other nonsense of the sort, that's what he'd be reading the following day under a picture showing him turning his back or waving his arms in an attempt to shoo the busybodies off, as one tries to rid oneself of a swarm of black flies.

He had known they'd turn up sooner or later, that bunch could smell blood from hundreds of miles away. Naively, he'd hoped that Boundary's isolation would keep them at a distance. Might as well wish for a wolf to spare a captive lamb. At first he thought he could get away with one of those all-purpose formulas you heard every day on TV, "No comment, guys, you know as well as I do that anything I say could compromise the investigation," but those formulas only worked when the investigation was being conducted in isolation. As it was, the reporters had already wormed information out of a dozen idiots all agog at the idea that their names would show up in the newspaper. Given that, better to bring them up to date, more or less, and get rid of them right away.

With his bad-day smile, he led the reporter and his photographer to the table carved with dozens of names, the tattooed table, beneath a maple whose leaves, curiously, were beginning to redden. An old tree that no longer knew how to gauge the light's intensity and thought itself already in autumn. He allotted them ten minutes, no more, during which he went over the broad lines of the affair, avoiding any mention of the letter M or W, as well as Sissy Morgan's sawed-off hair, as this detail, both morbid and sensational, was perfect fodder for the sort of headlines he abhorred: *Young Girl Scalped in Boundary Pond Woods, Stripped of her Hair, then Murdered*. Then he told them to go and finish their work in town and to let him carry on with his own. I've got enough people already underfoot, guys, give me a bit of air. But he knew he'd see them the next day, and that the appearance of their article would bring more scribblers in their wake. He was trying to buy time, just a little, before the affair hit the papers with the version of the first victim's neighbour alongside that of a housewife concerned about her children and an adolescent who had spotted a stranger going into the woods with his Stetson and a horse. If it were possible, he'd force all of Boundary to keep its mouth shut, but his powers didn't extend that far. No power did, other than that of violence. However much you asked everyone to be totally discreet, there'd always be someone yielding to the temptation of sharing secrets or making up stories.

Suddenly, the heaviness in the air didn't seem so comforting. He went back to Cusack with his head lowered, with no other desire than to go and stretch out under a tree and shut himself off, to be left in peace. But there was no peace and no absolute power and he had to be content with taking off his tie as he greeted Brian Larue, who arrived in an old red pickup truck that could have used a good wash. After parking, Larue jumped out of the truck, humming the tune of "Mystery Train," which he'd been listening to on the radio. He'd slept little, but he felt energetic this morning, which wasn't the case for Michaud, who seemed to be dwindling in stature under the weight of the clouds. Faced with others' misfortune, Michaud was one of those people who aged before your eyes, the way sponges soaked up the fecal matter of their fellow creatures. By the end of this investigation he'd have lost several years that he'd never regain, crushed by the hastening hours in a bad time, his life consumed as if by a huge black hole.

Still, Larue's good humour did perk up Michaud, who smiled when he recognized Little Junior Parker's old hit. Michaud liked Black music, and owned a small collection of blues albums which he sometimes dipped into on Saturday night, when Saturday nights were still Saturday nights, drawing Dottie's body in on his own to the sound of the guitar or harmonica. When it was all over… but he let the thought go in order to explain to Larue that they were setting up for questioning in the building facing the lake, a kind of refectory where the campers could take shelter on rainy days when there was nothing to do but play cards while waiting for the sun to return. Flipping through his notebook, he said he'd start with the campground's owner, after which he'd deal with Meyer, not yet seen since his return from West Forks at dawn, and he'd end with the campers.

As on the previous day, Michaud wanted Larue present at all the interrogations, whether or not it was necessary. He wanted him to know what was going on, and to hear everyone's version. His task was not simply to provide a word-for-word translation of the answers to questions, but to look for connections between different testimonies, or on the other hand, subtle contradictions. *Ready?* he asked Larue, then he signed to Plamondon, who was repairing a water pipe, to follow him into the refectory.

The room smelled of sand and humidity, a vacation smell that reminded Michaud of his last real holiday in July of '65, a week with Dottie on the shores of Lake Champlain, with nothing to do but go from the lake to the cottage rented for the occasion, from bed to hammock, from lunch table to that of supper, where were lined up the yellow or blue plastic plates and bowls, the July colours mingling with the odour of the sand. When he tried to bring back the memory of happy moments in his life, that week always turned up. In his mind, those few days next to the water were a dazzling yellow carved into by hard shadows and swept with the scent of trout and gusts of wind charged with blue and green perfume. In normal times, Boundary must have resembled those bright days when he'd been close to carefree with Dottie. He'd promised that he'd go back there this year, but he hadn't counted on a murderer crossing his path. Dottie would have to be content with her garden while he closed out his summer near a lake that had lost its lustre.

He came out of his reverie when Cusack opened one of the windows protected by the green-painted screens you saw everywhere, in the schools, the sheds, the community halls. Unfortunately, no breeze entered the room. The day was oppressive, just like the sky.

Coffee was dripping into a pot on the counter set up at one end of the room, and Michaud was happy to accept a cup, after which he placed chairs around a table in such a way that the people being questioned would be isolated on one side, and aware of who was in charge. Then he invited Plamondon to sit across from him. He had a solid alibi for the day and evening of 21 July. Mark Meyer had been off, and Plamondon had been taking care of the campground. At least twenty people had seen him moving about the property, stirring up the campfire, replying to questions, and helping a young couple put up their tent, after which he'd played gin rummy with a fellow who couldn't get to sleep. Zaza Mulligan having been murdered during the night of 21 July, Michaud could exonerate Plamondon as soon as he confirmed what he'd said, even if his alibi was less than perfect for the afternoon and evening of 12 August, an uneventful day that he'd spent for the most part in the caretaker's cabin. No problems, no tent carried off by the wind, no arguments over whose turn it was at the shower. Nothing. A peaceful day, a dull evening. No witness to his leisure time. It was as if all the men in Boundary had agreed among themselves to remain alone, each in his corner during that blasted day, Michaud thought, drawing one hand carefully over his damp skull, beneath which there thrummed the dim music of fatigue. How to exonerate all those people whom no one had seen? And Meyer? Michaud went on, wanting to finish things off with Plamondon as fast as he could. According to him Meyer was a good worker, punctual, quick, efficient, about whom he had no complaints. His biggest flaw was that he liked flirting a bit too much. There were lots of young girls on the property in summer clothes, soaking up the sun, it was hard to blame a young man for being drawn to those bare arms. But aside from that weakness, Meyer was a model employee.

Michaud then asked him about the trio formed by Zaza, Sissy, and Frenchie, and their behaviour on the night of 21 July. Young girls who were having fun, Plamondon replied, no more than that, and who'd drunk a bit too much. Perfect victims, Michaud thought, you just had to push them a bit for them to fall over. How many men had seen them in that state? How many had thought how easy it would be to trip them up? And which of them had his eyes on them, determined to shadow one of them, the lost lamb, the doe drinking innocently at the stream?

He'd never make it without solid proof, a misplaced object, a clue buried under a body. As soon as he had a moment, he'd return to the path or the clearing and he'd find, he had to, what the killer had forgotten. Meanwhile he let Plamondon go, and asked him to send in Meyer. Right away, he insisted, since he'd looked at the clouds, lower than before, denser, threatening from one moment to another to pour their darkness onto the mountain, also dark, with its monotone cast blurring the trees, transforming them into an inert mass. Two goldfinches, out of place in this gloomy décor, had just alighted on the top of a Virginia pine when Meyer arrived. Ill at ease, the young man lingered near the door until he was asked to sit down. The questioning lasted half an hour, at the end of which Michaud felt that it could go no further. What Meyer said matched to the letter what he'd told the sheriff of Somerset County the day before, a statement Michaud had received by telephone that morning. The father's version also agreed with that of the son. Meyer was at West Forks when the murders took place.

Michaud didn't know what he'd hoped to get out of that interrogation. A confession, perhaps, but Meyer was as innocent as a choirboy, if you excluded his adventures with Zaza Mulligan and Sissy Morgan. Ancient history, Meyer said, lowering his eyes, as if he regretted that those dalliances hadn't lasted. And Françoise Lamar? Michaud put in. Are you a collector or what? At the sound of the young girl's name, Meyer's red face went crimson, and he stammered something to the effect that it wasn't the same with Frenchie, she didn't make fun of him. Michaud grilled him a bit on the subject, but got nothing out of him. This cretin was in love.

He spent the rest of the morning interrogating the few campers who'd not yet taken off, with no result. No one had seen anything. Everyone had an alibi. He'd have to contact those who had left, seek out the ones who'd set up their tents in Boundary on the 21 July weekend, appeal to the police in other counties, a real puzzle, as his colleague Dave Leroy had said, one with numerous pieces spread all over the state of Maine and beyond. It was the beginning of the afternoon when he declared that it was time for a break, and then the sky opened up. The abrupt drumming of the rain swept down on the building at the same time as the wind, and he saw a woman go by, running past the windows, already soaked by the bath she'd just subjected herself to, running all the same, her towel over her head, as if the rainwater were threatening to bleach her tan.

Larue had left a few minutes earlier to pick up his daughter in Farmington, so he was alone in the refectory with Cusack, who was already attacking the sandwiches Laura had prepared for him. He had his own lunch as well, potato salad and mortadella sandwiches, along with a slice of blueberry pie Dottie had slipped into his lunch box despite his objections, but the mere prospect of having to chew on whatever it might be seemed beyond his capacities. He swallowed what was left of his coffee and advised Cusack that he was going to lie down in the car, come get me in half an hour.

Cusack watched him running beneath the rain, a sturdy man who carried his weight both like a burden and like his armour, and who would land himself a heart attack before he was sixty unless his brain exploded, spattering the walls with the horrific images collected there along with his childhood memories, Dottie's smile, the crazed colours of beautiful days. He dared not imagine what was in Michaud's head, and wondered whether that was what awaited him as well, the fatigue, the bulk, the constant torment. He was thirty-two years old, and he saw his future as a long corridor where there was a disaster lurking behind every door.

He closed the windows and gave himself a shake. All that would pass. All that was because of the two girls, their bodies stretched out in the forest, two bleeding dolls, oversize and anomalous, two elusive mannequins striding through his dreams. But he swore to himself that he'd forget them, Zaza Mulligan and Sissy Morgan would not be his Esther Conrad. He'd not let himself be entrapped by his chief's obsessions. He finished his meal listening to the rain drumming on the metal roof, another music that reminded him of the sweet fever of childhood, then he ran to wake up Michaud, hopping through the stones like a child, like a dog shaking himself off. Beneath his feet the water spurted, making tiny arcs that brought into focus his zest for life. That's what they'd see if his brain exploded in ten or twenty years, a gush of bright water.

Sitting next to me on my bed, Emma was admiring her polished nails, where a bit of the varnish had spilled onto the skin. I was looking at mine as well, which seemed to belong to another girl, a girl who would have worn a dress, and shoes as shiny as the nail polish. It was my mother who'd insisted that we paint ourselves like that. Come on, girls, I'll show you how to do it. On the instant, I almost cried for joy. My mother was giving me another promotion, she was giving me permission to rummage around in the little flowered plastic case where she kept her makeup, and also to go through her toilet articles, in a bag that had made me envious ever since I was little, one whose form and design changed with the years, but which always held the same treasure, with its bright and perfumed objects. I right away thought of Zaza Mulligan's long fingers flicking the ash off a Pall Mall in a flash of pink. Once I had the nails, all I'd need would be a cigarette to be able to say *fuck* Emma, raising my little finger.

Now that the polish was gleaming under the lamp, all I could think of was to remove all that junk, tear off the dress that would go with it, and go bury my hands in the mud that collected around the cottage where the gutters overflowed. I wasn't Zaza Mulligan, I didn't have the delicate hands of young girls smelling of perfume. I was the mite, the bug, the family's tomboy, and even if my breasts were beginning to tickle, a sign they were growing like Emma said, that was no reason for me to disguise myself as a doll. If that continued I'd end up looking like Millie's Barbie and walking on stilts. *No way!* In a minute I'd borrow my mother's nail polish remover, saying my nails were burning. Like it or not, she'd have to believe me, they were my nails after all, but for now I was waiting for Emma to show me her surprise.

Emma was waiting too. I could see her excitement by the suspicious light in her eyes, glimmering like those of a raccoon getting ready to topple a garbage can. After making sure that my bedroom door was tightly shut, she placed a manicured finger over her mouth, and pulled a pack of Alpine menthols out of her backpack. I stole it from my mother, she whispered, there are five left.

Foreseeing in a flash the look in my mother's eyes if they were to come to rest on that little turquoise cardboard square, embodying, after sex, swearing, and alcohol, the be-all and end-all of what was forbidden, I too ran to the door to lock it quietly, and a whole raft of pictures of girls with their fingers in the air rushed into my head. I was again the disciple of Zaza Mulligan and Sissy Morgan, the girl who walked around swaying her hips, and already I saw the cloud of smoke that would soon envelop us, Emma and me.

We have to find a hiding place, Emma whispered again, and I thought right away about my cabin under the pine tree, where the branches protected us a little from all the rain. We'll take my poncho and my brother's, then we'll say we're going to pick up insects knocked out by the rain, my mother won't be able to say anything.

Then Emma slipped the pack of Alpines and the matchbook into the back pocket of her jeans, and pulled on my rainproof poncho. No one the wiser, we left my room whistling,

Brownie at our heels, while over our heads there floated a huge grey cloud on which was written the word "guilty" in block letters. The two greatest conspirators of all time at work.

In the kitchen, Mama was rolling out pie crust, giving a push to the right, a little less to the right, then to the left, following the invisible curve of the circle that was slowly forming. Seeing us, she screwed up her eyes, including her third eye, which could see even in the dark, like God, omnipotent and omniscient, and she asked us what we were up to.

Nothing, I replied, a bit too hastily. We need a plastic dish, we're going to save dying butterflies. Her three eyes still narrowed, she dried her hands on her apron, getting flour on the big mushroom face displayed there, and took from a cupboard an empty Crisco jar that she held out to me as if to say that she knew I was lying, and that I knew she knew. You can't beat mothers for telepathy. That must come from the fact that they made our brains at about the same time as all the rest. Tough. I grabbed the jar and Bob's poncho, which was hanging on the veranda, and ran out with Emma, who ventured a quick thank you, Madame Duchamp.

Your mother knows, Emma whispered, as we installed ourselves in my pseudo-cabin, to which I replied that she maybe knew something, but didn't know exactly what, so we were safe for the time being. Get out your cigarettes, she's not going to come spying on us, she's too proud.

A bit hesitant, Emma extracted the half-crushed pack of cigarettes from her pocket, and we first studied the effect of the Alpine king-sizes sticking out from between our bedaubed fingers. You'd think we were movie stars, Emma giggled. For my part, all I could see were the fingers of a girl who wanted to see herself as a real girl, when there were traces of spruce gum, scratches, and insect bites on every digit. Nothing at all like Zaza Mulligan or Sissy Morgan, whom I didn't want to allow into the cabin, for fear of depressing myself thinking that Zaza Mulligan would nevermore snap down the cover of her gold lighter, that Sissy Morgan would never again stub out the butt of her Pall Mall under the heel of her white patent leather shoes, all of which made no bloody sense and I couldn't get it all into my head, as if death gave a damn whether anything meant anything, good or bad. A drop of rain fell onto my hood in a steady rhythm, and I got a sense of the world's injustice thanks to an unlit cigarette that was trembling just enough to accuse me of being there, alive and well, ready to take the place of two girls who were no longer breathing.

So I made myself think about Marilyn Monroe, Elizabeth Taylor, Jenny Rock, who didn't act but must have smoked, and about Donalda, Séraphin's wife, who might well have allowed herself to smoke before being canonized, anything to erase Zaza Mulligan's likeness from my cambered nails, then I asked Emma to light me up, fast, before I changed my mind. The scrape of the match sent its sulphurous odour out under the pine, I breathed in deeply and found myself coughing my lungs out in the midst of a cloud of smoke that had exploded into the humid air to hang there like an early morning mist. It smelled awful, but because it was supposed to be good I took a second puff, not inhaling this time, so I was able to vent the *fuck* I'd been holding in reserve for so long, with my lips rimmed in smoke and my head absurdly tossed back, like Marilyn Monroe, all the while thinking of Donalda.

Don't breathe, I said to Emma as she lit up, and her smoke mixed with mine, like blood flowing from the wrists of those who make a pact for life and until death. I stuck the end of my cigarette onto the end of hers, tchin tchin, and Emma had a good coughing fit too, while still managing to swear eternal friendship. She was just catching her breath when one of the policemen scouring Turtle Road and its vicinity parked his car at the McBains' and ran onto the porch with a plastic bag whose contents we couldn't make out through the pine branches, but which had to be some kind of evidence. The investigation was heating up and we craned our four ears in the direction of the McBains' open windows, where there was a meeting going on that included Emma's father. Forget it, all we heard was a scream, *what the hell*, after which fat Flora Tanguay, who took herself for Miss Clairol and did her hair just like Mary in *The Family Stone*, came out escorted by Jim Cusack onto the McBains' porch, babbling over and over that this butchery was the work of Pete Landry. It's him! It's him, the damn trapper! Cusack was trying to calm her, but she was all worked up and fanning the air with her soft arms, a bonnet askew on her head, making her look like a parachutist struggling to disentangle his cords. Cusack nevertheless managed to get her into his car, and left to drive her home, I suppose, or to drown her in Ménard Bay.

Flora Tanguay might well have been loopy, but her reference to Pete Landry hit home. What if it really was him, Pete Landry, who was following us near the Chauves-Souris Falls? Our last puffs weren't happy ones, and we were wondering if we should tell the police about our trek to the falls in case our pursuer might have left a trail, even though ghosts, in theory, don't wear shoes, when we heard an "Ahem" from behind us. We almost swallowed our butts, and spun around lightning fast, two panicky heads pivoting a hundred and forty degrees.

Below the branches closing off access to the cabin, there was my mother's face, as white as the kindly smiling mushroom on her apron, but without the smile. She was gunning for me, but I didn't try to dodge the bullets. I knew my mother used blanks, otherwise I would have been dead a long time ago. Still, I tried to hide what was left of my cigarette under my poncho, stifling another coughing fit behind the smoke drifting up from under my collar.

That day, Emma had to go back home to sleep, contrary to what had been planned. As for me, I was promised a session of family therapy, in other words a good bawling out, once my father returned on Friday night. Meanwhile, my mother sat us down at the kitchen table, an all-purpose table that was the cottage's nerve centre across which passed, after the patties of ground beef and the High Liner fish sticks, all our good news, dramas, reprimands, and praise, in short, everything requiring that we sit face to face.

My mother quickly passed over the question of cigarettes, our respective fathers would deal with that. But we had to describe in detail our nocturnal outing to the Chauves-Souris Falls, which merited me two new salvos, including one from Bob who was firing wide of the mark from the living room, but firing all the same.. Since we had no choice, we gave a long account of our hike, long but not wide, we weren't so dumb as to talk about how we'd been followed. My mother was pale enough already, pale and flushed in fact, a curious blend of anger and retroactive fear, the angry red accentuating the pallor induced by what it would have been better for her not to know. We weren't going to say more and risk seeing the red bleeding into the zones of white that in fact worked in our favour. No, that part of the story was Emma's and mine alone, that of two girls who'd made a pact not unlike the one, I imagine, that bound Zaza Mulligan to Sissy Morgan, for life and unto death.

Brian Larue had made the trip from Farmington beneath the pouring rain, answering as frankly as he could the questions posed by his daughter, who wanted to know all about what had been going on at Boundary during her absence. And he was exhausted. If he'd had the choice, he would have stretched out under the table, on the soft carpet patterned with diamonds, and he would have let the rain lull him to sleep, but there was this woman facing him with a wet plastic bonnet on her head, Flora Tanguay, old Pat's daughter-in-law, waving her arms and discharging a frenzied torrent of words. She'd knocked at the McBains' door just as he was dropping Emma off at the Duchamps, and had burst into the dining room with that ridiculous turquoise bonnet whose ties, tightly knotted into a bow, tripled her double chin.

It's him, she repeated, flapping her arms, it's him, Pete Landry, and Michaud had to raise his voice to calm her a little. *Have a seat*, he ordered, pointing to a chair. Flora Tanguay obeyed, a bit confused, while accepting a glass of water offered by Cusack. While she took off her bonnet and arranged her hair, ill at ease with the three pairs of eyes focused on her, she appraised the furniture, of a quality she could never afford, the highly polished candleholders adorning the buffet, casting their silver shimmer onto porcelain while the guests shared their Sunday lunch, roast beef or roast chicken, and she was ashamed of her intrusion. With the end of one of her sleeves she tried to wipe away the drops fallen from her bonnet onto the table, but she only managed to spread them out, her jacket's waterproof material unable to absorb the liquid that the table's varnish couldn't soak up either. Aware of her clumsiness, she sighed, seeking a bit of sympathy in the gaze of Cusack, the courteous policeman with the hazel eyes, then she began again, it's him, it's Pete Landry, rubbing her plump hands over the streaks formed by the water until her skin emitted a faint squeak on contact with the wood, dry at last.

*Tell us what you know,* Cusack asked softly, and Flora Tanguay's shyness disappeared. She opened her mouth and a rush of words came pouring out like a dammed-up torrent suddenly free to sweep down on an arid world. Whenever he could, Larue interrupted her to translate, and then she was off again, throwing the past in with the present, reviving the dead and mixing her own blood in with that of the victims, blood flowing from her womb after the hysterectomy that had prevented her from spending the summer at Bondrée as she usually did. She'd arrived the day before, and had only learned about the dramas at noon today. Right away she knew, right away she saw the connection, those murders were the work of Pete Landry, a monster whose first victim was a poor little dog, Sugar Baby, caught in a trap the same way, a maniac who'd been declared dead when the body found in his cabin was so decomposed that it was unrecognizable. At the time no one bothered to check the fingerprints or the shape of the skeleton, as one would today. Landry was recognized beneath his blackened flesh, distended, ready to burst, the corpse was linked to the shack but Flora Tanguay always had her doubts, which increased when the wind blew over Bondrée and hands scraped at her window panes. Zaza Mulligan's and Sissy Morgan's deaths confirmed these doubts: Pierre Landry wasn't dead. Pierre Landry had come back to take his revenge on everything beautiful.

During this whole account, the three men sitting near her were sending each other meaningful looks, not knowing how to stem this renewed deluge nor how to get rid of this woman without triggering a hysterical episode. Luke Stanfield saved them by bursting into the room to set down in front of Michaud a clear plastic bag inside of which you could see a thick mass of blond hair. *What the hell!* exclaimed Michaud, signing to Stanfield that he remove the damned bag. There was a witness in the room whom he didn't want too involved in the affair, but Flora Tanguay had seen the hair and gone white in the face. Pointing her finger at the bag, she started to scream, describing the pelts hanging on Landry's walls, piled up on his filthy cot, just like that horrible thing in the plastic bag, and Michaud felt his own blood drain from his face. That madwoman thought, as he did, that the killer was a man of the woods, the difference being that he wasn't so crazy as to believe that Landry had risen from the flames engulfing his shack in order to seek vengeance. He'd heard enough, and he wanted this Flora Tanguay gone from the premises. *Va chez vous, speak avec nobody*, he told her with a wink of his eye, as if in confidence, not caring whether he was butchering his ancestors' language, then he handed Cusack the keys to his official car so he could drive her back. Meanwhile, he'd have to talk to Luke Stanfield.

A wave of pain fanned out through Michaud's head when he looked at the bag and saw there was an earring still caught in the hair, Zaza Mulligan's earring, *a tear, a drop of pink rain*, which the little Duchamp girl, recruited by Sissy Morgan, had found in the forest. Sissy Morgan had been wearing her friend's jewel as one wears a mourning ring, as one dons the old clothes of a lover who's disappeared. That realization intensified his rage, but also the tenderness he felt for the young girls, Sissy, Zaza, Esther.

*Where did you find this?*

And Stanfield described to him the heap of boards piled up in a vacant lot where the woodcutters' road began. Apparently the land belonged to Gilles Ménard, the man who'd found Zaza Mulligan. Ménard had torn down his old shed at the beginning of the summer, and stacked the wood up there. Stanfield's team was still searching through the pile of boards, in case there was more to find, the hunting knife for instance, which was responsible for Sissy Morgan's hair ending up in the bag.

The first time Michaud had met this Ménard, he'd immediately struck him off the list of suspects. He was too overwhelmed, too stunned to be the killer of a young girl whom he'd discovered, he said, by chance. But was it by chance?

His name was turning up too frequently in this investigation, always where blood was involved, the blood of a fox or a young girl, and hair cut off, and limbs torn away. Of course, anyone could have hidden Sissy Morgan's hair under the pile of boards, but he wanted to know what Ménard thought. We're going to Ménard's, he said to Stanfield and Larue, just as Cusack returned, shaken by Flora Tanguay's verbal frenzy.

As the Ménards lived on the bay, they'd have to take the car, even if Michaud would have preferred to walk, thereby putting off the moment when he'd have to confront Ménard. He always felt that way when things began to accelerate and he stumbled on a factor that might bring an investigation to a head. He was scared stiff, afraid of making a mistake, or finding that the killer, the thief, the rapist, or the swindler, was his wife's nephew, his neighbour's son, his dentist or garage man, afraid of losing his grip and beating him to a pulp, or, on the contrary, backing off and apologizing. During the trip no one uttered a word, no one tried to say anything about Stanfield's discovery. They all felt weighed down by the same apprehension, by the prospect of gazing into the eyes of a murderer. They all thought the nightmare might be drawing to a close, but there would be no happy ending, the awakening would not free them from the pall this nightmare cast, from its rank and fetid aftertaste.

Jocelyne Ménard was altering an old pair of pants and listening to the radio when she heard the car parking in the driveway. The engine's growl superimposed itself on Frank Sinatra's voice singing "Something's Gotta Give," as, humming, she lowered the volume. Seeing the police car, she went out on the porch immediately, as women do when they're welcoming trouble as well as joy, too impatient to wait for the one to creep its way towards them or the other to throw itself into their arms. With what was happening in Bondrée, a visit from the police did not bode well, but she graciously invited the men inside, telling them not to bother removing their wet shoes, as she'd be washing the floor in any case.

At a sign from Michaud, Larue informed her that they wanted to talk to her husband. As he had gone out for an hour or two, Michaud immediately assumed that Ménard had left on one of his walks deep into the woods. But he was wrong. Ménard no longer went into the woods. He was afraid of the hazy light that could turn a fox lying on a bed of moss into a half-animal, half-human creature. Since he'd found Zaza Mulligan, since he'd stumbled on the disembowelled fox on the slopes of Moose Trap, since he'd taken part in the discovery of Sissy Morgan, Ménard just mooned around the cottage like a lost dog. At most, he sometimes ventured onto the woodcutters' road that went up behind the cottage. Too much blood, he'd mumbled to his wife, too many pictures filtering through the green light and giving the spruce buds the taste of rusted metal. No. Gilles had simply gonc to buy some materials to rebuild the cabin, the old shed he'd torn down in June. He wanted to use his two weeks of vacation to finish some work. The police were lucky. Normally, he'd be in town, at his job.

Michaud was lucky indeed, because Boundary lost most of its men as of dawn on Monday mornings, except for vacationers and retirees. He'd imagined the scene more than once, the women in nightgowns embracing their husbands on the doorstep, car doors slamming, engine noises fading into the distance, then calm returning to the little community where all you heard was women's voices. An idyllic society, they said, where a male presence was not needed for the rain to keep filling the wells with water, where women easily learned to deal with a lawnmower, a hammer, or a chainsaw, far from the confusing world of the opposite sex.

He was unhappy at not being able to talk to Ménard right away, but he'd wait. He sent Stanfield onto the property, and asked Cusack to go with him, to see what was going on with that pile of boards, and he sat on the wide porch with Larue, despite Jocelyne Ménard's insistence that they stay inside where it was dry. But Michaud didn't want to get too close to Ménard's wife, in case things took a bad turn. He preferred to stay with the rain, whose spray would perhaps make him feel like it was washing away the thick layer of grime that had built up on the old cop's skin. He was telling Larue that this investigation would probably be his last, when Ménard's car drew in near the cottage. Immediately a little girl in a yellow raincoat jumped out and ran to Michaud to show him the plush kitten her father had bought her. Look, mister, he's called Pixie, you can pet him, but Michaud understood nothing of what the child was saying, no more than he understood what he was doing on the porch of a man he was getting ready to destroy.

Sitting on a leatherette hassock that crackled every time he moved, Gilles Ménard held the plastic envelope in his hands, rigid, as if inside it were a child's remains. On a low table there sat another envelope, this one containing a blood-stained shirt that one of Stanfield's men had just fished out from under the pile of boards. Cusack had immediately brought it to his chief and Ménard confirmed that it was indeed one of his shirts, because of the last button, at the bottom, different from the others. He hadn't said a word after that, too shaken at the sight of the hair, a blond foxtail, cut off by a madman. In front of him, Michaud, Larue, and Cusack waited while Jocelyne, his wife, begged him to talk. Say something, Gilles, tell them that this can't be.

The atmosphere in the tiny living room into which they were crammed was as sombre as that of those long hallways down which condemned prisoners are led, their wrists and feet chained. The heat was such that the men had to mop their brows with their shirtsleeves. The rain had not eased the humidity, and they heard it rattling on the roof, heightening the oppressive silence. Only Gilles Ménard was motionless, letting the sweat run down his face, indifferent to the salt burning the corners of his eyes. He looked at the window, where drops of condensation were tracing paths that snaked left or right in response to some obscure resistance, a bit of dust perhaps, or an oily fingerprint easing the water around its circumference.

Take Marie to the Duchamps', he told his wife finally, in a low voice. Inside his head a sequence of words, always the same, was overlaying his incredulity, not in front of Marie, not in front of the little one, not in front of my angel, and he gave Michaud back the bag containing Sissy Morgan's hair.

Lost in thought, he heard Marie say to him, see you soon Pappy, I'm going to play with Millie. Raising his eyes, he saw Marie hand in hand with Jocelyne, her face serious, darkened by the presence of all those adults looking equally solemn, and he longed to throw himself into her arms and hug her until the nightmare was over, but he didn't want to cry in front of her or wet the hood of her raincoat with tears that would never dry. See you soon, my angel, he replied, managing to draw from the love the child inspired in him a smile born from the stuff of real smiles, I love you, then the girl went away with her mother, leaving him alone with men who had to settle among themselves some man-to-man business.

The shirt, he finally managed to say, that's the one I took off to put over Zaza Mulligan. That's the one I was wearing that day, but I'm not the one who hid it. Why would I have done that?

That was the answer Michaud expected. Why hide an object that doesn't incriminate you? Either Ménard was a damned good liar, clever enough to have orchestrated the discovery of Zaza Mulligan's body, or someone else hid that cursed garment, but who, *for Christ's sake*, and when, how, why? The hypothesis was absurd, because it supposed that the killer had returned to Zaza while Ménard was racing down Snake Hill to go and knock, white-faced, at Sam Duchamp's door, or that he was still in the vicinity when Ménard was covering up the young girl's body. But good God, why take the shirt? Michaud didn't understand, and Ménard neither, he was turning himself inside out trying to remember if the damned shirt was still there when he came back to the woods with Duchamp and the police. He was so disoriented at that moment that he'd forgotten about the shirt. Duchamp hadn't said anything about it either, but it wasn't his shirt. In any case, Duchamp was as shaken as he was. When he'd seen Zaza under the floodlights he'd given Ménard a fright, looking like he was going to pass out and that they'd both find themselves in a dead faint, arm in arm, in that mushy place men go when they've had all they can take of being a man. I don't know what happened to that damn shirt, he repeated, but one thing is sure, it's someone around here who took it, someone who knew my property and wanted to pin Zaza Mulligan's murder on me. I don't see any other explanation.

That could make sense, Michaud thought. If this mysterious and hypothetical unknown's purpose was to incriminate Ménard, he's succeeded, because everything points in his direction. If there was only the hair, you could think that anyone might have put it there, but the shirt led them straight to Ménard. *Sorry, Menarde,* I have to take you in, *I have no choice.*

Hearing those words, Ménard wanted to slam his fist into the wall, just so as to hurt, just so as to feel something other than this curious numbness that weakened his legs and thickened his tongue, as if he'd just fallen from a rooftop into a nightmare already well under way, but he obeyed. When he got up, the others all lowered their heads, Michaud, Cusack, Larue, feeling obscurely guilty about the situation, not able to be there before the harm arrived, to head it off, to disable the machinery that in the end grinds us all up, one after the other. They experienced no sense of achievement, no feeling of relief. All they saw was Ménard's distress, the distress of all men unable to walk side by side without one cretin pushing the other face down in the dirt so the herd can walk over him. No one was proud of what was happening in that humid cottage, no one relished his role, but no one would have traded places with Ménard, who would never recover from his fall, guilty or not.

Michaud placed a hand on Ménard's shoulder to lead him out, and at the same time to have him feel the warmth of another man, one of those who walked tall and took no pleasure in tripping up his neighbour. Just as they were leaving, Jocelyne Ménard drove into the cottage yard in their metallic blue Ford, its tires squealing under the driving rain. She leaped out of the car and ran to throw herself into her husband's arms, limp arms, inert, barely able to graze her lower back. As they were easing the suspect into the police car's back seat, she began to shout, but Ménard wouldn't remember what she was trying to tell him, only her face, her outrageously blue eyes withdrawing into the darkness of her cries. And the rain, the rain creeping round the first furrows on her cheeks.

They think it's Gilles, Jocelyne Ménard whispered to my mother, can you keep Marie, then she left at a run, her beautiful white blouse all wet, her lovely blond hair half undone. Twenty minutes later she was back, her skirt and blouse even wetter, glued to her thighs and her stomach. Mama made her tea and gave her a towel, but Jocelyne Ménard, the towel over her shoulders, couldn't drink. Every time she brought the cup to her lips she was seized with hiccups and started again to cry, clouding the mirrors, the silvered surfaces of certain objects, the water pitcher, my mother's compact way back in her bedroom, everything that reflected the world and her red eyes. Kleenexes piled up on the table, forming a sad white little mountain that reminded me of those eternally snowed-in summits where the sun is cold all year round. Unable to console Jocelyne Ménard, my mother took extreme measures. She brought out the Dutch gin and filled two mustard jars right to the tips of the red diamonds that ringed them round.

You could hear Marie and Millie in my room putting on ladies' voices and telling stories about their babies, whose diapers they had to change, and whom they had to bathe. I would have given up my whole collection of Bazooka Joe jokes to be in their place, patting my doll's behind while covering it generously with talcum powder, but after she had surprised us in my smoke-filled cabin my mother had kept Emma and me in the living room, where we pretended to read *Lucky Luke* without turning the pages, totally stunned by Gilles Ménard's arrest and by the suffering of his wife, who swore every ten seconds that Gilles hadn't done it. Gilles Ménard couldn't even stick a worm onto a fishhook without feeling sick to his stomach, he couldn't even set a mouse trap, Jocelyne Ménard had told my mother at the beginning of summer, he couldn't even set a mouse trap, so how could he have massacred two girls? It didn't hold water, and the only thing I could think was that Gilles Ménard was maybe like Doctor Jekyll and Mister Hyde, whom I'd discovered over the winter in an old film starring Spencer Tracy, with the face of a poodle on one side and a bulldog on the other. But that didn't work either. A bulldog's face is too big not to stick out behind that of a poodle.

I was racking my brain when Stan Michaud turned up on the veranda. Seeing Jocelyne Ménard and her mountain of Kleenex, he bowed his head, that was the best thing he could do since he was too big to get under the carpet, then he apologized for arriving unannounced, but he had to talk to my father about a shirt that had disappeared as if by magic, or that went wandering off all by itself in the bush, as I understood it from his mutterings, which were not very enlightening. Seeing him, Jocelyne Ménard jumped up, imploring him to give her back her husband, but Michaud, glumly, just managed one of those shoulder shrugs that are as painful for the person who's trying to justify himself as for the one who's wailing in front of him, and that was the end of it. My mother coldly informed Michaud that my father had gone to work in town and that he wouldn't be back until Friday night. Michaud turned around and left under the carpet this time, a proof that shame really does make you smaller, after which Jocelyne Ménard threw herself into my mother's arms, which were wide enough to embrace half of Bondrée's population, and the two women went back to sit down with their bottle of gin.

I'd never seen my mother drunk, but at the rate she was emptying her glass this would soon be a first, proving that mothers are human. A lousy day. A damned lousy day. For a while, all we heard was the noise of the rain on the roof, then Marie, in the next room, commanded dodo, baby, dodo. That was all it took for my mother to burst into tears, tears copious enough to drown half of Bondrée's population.

Jocelyne Ménard stayed at the Duchamps' until nightfall, then she took Marie home and was able to put her to sleep by telling her for the hundredth time the story of Snow White and the Seven Dwarfs in a version where the prince was replaced by the king of the dwarfs. She then went down to sit by the lake, where she lit herself a cigarette she'd scrounged from her neighbour, Martha Irving, who smoked like a chimney and didn't care, since no one was interested in her mouth anymore. But who, in any case, would have wanted a mouth attached to a body that was falling to pieces? Jocelyne Ménard saw her smoking on her patio when she got back, and took the opportunity to bum a Player's. It was her first cigarette in months, and that, combined with the gin she'd drunk with Florence Duchamp, made her woozy. That was what she wanted, to drown her sorrows, to lose herself in the cloudy sky so as to stop thinking about Gilles, his eyes, his helpless arms the length of his body, gone suddenly limp. A pointless effort, as the picture of her husband descending the stairs surrounded by policemen kept coming back to her. It was a nightmare, she thought, but a very real nightmare, the roughness of the sand on her bare thighs was not at all like the feelings she associated with bad dreams, any more than the nausea coiling around her throat along with the smoke.

At least she wasn't crying anymore. Her eyes had gone dry after her second glass of gin, and she no longer saw the world through a hot veil of tears, but with the sharpness that comes in the wake of panic, the exaggerated clarity that makes everything seem unreal. She even managed to make out the mountain's peak, black on black, silhouetted on her left. If she'd been able, she'd have gone to stretch out on the mountain's slope the way you lie full length alongside a lover, and she'd have wrapped her arms around it. She was so tired that she felt as if her body were as heavy as that mass of rock pointing to the sky. She knew she wouldn't sleep that night, and to imagine her head in repose leaning against the Moose Trap summit gave her a deep feeling of peace.

That was what she'd planned to do over the next two weeks, to lie in Gilles's arms with their odour of spruce when he wasn't busy rebuilding his shed, to lie next to him, here, while Marie built sandcastles or buried their feet in the sand with her plastic shovel. She'd been waiting for her husband's two weeks of annual vacation since the beginning of summer, and here a bloodstained shirt had dropped onto their outstretched bodies before they could even savour the sweet sigh of weariness that comes with too much heat and sun.

How could the police have got it so wrong? How did they come to believe that a man who gathered water from streams with his grass-stained hands could attack young girls? There was such ardour in the act of gathering water, a silent ardour, full of respect for the millions of tiny units of life slaking our thirst. A man infused with such faith could not be bad. The police would soon see the error of their ways, nothing else was possible, and life would carry on as before between green leaves and the sand.

But Jocelyne Ménard knew that wouldn't be, that a normal life was from now on out of the question. Even absolved of all suspicion, her husband would bear to the end of his days the mark that comes with doubt, the mark of the pariah. Martha Irving, who was not, however, a gossipmonger, had just looked at her as if she were a poor soul, the wife of a condemned man reduced to asking for one last cigarette before the axe came down. She regretted now not having pressed her for two or three more, to dizzy herself again and feel alive thanks to her nausea.

She doused her cigarette butt in the sand and removed her shoes, then she advanced down the lake's gentle incline, wetting the bottom of her skirt, the top of her skirt, wetting her white cotton blouse, which billowed out from her torso like a liquid flower. The water was just reaching her hair when a cry rang out, echoing from the bay to the mountain to the Millers' and the Lamars', the Morgans' and the Mulligans'.

The killer's wife, they all said to themselves, trembling, she's expiating the sins of the monster she'd wed before God.

Once in the clearing, he set the girl down on the ground and threw water from his flask into her face. The cold water woke her, and she wondered for a moment who she was, where she was. He'd already seen that in the trenches, soldiers who only came to themselves to realize that they were going to die. Fear flashed through their eyes, and it was all but over. Some cried out, others struggled, still others took their guns into their mouths, but the result was the same. The trenches were red and death carried them off.

He didn't have to wait long for the flare to ignite in Sissy Morgan's eyes, followed by cries and insults. After that, he had only to push the girl into the centre of the clearing, and the trap snapped down. He was about to leave the carnal remains for any interested party, when he noticed the hair, which, spread out on the grass, looked like a young fox coiled around the girl's head and shoulders. Without thinking, he took out the knife he used for stripping off fur, not unlike the pelts Landry lovingly groomed on the table in his shack, while offering a prayer to the earth god.

Smoothing the hair, he regretted not having taken that of the other girl, fox red, but he'd been afraid of the open eyes, of the frightened hand convulsively beating at the air amid machine gun bursts. Today, however, he was so calm that nothing would be able to trouble him. The shooting was over. The world was at peace once more. He left the clearing holding Sissy Morgan's mane at arm's length, a long, strangely blond animal tail, saturated with dew.

# DAY 4

Up at dawn, Mordecai Steiner was preparing a full pot of strong Arabica before going to pick up his newspapers, which a paperboy insisted on throwing onto the wet grass. Michaud was on the front page of the *Bangor Daily News*, offering to the camera his profile of an angry cop. Steiner skimmed the article, certain that Michaud had only told the reporters what they knew already. Two girls were dead, the police were investigating. However, on page four, two long articles quoted a number of people interviewed at Boundary Pond. They'd spared no details, no matter how lurid, and the press was quick off the mark to rehash Pete Landry's legend, which it had already been onto for years.

*Words, words, words*, Steiner exclaimed, closing his paper, *words and blood*, the perfect combination to sell copy, then he poured sugared water into the hummingbird feeder hanging in front of his kitchen window, where at breakfast he could watch the little creatures, whose brightly coloured thrumming relieved his morning torpor. He drank his first coffee amid this buzz, thinking about the dead bodies waiting for him that would not all make the front pages, then he turned on the radio in case there was fresh information concerning what the reporters had called the Boundary Pond affair.

After the weather report he was treated to one of the summer's hits, a song in which a certain Lucy flew away surrounded by diamonds, or at least that was what he was able to deduce from the lyrics whose meaning he couldn't really grasp, being too old, probably, to share in youth's boundless enthusiasm. Zaza Mulligan and Sissy Morgan must have hummed this hit before themselves becoming Lucys in the sky, but he doubted if today they were crowned with diamonds. Elisabeth's and Sissy's diamonds had the consistency rather of stone, the richness of black earth, *Zaza in the soil with stones, Sissy under the ground with sand.*

He was pouring himself a second coffee when the radio show's host passed the microphone to the newsreader, who informed the listeners that there was a new development in the Boundary Pond affair. A suspect had in fact been arrested, a certain Gilles Ménard, he who had apparently discovered the first victim's body. No accusation had yet been brought, but the police finally had a trail to follow.

Djill Menarde, murmured Steiner, Djill Menarde... then he remembered the man pacing up and down on the path the night he'd been called to confirm the death of Elisabeth Mulligan. A man who had practically no more face, so sunken were his features, a man hunched in on himself, who must have been six inches taller under normal circumstances. *Absurd*, he thought, *totally absurd*. If this Djille Menarde was the murderer they were looking for, then he, Mordecai Steiner, was Jack the Ripper's illegitimate son. *Absurd, totally ridiculous!* How could a cop like Michaud be so blinded by his investigation, and what reason did he have for arresting that man?

He had to get this off his chest right away, at the risk of being put in his place, because this Ménard was a victim, that was obvious, just like Landry, about whom people were still obsessed years after his death. He quickly dialled the number of the police station and asked to speak personally with Michaud. He claimed it was urgent.

The inspector was in a foul mood, as he expected. The telephone had not stopped ringing since dawn, the state governor wanted a complete report on the investigation within the hour, and Michaud was going to have to organize a press conference for the next day, though there was nothing he hated more than playing the fool in front of a pack of hyenas ridiculing his idiocies. Steiner let him shoot his wad, then said *you're wrong, Menarde is not your guy.* A silence followed, during which Steiner heard the inspector sigh. Michaud knew the goddamn examiner was right. He knew well that Ménard was not his man, but how to let a guy go whose guilt everything pointed to, without getting himself lynched and sending the poor innocent to the scaffold? *I know, Steiner, but I have no choice.* Before hanging up, he advised Steiner to barricade himself inside as if the Third World War were going to break out, and to keep his mouth shut: *you say nothing!* This was not Steiner's affair, he was taking care of Ménard, who for the time being was better off under lock and key.

His hand on the receiver, the examiner thought to himself that his adopted country was still living in the age of the Far West. He felt sorry for Michaud's having to draw his gun every time a dog barked and to always be pitted against the dead who continued to show signs of life, demanding justice and compensation through the medium of their survivors. His own dead were at peace in the whiteness of the morgue. The horror of their last moments, to the extent that they were horrifying, now faded away behind them, and their faces expressed only the affectless wisdom of letting go.

Michaud, for his part, didn't envy Steiner. He could never have borne sawing into skulls and manipulating organs all day long amid the odours of formalin and disinfectant. That morning, however, he would have liked nothing better than to have changed places with the man, who seemed always just as composed as his cadavers. Since he'd awoken he'd tried to breathe deeply, closing his eyes over neutral or restful images, as Dottie had advised him, upset at seeing him struggle like a marionette being strangled by its strings, but he couldn't do it. No image was neutral enough to loosen the knots in his stomach. He'd been able to put the reporters off by promising them a press conference, but he didn't know how to broach the affair. The budding genius to whom he'd granted an interview the day before had taken Peter Landry and the traps he'd left behind as the focus for his first article, as if Landry, before passing the rope around his neck, had orchestrated a Machiavellian plan whereby some sicko would come along and dig up his traps fifteen years after his death, all in order to poison the lives of those who'd survived him, why not, and to sow chaos among the Boundary intruders, allowing Landry to treat himself to a bracing laugh from out of the depths of his rotting coffin. Nonsense! Today, however, it would all be about Gilles Ménard, who'd be pilloried, even though no formal accusation had been made against him.

He almost regretted having arrested the fellow, just as he regretted not having listened to his mother, who'd dreamed that he'd become a lawyer and defend great causes, but he didn't have it in him to be a John Adams or a Perry Mason. He dispensed justice far from the courts, in the field, where he stoically endured the insults that came with the territory, along with the clichés associated with the police. This job never promised him a great future, but glory and success meant nothing to him. His causes were called Esther, Zaza, Sissy, and he gave himself to them body and soul, receiving in return, for the most part, only anguish and reproach. Whatever happened, in the eyes of the public, the police always did its work badly, and never acted fast enough.

He foresaw the questions that would be put to him during the press conference. They'd start by asking him, typically, what his men thought they were doing, how it was possible to allow a murderer to strike a second time, and whether they were waiting for all of Boundary's young girls to be killed before collaring the perpetrator. These classic attacks were articulated by people who didn't know what it means to stalk a man who seems to be a familiar of the wind and the rain, and whose tracks vanish as he goes, as if he could fly or materialize only long enough to bring out his instruments of murder. He wouldn't be surprised if he was accused of not having arrested Landry while there was still time, the depths of idiocy being limitless, while Landry's only sin consisted in his having forgotten who he was. That trapper was but an instrument in the hands of the killer, who could have used him as a perfect alibi had he stopped at his first murder, or had not used the same weapon to kill Sissy Morgan, faking instead a suicide or a second accident everyone would believe, young Morgan being only a shadow of herself since the death of her friend. The man was following a plan that eluded Michaud, a logic that only madness could fathom.

Michaud was rapping on his desk with his pencil, *what did I miss?* when Anton Westlake informed him that the governor was on the line. Michaud planted his pencil in his eraser, which tipped over onto its side, took a deep breath, and picked up the receiver. The real shit was hitting the fan.

The rumour had spread like wildfire. Gilles Ménard had not yet been led off by the police when already it was on its way, rounding the bay at high speed to head up Turtle Road and sweep along in its path everything that could feed into it: Ménard's face, deathly pale, his too-frequent sorties into the forest, the likely frigidity of his wife, who at the age of twenty-nine had brought into the world only one little girl, and then his hands, big and heavy, which one could easily imagine crushing the head of a cat. After having circled the lake, the gossip left Boundary by the main road, arriving at the office of the state governor, who declared on the radio that a suspect had been arrested in the Boundary Pond affair.

Emma translated for me the broad lines of the governor's statement, then, too depressed by the speed with which you could transform an innocent harvester of blueberries into a killer, we changed the station for one that broadcast rock 'n' roll. Eric Burdon and the Animals were singing "Don't Let Me Be Misunderstood," a song that would make me swoon the following year as I became aware of Burdon's frankly animal sensuality, when Emma's father, just like that, came to see whether we might not be plotting another coup. Since my mother, unable to hold her tongue, had told him about our expedition to the Chauves-Souris Falls, he hadn't left us alone for ten seconds. He'd sworn that that wouldn't happen again, and that we'd best keep our noses clean, because if we got out of line we'd find ourselves inside a ring of poles held together with boat rope and three hundred and sixty knots.

Brian Larue had nothing to fear, we'd been bored stiff since morning, and people who are bored don't have enough imagination to plan actionable stunts. They're as boring and inoffensive as pious images, where you won't catch little Jesus or one of the angels scurrying about, conspiring behind the Holy Virgin's back. Even Brownie found the day interminable. She remained slumped at Emma's feet, sighing constantly, like someone who looks at his watch every two minutes and is stunned by time's inconstancy.

Seeing that we were down in the dumps, Monsieur Larue suggested we go for a swim, the weather was too good for us not to take advantage of it, but our hearts weren't in it, our hearts weren't in anything, you could even say that we had no hearts at all. What we would have wanted was to launch our own investigation. With an adult hovering over us all the time, we might just as well have tried stripping bare naked and shouting out obscenities, hoping no one would notice. In the morning, we'd started from the premise that we weren't any dumber than Sherlock Holmes, who was able to solve complex mysteries while smoking who knows what between the four walls of his office, but we soon got discouraged. In the first place, we didn't have an office, and secondly, our three last cigarettes had been confiscated by Emma's father, who'd probably smoked them behind our backs. Anyway, we were girls who worked in the field, more like Miss Marple minus the girth, and even she wouldn't have got anywhere with three or four parents underfoot.

As Monsieur Larue was anxious for us to rouse ourselves, we went down to dip our feet into the lukewarm water sliding over the sand. The sun was going down behind the mountain, and a large candy-pink band bobbed up and down on the lake, where a few clouds were reflected, cleaved by the ducks. It had been a long time since I'd been able to savour this beauty without a girl's panicked cry or a corpse's leg, hard as wood, coming to hit me full in the face and ruining the landscape. Since Zaza's death, since Sissy's, we saw things differently, colours had paled and the loons' song was but a funereal lament. Beauty wasn't forbidden us, it had just become as unbearable as the wailing of a child abandoned by its mother by the side of a gravel road, as disturbing as beauty can be when you don't know how to handle it. I was telling Emma that I was in a hurry to get old so as to remember nothing, when her father called us in for dinner.

Exceptionally, Monsieur Larue had gone to some trouble, and had made us macaroni and Kraft cheese, rather than his usual grilled cheese sandwiches. We also got a few cocktail wieners marinated in oily ketchup sauce. A feast worthy of a special day, to which I did justice, as my mother would never have let me gorge myself on sausages before supper. Even Brownie got hers, which she swallowed whole without chewing it, you'd think dogs had teeth in their stomach.

This brief gastronomic interlude revived us a little, and we washed the dishes without complaining, even doing imitations of Jerry Lewis, one foot in the nose or in an ear. After the dishes, the kitchen floor looked like a pond after a soapy rain, and Brian Larue was missing a "Drink Coca-Cola" glass. *Never mind*, because we were ourselves once more, two girls ready to unmask the Bondrée murderer.

We were almost done mopping the floor when Brian Larue came to tell me he was taking me home. My mother had made rules for the week, while waiting for my father to come and lower the boom on Friday. We could see each other under strict supervision during the day, but there was no question of sleeping over. Talk about trust! If it had occurred to her—but one woman can't think of everything—my mother would certainly have hired a Pinkerton agent to guard my bedroom door.

I got my stuff together and climbed into Brian Larue's pickup truck, where I sat beside Emma, who held Brownie on her lap while Monsieur Larue belted out "Edelweiss" at the top of his voice. After a few moments of excusable hesitation during which I wondered whether Brian Larue had lost his mind, Emma replied in coded language that he did that kind of thing sometimes, and we made the best of it, following his lead in braying life into that song, the better to demolish it. The Trapp Family version, in miniature. When we parked on Turtle Road behind my parents' cottage, I told Monsieur Larue to stay in the pickup truck, hoping for a few minutes of freedom, but he insisted on accompanying me, as stubborn as my mother and father put together. On the way we ran into Frenchie Lamar, who was pacing up and down on Turtle Road. She'd been crying, that was obvious, since her cheeks were mascara-black, and she didn't seem to be doing well. You could understand that, given what had happened to her friends and given the sword of Damocles hanging over her head if the killer was still free. In her place I would have done the same thing, I wouldn't have wanted to be in my shoes, and I would have been walking all crooked.

Seeing that she didn't turn and run, Monsieur Larue went up to her and said hello, with Emma, Brownie, and myself in single file behind him, Indian-style. The Trapp family among the Iroquois. Below Côte Croche, we'd glimpsed Mark Meyer, who was walking towards the campground, kicking the dirt up in front of him. That probably accounted for Franky-Frenchie Lamar's black tears. She and Meyer had had a lovers' quarrel, one of those set-tos that always end up with the girl crying and the boy in a foul mood. Monsieur Larue asked her if she was all right, out of politeness and as a way of breaking the ice, because it was clear that something was wrong, even a blind beaver would have seen that. Frenchie tried to answer yes, but her face turned into a huge grimace, like a balloon that doesn't quite know if it should explode, then she burst into tears and ran towards her parents' cottage. We stood there with our arms dangling, Monsieur Larue, Emma, Brownie, and I, the Trapp Family discomfited, until my mother, whose frontal blotch was certainly endowed with a seventh sense, given that mothers already have six senses, appeared on the balcony upstairs.

That night I went to bed early, general's orders, but I didn't sleep for all that. My eyes open on the inky black where Millie was breathing serenely, I thought of what I could do so that my little sister would continue to sleep peacefully, so that Gilles Ménard might go back home and spin Marie around under the greenish light of the trees that touched the sky, so that my mother would stop jumping every time a curtain flapped, so that life would go back to normal, that was all, the way it was before death got in the way. But there was nothing to be done, of course. Everyone knows that death stains, that it leaves marks everywhere it goes, big dirty tracks that make us lurch backwards when we're about to step right into them.

Coming out of the woods, he saw Victor Morgan pounding frantically on the Mulligans' door and grabbing the shoulder of Jack, the eldest of the two sons, crying in his face *Sissy's gone, my daughter's gone. Please help me find her, Jack! Please...* The man's distress shocked him, and he went up to him, Sissy's hair in his bag, to promise him that he'd help find his daughter. It was only the next day, after witnessing the spectacle of Victor Morgan weeping in the clearing, *open your eyes, Sissy darling,* the same words he'd uttered himself, *open your eyes, Pete, open your fucking eyes, Latimer,* that he'd brought Sissy's fur to Landry, there where his first shack used to be, near Ménard Bay. Coming close, he saw Landry, scrawny and half naked, swaying at the end of a rope, skin and bones, hair long and dirty, a body stripped of all fur to ward off the cold to come. He saw the glassy eyes of Boundary Pond's hanged man imploring *Maggie darling* to accord him one last look, and he congratulated himself on having settled their account with the two new Maggies of Boundary, while war machines tore Landry to pieces and reduced his world to dust.

Where the old shack had been there was now only a pile of rotten boards, beneath which he slid the fur so Landry could cover himself up. He then went and sat on a beam, there where the shaky deck once stood, and he looked at the stars with Landry, trying to make the man talk, he who had only a few words left on his lips, *Maggie, sweet Marie,* Tanager of Bondrée.

# DAY 5

Stan Michaud was furious. Anxious to calm public opinion and at the same time to boost his political capital, the state governor was virtually placing a noose around Gilles Ménard's neck. But Michaud's face didn't go red for just that reason. Not satisfied with barging into his investigation, the idiot governor was threatening to set the feds on his tail if it turned out that Ménard was not the murderer they were looking for. Fortunately, Michaud only had the fellow on the telephone, because otherwise he'd have probably scuppered his career with one of those fits of gratifying exasperation when you grab a guy by the tie just to make yourself feel better.

He arrived in the room where the press conference was taking place in a state of irritation close to a nervous breakdown, and almost strangled a reporter who wanted to pull him aside to obtain some exclusive information. Get this asshole out of here, Westlake, he ordered his subordinate, and he plunged headfirst into the lions' den. The atmosphere in the jam-packed room was so electric that it could have supplied power to a pumping station. Michaud had to force his way to the table reserved for him, and it required the intervention of three other policemen to obtain a modicum of silence. Immediately, Michaud tried to set things straight. In vain—the harm had been done: as far as everyone was concerned, the culprit had been arrested. Not once had he uttered Ménard's name, but it was already in the wind, borne beyond Boundary in a reporter's Volkswagen or the van of a television crew wanting to do some sightseeing around the countryside.

The conference lasted only half an hour, but Michaud was still dizzied by the flash bulbs, the questions coming from all sides, the microphones held out like so many vipers thrusting their way out of a swamp on whose surface there floated white shirts and summer jackets. He tried to focus on that picture, the lightness of summer clothes, but his head was full of the governor's voice and the pleas of Ménard's wife, who turned up a bit later with her red eyes, holding her daughter by the hand, a sweet little thing with ice cream on her chin, casting her eyes over the police station's yellow walls and trying to figure out why her mother always had her nose buried in her handkerchief, and yet was treating her as if it were Sunday.

Michaud tried to reassure Jocelyne Ménard, swearing that he was only keeping her husband locked up in order to prevent him from being torn to pieces by the mob waiting outside. But she didn't see it that way. There are laws, she insisted. You can no more incarcerate an innocent man than you can hang him in the public square without a trial. Uttering these words, she struck the reception counter with the flat of her hand, setting Westlake's pencils rolling to the floor, and she left, declaring that she'd be back with a lawyer. Michaud looked at the pencils rolling on the ground, then at little Marie, who had to run to keep hold of her mother's arm, uncertain if she should cry or look pretty, as one often asked little girls to do who didn't know how to dance. Still, there was a tear on Marie's cheek as her parti-coloured dress disappeared through the creaking door that led to the parking lot, leaving behind a whiff of innocence in which Michaud would have liked to lose himself.

He picked up the pencils, put them back where they belonged, gave a blow to the counter himself, then left the reception room to the sound of dry wood clattering onto the floor, and shut himself up in his office. He only had a few hours to deal with this affair to his satisfaction, and he couldn't let himself be distracted by a child's dress. He asked Westlake to bring him all the files on the two cases, those of Elisabeth Mulligan and Sissy Morgan, and he buried himself in them, advising Westlake that he was there for no one, not even for that bastard, the governor. The afternoon was drawing to a close when Westlake dared to open the door a crack and tell him there were men waiting for him in the conference room, and that the day, in fact, was far from over.

Millie and Bob were still sleeping when a van bearing the logo of a television station parked beside the cottage. Seeing it, my mother, who spent half her life over the kitchen sink, dropped her dishcloth in a big splash of tiny multi-coloured bubbles, some of which burst in contact with her head, before uttering three or four bad words that mothers, in principle, never pronounced in front of their children, an indication that she'd forgotten about me. Forgetting, however, that a mother never forgets, I tried to slip away, but she ordered me to go and get dressed and she assumed the stance of a dignified woman before going to confront the reporters, whom she didn't want to see inside her cottage. I quickly pulled on my shorts, not wanting to miss the scene to follow, and I grabbed my dirty T-shirt from the day before, certain that my mother wasn't going to scold me in front of the television stars. Anyway, she was the one who wanted me dressed, she'd just have to take me as I was.

Super Flo, faster than lightning, was already in the yard when two technicians armed with microphones got down from the vehicle, along with a man who was carrying nothing, just a clean suit he wasn't going to get dirty toting dusty cables. I caught up with Super Flo just as she was telling them to put their camera aside and explain what they wanted. A short interview with Monsieur Duchamp, replied the man in the suit, as if that wasn't crystal clear, to which my mother answered that Monsieur Duchamp wasn't there, and they could pack up their equipment.

Not yet clued in on Florence Duchamp's determination, the tallest one, I mean the cleanest one, insisted on interviewing her. With the kid beside her that'll make a good shot, he said in a low voice to the others, indicating that they should get ready. One of the underlings was putting up his tripod, when my mother grabbed the camera and went to deposit it in the truck. We've nothing to say to you, she added, smoothing the apron she'd forgotten to take off, which must have infuriated her and at the same time given her the energy to repulse the enemy, then she dragged me with her into the cottage, where her third eye, which she could no longer suppress, was able at last to display its anger.

Since Gilles Ménard had been arrested and she'd brought out the bottle of Dutch gin, my mother had become a real fury, more prickly than ever. She made everyone who approached her understand right away that they'd better not step on her toes, which made me keep my mouth shut, because I might have had something to say to the reporters. Don't even think of it, Andrée Duchamp, she ordered me, before I'd even had the chance to finish my thought, we're not gossips, and we're saying nothing. Okay. I got my things and went to meet Emma, but I had to make it through the general's office before leaving: no, I wouldn't talk to reporters, not those and not others who might turn up later, no, I wouldn't go near them, no, I wouldn't make her ashamed of me, and I wouldn't pee in my pants, and yes, I'd pass a lie detector test when I got back.

Fifteen minutes later, I threw my bicycle onto the Larues' lawn and ran to tell Emma that there were reporters everywhere. She threw the rest of her toast and peanut butter to the crows and promised her father we wouldn't leave Turtle Road, that we'd be careful, that we'd cry like banshees at the least sign of anything, that we wouldn't pee in our pants, and we mounted our bicycles, raising a cloud of dust worthy of the best westerns.

All morning we spied on the reporting team from a distance, and you could bet that in every interview broadcast on television you'd see the heads of two dishevelled girls in the background, planted behind a bush or a tree trunk, which wasn't too serious, as our parents had refused to install a TV set in their cottages. If they learned that we'd made the headlines, it would be from the mouth of a Bill Cochrane, who liked nothing better than to cause trouble, or a Flora Tanguay, who'd by the way put on her loudest dress to greet the reporters. They'd interviewed her beside her cottage, sitting in front of a clump of dahlias that blended in with the flowers on her dress, so much so that on the screen you'd probably see just her head sticking out of a brightly coloured mound, then our two heads, behind, poking up from a clump of rhubarb gone to seed.

We didn't hear much at the Tanguays' other than Pete Landry's name, which popped up over and over with Flora's gesticulations and the dahlias that received some good whacks from time to time, but other than that it was the name Ménard that we heard, which punctuated the accounts like a dirty word people uttered unwillingly, or spat to the other side of the road, not even wanting to wait for Ménard to be judged. The hypocrisy was one with the stream of coarse murmurings that issued from angry mouths: "I never trusted the guy," "goddamn two-faced," "we should've known," a pack of lies that dilated their pupils until they almost reached to their foreheads, and darkened their eyes with mortal sins. The way some people were having at Ménard, they'd soon be blaming him for World War II.

At the end of the morning, the reporter who'd been sent packing by my mother approached us, figuring by our behaviour that we must be in the know. We hesitated an instant, it's not every day you can get on television, but the thought of seeing my mother turn up with the flour-covered face on her apron got the better of me. So we took off in a cloud of dust, Calamity Jane and Ma Dalton, but pursued by the name Ménard, which we'd spell out with our peas in my mother's mashed potatoes, wondering if the real killer was also having hamburger meat for lunch.

Coming out of his office, Stan Michaud saw little Marie's dress all over again, flying away at the end of the hallway, the lightweight garment floating free of the child's body, which looked just too sad. Suddenly his immediate future appeared to him with astonishing clarity: this would be his last case, Sissy Morgan his last ghost. There was not enough room in his head to accommodate another. He'd take with him the three girls, Esther, Zaza, Sissy, and would leave them by the side of a road where he could come back to visit them whenever a stray boomerang caught up with him. Who, Esther? *Why?* He'd made his decision, as soon as the case was over he'd take Dottie to Lake Champlain, far from the road where the girls would be waiting for him. They'd pick up their last vacation where they'd left off, in the late summer light. They could also get themselves a motorhome and embark on an adventure, drive all the way to Arizona or Texas, with no ties and no obligations, like those hippies crisscrossing the country. Dottie would buy herself flowered dresses, and he too, why not, robes in which he would greet the rising sun, intoning a mantra. Rubbish, he said to himself, and he headed for the conference room.

Ten or so men, with whom he'd shared the governor's demands, were assembled in the room. If they didn't move their asses, Ménard could say goodbye to his family. A heavy silence descended on the room, along with sighs and the clearing of throats, tired looks that didn't dare focus on Michaud but took refuge in the tiling on the floor. Jim Cusack, more than the others, seemed overwhelmed by the situation. His elbows on his knees, he held his head in his two hands, he too staring at the floor. But he didn't see that it had been polished the day before, and that reflected in it was the joyous light of a cloudless sky that harked back to his childhood, floors smelling of wax to herald the weekend's arrival. All he saw was Laura's face, the angry beauty of his wife, who'd left the house slamming the door when he came home the night before, rebuking him for not having telephoned, for having left her high and dry in front of a cold oven, staring at a roast that ended up in the garbage along with the tomato pie she'd gorged herself on out of her bare hands, in the process dirtying her white dress, the freshly polished floor, her patent leather shoes. He searched for her part of the night, alerting half the town, including Michaud and Dottie, until the front door creaked open and he saw her reappear, her hair dishevelled, her eyes on fire, her pretty dress covered in dust and blotched with red. He immediately threw himself into her arms, from where Laura shoved him away to go up to their bedroom and lock herself in after banging shut the door. He tried to make her open the damned door, begged her to talk to him, but she didn't come out of the room until morning, only to tell him that he had to choose between her and those girls, *those dead whores*, she blurted out. The word "whore" hit him like a slap, incongruous in Laura's mouth, like a bug running across her tongue that she had to spit out, a cockroach slipping into a corner and defying you to squash it. When he tried to answer, Laura locked herself in the bathroom and stayed there until he left.

He'd hardly slept, lying on the hall rug in front of their bedroom door, and felt like he'd been hit in the lower back by a truncheon, one of those blows you don't see coming that shatters reality and thrusts into a kind of heavy fog everything a broken individual has grown used to hanging on to. The governor's interference, together with the echoing of the word "whore," had been the last straw. Ménard was a guy like himself, incapable of attacking young girls, or women, or children. Yet he himself had hurt Laura, had sullied with dust and blotches of red her loveliest summer dress.

He was trying to imagine what his life would be like if he were to quit the police when Michaud asked him for news of Laura, whom Dottie had gone looking for during the night, making the rounds of the places they went, the park, the little hill where they sometimes picnicked in the town's east end, the fast food place that was open twenty-four hours a day, while Michaud made calls and alerted his police cars, all for nothing, as Laura was brooding over her pain right behind the house, sitting in the shed among the carpentry and gardening tools.

*Good, she's good*, Cusack replied. Michaud hadn't pursued the matter. This affair concerned only Cusack and Laura. He passed a hand over his brow and left the meeting room, grumbling. It was time to tell Gilles Ménard that he'd be eating canned stew for days, or maybe weeks to come.

Gilles Ménard had covered Zaza Mulligan's body so she wouldn't be cold. Death could be so cold in the middle of summer. His gesture was also prompted by modesty, the bared torso, the arms, too much skin exposed. But there was no blood on Zaza's torso, no. The shirt must have slid down to where there was blood, pushed by the wind, displaced by an animal. It was the same animal, or perhaps the wind, another wind, that had dragged the shirt under the pile of boards, unless the killer had still been there nearby, unmoving in the shelter of the underbrush, his eyes on Ménard and the young girl. He would have waited for Ménard to leave before stealing the shirt to swab the ground, to wipe his hands.

In Gilles Ménard's mind, you had to blame the animal or the wind, you had to find the man hidden in the woods, but he could no longer say who, the wind or the man, had landed him in this cell. All he knew was that he was innocent. Only a deranged individual could have unearthed Pierre Landry's traps, and he wasn't yet crazy, not then, not at the beginning of summer. It was now that he was coming unhinged, unable to see things clearly, and unable to take his eyes off the drop that, every ten seconds, was falling to the bottom of the washbasin. He stared at the tap, imagining the progress of that minuscule thread of water through the piping, saw another clear small bead form under its rusted outlet, swelling, elongating, then dropping into the drain through the force of gravity, where its echo resonated between the grey walls. Plock. That drop obsessed him and kept him from thinking, which was perhaps all for the best, because this constant drumming seemed to be protecting him from true madness.

Seated in front of him, Michaud watched Ménard eyeing the drop, and felt as if he was going to lose his nerve. If he couldn't stop that damned leak he'd end up tearing the sink off the wall. He got up abruptly and wrapped his handkerchief around the tap. As soon as he left that cell, he'd call a plumber. Ménard was distraught enough without this torture being imposed on him. Yet he seemed let down when Michaud stemmed the flow of the drop that connected him to the passage of time, to the eternal return of suffering and death. Still, Michaud pushed his chair in front of the basin so that Ménard would have to look at him at last. He'd have preferred him to throw a fit, to smash his chair against the wall and protest his innocence, but he seemed drained of all energy, as if he'd been walking for days in the desert only to see a thread of water appear at the foot of a dune, which he knew, however, was an illusion.

Unable to draw anything out of Ménard, Michaud closed the cell door behind him. Passing in front of the reception desk, he asked Westlake to summon a plumber, then went to sit in the parking lot, where he directed his attention to the iridescent mirrorings in a patch of gas, reminding him of pieces of marble or onyx run through with veins, stones whose formation evoked stratified reliefs crisscrossed by streams of lava. The earth's history was concentrated in those stones and in this pool of gas slowly evaporating. Billions of years to end up in this parking lot, in these leather shoes, in this creature on two legs with no other option than to invent God in order to defy time.

What a mess, murmured Michaud, who nevertheless got up to go back to his job. He could tell himself that every action was meaningless, since the tree, the parking lot, and the shoes would all disappear in short order, but he saw no better way to get through this life than to keep putting one foot in front of the other. For him, the illusion of going forward took the place of God, and he would try to maintain this illusion for as long as his legs obeyed him. *Hurry up*, he added, without conviction, then he made his way towards the building. Many tasks awaited him, many men as well, who'd learn to do without him once he'd turned in his badge and walked away. Yet he'd phone the governor when he arrived, he'd curse the press, and he'd wait for Gilles Ménard's trial to be finished before emptying out his drawers. In a few weeks, it would all be over.

The girl wasn't dead, he said over and over again, as the shower spray struck his chest. The girl's eyes were open. The girl wasn't dead. A wave of panic swept over him, and he bolted from the shower to throw his clothes back on. Two minutes later, he slammed the door and jumped into his car to make it look as though he was going into town. He parked at Juneau Hill behind an abandoned building, and took to the woods in the direction of Otter Trail. His heart was beating in his temples, and he felt as if he were back there, under fire from the German Maschinenpistolen, with the ground breaking up around him. Skirting a fallen tree, he tripped and heard the bullets whistling over him. *Run, Little Hawk, run!*

Out of breath, he finally made it to the spot where he'd left Zaza Mulligan. He saw the red hair, the shirt draped over her chest, and he almost turned back. Someone had come, someone was perhaps watching him at that instant, and the young girl was still alive. Beneath the shirt that had appeared, he didn't know how, he saw her heart beating, he saw her breath coming and going, shading the white garment with lighter or darker greys depending on the slant of the light. He swiftly scanned the trees around him, seeking an enemy in ambush, and he crawled towards the girl. As soon as he placed his hands on her neck, he felt the cold skin and saw the closed eyes.

*Who's there?* he demanded, his voice on edge. *Who's there?* But no one answered Little Hawk. He scanned the forest again, where a few birds were cheeping, tits or robins, and perhaps tanagers, Zazas with red wings. He took away the shirt to be certain the breast was stilled, and in a surge of tenderness out of the distant years of the war, *don't cry, Jim*, he swabbed the girl's wounds. A crack rang out, *who's there?* as he was dabbing at the torn leg, and the rain began to fall, which would wash away his tracks, would undo the sound of his footsteps.

Taking advantage of this providential rain, he made his way back through the trees. Without thinking, he'd brought with him the garment left behind on Zaza Mulligan's body by another man, a wanderer who had found the adolescent and had perhaps finished her off.

# FRENCHIE

The Morgans left Bondrée at the same time as the Mulligans. Autumn's on its way, my mother murmured, seeing the Morgan station wagon go by, fully loaded, in the rear window of which a box bearing the inscription "Fragile" was shoved into a corner next to other boxes that must have contained Sissy's personal belongings, clothes, jewels, 45 and 33 RPM records. All the things their owner's passing had rendered vulnerable, ready to crumble at the slightest touch. My mother well knew that the Mulligans' departure was not just due to the coming of autumn, that there were a few weeks left before the clouds would be swollen with the darkest of greys, but she preferred to associate this departure with the changing seasons, rather than the dramas that had marked the summer. In two weeks we would also leave for the start of the school year, but the summer, what I called the summer, with its odours of cut hay and the schoolgirls with scabs on their knees, would go on until the end of September. It was in Bondrée, only in Bondrée, that autumn had arrived prematurely, swathed in mourning clothes, and with its store of traps covered over with dead leaves.

After Gilles Ménard's arrest, the mood did not lighten. On the contrary, it was as if Ménard had been taken away in a hearse, not a police car. Death had struck a third time, leaving us all in state of incredulity or the same anger. There were those who were convinced of Ménard's guilt and sullied his name in front of television cameras, those who swore that his arrest was an error, and those who remained open-mouthed, like the fish expiring in Pat Tanguay's wicker basket. My parents were among those who refused to believe that Gilles Ménard was harbouring the face of a maniac behind his own face, deathly pale. When my father got back to Bondrée, Thursday morning, moving his weekend up by two days after hearing that Ménard had been taken away, he arrived in a state of fury. The police had screwed up, Ménard would have burned his shirt if it was him, he's not such a sucker as to walk around with a sign saying "guilty" on his forehead! In any case, it can't be him, it's all he can do not to faint when he sees a drop of blood.

My father spewed out what he had to spew to rid himself of the nastiness, the bile burning his stomach, then he went to see Jocelyne Ménard to try to cheer her up. During his absence, unable to sit still, my mother threw herself into cake making. She disappeared into a cloud of flour, and I left before I got asphyxiated.

It was a beautiful day and no one seemed to notice. Not even Franky-Frenchie was lying out on the beach with her radio and bathing suit. She must have been mulling over her argument with Meyer or coming to terms with her heartbreak, depending on whether their set-to was fatal or not. Since I still didn't have the right to wander off, I went into my cabin, under the pine, to depress myself a bit more I suppose, because the place no longer resembled the dark, odorous grotto where nothing could touch me. I suddenly felt constricted there, and I had the feeling that the heavy branches were forcing me down rather than embracing me. Maybe I'd grown, but what bothered me the most was that I'd got older, I was starting to lose my capacity to crawl under trees. Since my manicure session, becoming a young woman didn't interest me any more. I looked at the ground flattened by the weight of my body, saying again that I didn't want a bra or nylon stockings or nail polish or blood between my legs. I wanted trees to climb, I wanted dirty running shoes that go a hundred times faster than new running shoes and girls' sandals, and I especially didn't want to feel that what up to then had got me out of bed every morning was going to leave me cold, while life went on without me. It hurt too much to think that old age planed down the mornings, and left slivers of new wood at your bedroom door.

I angrily dug up my tin box, in which there remained a few candies glued to their wrappings, as well as a melted mint patty stuck to the bottom under duck feathers and snakeskins. My treasure chest had lost its magic. No fairy, no genie out of the woods, could ever emerge from it any more. Still, I slid a mallard feather into my hair, and I unwrapped a caramel, *here, littoldolle*, but it stuck to my teeth and had a bitter taste. My mother was right, summer was over and had only lasted a few seconds, all condensed into this rusted tin container. If I could have, I would have jumped on my bicycle and left Bondrée right away, instead of which I put the box back, for Millie, and dragged my running shoes to the edge of the lake.

It was only ten o'clock and I was already turning in circles, which is just a manner of speaking because my circles were all askew. I was navigating, rather, through a kind of pale grey that spread itself out all around me, powerless to take in the smells that always unblocked my ears and opened my eyes wide in the wind's direction. I was suddenly at a loss in the presence of a familiar beauty, and a magnificent day was being spoilt by states of mind, adult states, children's souls were not so complex, too new to the world to fall all to pieces when a day goes wrong. As this one had. Emma was in town with her mother and would be back only on the weekend, Bob had gone off with Scott Miller to cut wood on Juneau Hill, and Millie was playing with Marie Ménard in the Ménards' sad cottage. That left my mother, and Jane Mary Brown, still fanning herself on her porch and reading useless novels and getting fat on cheese curds. A lame day, where even the fish had to drift with their heads down, their eyes brimming with salty water.

I was getting ready to give myself a kick in the behind, literally, a good blow with my heel between my two buttocks, to go and put on my bathing suit so as to cheer up the fish, when I heard someone cry out in the Lamars' cottage, where they were also getting ready to leave. Frenchie came out right after, slamming the door with her mother on her heels telling her that if she knew anything at all, then she should talk. *Fuck, mom,* I've told you a hundred times that I don't know anything, she shouted. With that she went off at a run, barefoot on the Turtle Road gravel. Madame Lamar was left with her eyes glazed over, so tired that they didn't even want to move, or to see, or to want to do their work. Finally Butterscotch, the house tomcat that seemed to weigh forty pounds, slid out through the half-open door to rub against her legs, at the same time bringing her back to life. Come, my lovely Butterscotch, Suzanne Lamar sighed, taking the cat in her arms, and she went back inside.

I was frozen in place. The scene I'd just witnessed was as wretched as this listless day. Frenchie Lamar had said *fuck* to her mother, her mother had lost three or four minutes of her life while her body went on strike, but at least something was happening, and that thing had something to do with Zaza's or Sissy's death, or both of them, I'd have bet my life on it, because what secret could she be hiding that was so important that it was making Frenchie Lamar's mother cry, if it wasn't a secret having to do with the murder of her friends. I figured that if Franky-Frenchie was hiding information about that, then Gilles Ménard wasn't guilty. That also meant that she was still in danger, even though the policemen standing guard in front of her house had been recalled after Ménard's arrest. Her father must have thought the same thing, because he spent his time watching Frenchie to be sure that she didn't leave their yard. I'd seen him talking to my father when he left our cottage to go and see Jocelyne Ménard. The two men spoke in low voices, making gestures in the direction of the bay, then they shook hands. A little later Monsieur Lamar got into his car and told his wife to keep an eye on Frenchie, *look out for my baby, honey*, and the argument started. Frenchie cried *fuck*, slammed the door, and left just like that, shoeless, with her long legs exposed to thorns and branches. If I hadn't been certain of being given the bum's rush, I'd have run after her to tell her to go and lock herself in, but Frenchie Lamar would have sent me packing, just like she'd sent her mother packing, and I'd have been flat on my back. I had no choice, I had to bring my mother into this. If I buried my head in the sand while Frenchie was being chopped to pieces, I'd never forgive myself if I lived to be ninety-nine, and I'd end up in the hell for those sinning by omission, where the innocents pound their chests all day long with their mea culpas.

My mother was just then going down to the beach, in her pink-skirted bathing suit, her towel, pink as well, and her rubber sandals. I wasn't used to seeing my mother like that, half naked. Exposed to the light, her white skin made me admit to myself that she had a body under her clothes, a body out of which I came nine months after my father had lain on it, and I preferred not to think about that.

Coming near me, she stretched her towel out on the sand, and lay down facing the sun, asking why I wasn't trying to teach sign language to the squirrels, or something like that. It was a good idea, I'd think about it. Meanwhile, I concentrated on the bruise on her left ankle so as not to have to look at her too-pale thighs, trying to figure out how to bring up the subject of Frenchie. It was the first time for weeks that my mother had settled down to tan herself, probably waiting until the Morgans and Mulligans had left, in front of whom it would have been indecent to be seen enjoying the pleasures of summer, and I was getting ready to spoil it all. You don't look too happy, my mite, what's going on? she added, placing a white silk scarf over her face, and I took the plunge, I told her about Frenchie's argument with her mother, Frenchie's *fuck*, the downcast look of poor Madame Lamar, insisting on the fact that even if Frenchie deserved a pair of slaps, she was in danger.

Since she was convinced of Gilles Ménard's innocence, my mother knew perfectly well that Frenchie was not safe from the murderer, which was the reason she spent her time keeping her eyes on her from the kitchen window, but she hadn't heard the argument because of the radio, which she'd turned up to hear Chet Baker singing "My Funny Valentine." I'll go and talk to Madame Lamar, she said, letting her silk scarf slide onto the sand, then she took my hand and smiled. The sun was making the watery yellow circles around her irises sparkle like a ring of minuscule molten gold nuggets. There was such love in her eyes that I thought that never, in all my life, would I see anything so beautiful. I turned away so as not to be transfixed, and again I focused my eyes on the blue, or the purple rather, discolouring her ankle.

I'll put a dress on over my bathing suit and we'll go, she said, getting up. I watched her climb towards the cottage, not even mad that I'd disturbed her tanning session, and I felt a pang in my heart, a pang of love, seeing her little skirt fluttering over her hips. I was getting older, there was no other explanation, and I was gradually becoming aware that it could be not just a bore, but downright painful.

By the time she knocked at Suzanne Lamar's door, my mother had lost her self-assurance, and was smoothing the sides of her dress, since she didn't have any belt to twist. Leaving the cottage, she warned me to be quiet and to let her talk, but I'd have bet my life that she was too wound up to think straight, that she'd forgotten the words she'd planned to start with as she was pulling on her dress, and that she was groping for them frantically in that recess of memory that whites out from shyness when your nerves start short-circuiting. Still, I had confidence in her powers of improvisation, my mother always knew what to say, even when there was absolutely nothing to be said but you had to talk anyway.

I took a step back when Suzanne Lamar opened the door in a dressing gown that must have dated from her wedding night, close to transparent, with lots of frayed lace. I'd only seen her from a distance earlier on, but she was so pale it was scary, with circles around her eyes down to her chin. She'd applied mauve eyeshadow to her bloodshot eyes, which didn't help at all, and by her puffed-up nose you could tell that she'd been crying to beat the band. Taken aback by her look of death warmed over, my mother right away put a hand on her shoulder, and Suzanne Lamar started to cry again. Without waiting for an invitation, Mama went in, bringing me along, and sat Madame Lamar down while she made some tea. I stayed standing near the door, not too sure if I wanted to hear Suzanne Lamar's outpouring, she'd end up stark naked if she didn't leave the sides of her dressing gown alone. I didn't know why women were always playing with a bit of skin or a fingernail or crumpling a piece of cloth. Hormones, probably.

Come help me, mite, Mama whispered to me from the counter where jars of jam and pickles were lined up, and I looked for cups in the cupboards, happy to be able to rummage around without being reprimanded. While the tea was steeping, Mama brought some handkerchiefs to Madame Lamar, she was always ready to help others, strangers or not, at her own expense, because she must have longed, sometimes, to bask peacefully in the sun without one of her three little brats coming round. But it was too late, the brat-in-chief had shown up, and my mother had left her beach towel to take the sun all by itself. She was a mother in the real sense of the word, who forgot herself as soon as a child cried or another woman needed help. Seeing her putting herself out that way, I'd long ago promised myself that I'd never have a child, and so would never be able to forget that I existed.

I finally found two cups with geese on them, and others with a picture of the queen, but I chose the geese, the queen reminding me too much of old-fashioned fairy tales. I took the quart of milk out of the refrigerator, and brought three cups to the table. My mother, sitting on the edge of her chair, took Suzanne Lamar's hands, hands faded too soon, slightly plump, the shininess of whose nails contrasted with the wrinkled skin, and Suzanne Lamar, touched by my mother's solicitude, gasped out that she couldn't sleep, that she was worried about her daughter, who refused to confide in her, that she didn't know any more what to do.

With all the tact and gentleness of which she was capable, Mama talked to her about the scene I'd witnessed, making it clear that if Frenchie had any information, she ought to alert the police. At the mention of the word "police," Suzanne Lamar abruptly pulled her hands out of those of my mother, almost shouting that there was no question of involving the police because Françoise hadn't told her what was bothering her. There was fear in her eyes, and more than that, terror, which prompted my mother to pull away from the cold blast of wind that had entered the room. For myself, I lowered my eyes to Madame Lamar's slippers, because the dread distorting her face, already disfigured by pain, hit me like a ton of bricks.

We don't need the police, she added, then she told my mother she could leave, the crisis had passed, and she'd be able to manage. We'd hardly had time to take a sip of our tea when Suzanne Lamar ushered us out, apologizing for getting carried away. This woman wanted to protect her daughter, that was clear. Mama didn't protest, she would have acted the same way had I been in trouble. Saying goodbye, Madame Lamar repeated that everything was fine, that she was just overwhelmed, it wasn't surprising, but her eyes were flitting back and forth, unable to focus on a single object while seeking help where none was to be found, in the crazed void into which the lake, the trees, and the mountain were being hurled, all pitched into a torrent of water and greenery deep in the abyss that was pulling them down.

Mama was just going down the porch stairs when Millie, coming back from the Ménards' with our father, ran towards her. Seeing the doll hanging from Millie's arm,

Suzanne Lamar opened her eyes wide, stifled a cry with her pudgy hands, and fled into her cottage.

Outside, Mama, Papa, Millie and I were left open-mouthed, wondering how Bobine could have made Suzanne Lamar take flight as if she'd seen a ghost.

Sitting at the kitchen table, my father slammed his newspaper down on the plastic tablecloth with its fruity design, crushing a green grape already punctured by a cigarette burn nobody could stop picking at. He'd made a decision. He'd go and phone the police as soon as Millie was put to bed.

While preparing supper, he and my mother had discussed Suzanne Lamar's attitude, that of Frenchie, and that of Bob Lamar, who didn't leave Frenchie's side for a second when he was in Bondrée. Those people knew something, there was no doubt about it, but my mother was hesitant. She was convinced that Suzanne Lamar wanted first and foremost to spare her daughter more suffering, and she felt she'd be betraying her by calling the police too quickly. But Bobine clinched the argument. When my father asked me where I'd found her, he and my mother almost choked on their corn. The bloodstained shirt had been pulled out from under the same pile of boards, plus a bag full of hair that had apparently been Sissy Morgan's, news that just about did me in—a scalp, for Pete's sake! All this was information the adults had kept to themselves, thinking maybe we had some special fondness for that pile of boards, or that maybe we'd start losing our hair out of solidarity with Sissy or start tearing it out at the roots from sympathy, who knows?

My father ran to spit his corn into the sink, my mother ran after him, and I spilled my glass of Fanta onto the tablecloth, drowning the tortured grape at the same time. I didn't bother going for a rag, the grape would recover, but I cried out why didn't you tell me? A question for which no one had an answer. Because I was an idiot, I suppose, too stupid to draw a line between point A and point B without tripping over some other letter. If I'd known, I'd have spoken up sooner, the police would have examined Bobine and turned the pile of boards upside down, which might have prevented Gilles Ménard's arrest, Suzanne Lamar's collapse, the zombification of Franky-Frenchie, the sadness of little Marie, and the loss of two dozen ears of corn.

In the dead silence that came over the room, Bob let loose with a stupefied Jesus Christ, which got a rise neither out of my mother nor my father, too stunned to react. The ticking of the teacup-shaped clock over the stove was the only audible noise, until Millie asked if her doll had bled. Mama reassured her, swearing that Bobine had not lost a drop of blood, but her look contradicted what she was saying. Given her state, Bobine had certainly bled, after Zaza, before Zaza, it didn't matter, captive to the slimy hands that had gouged out her eyes. No one knew what role Millie's doll had played in this story. We were all certain, however, that it was hidden under the pile of boards by the person who had also deposited there Ménard's shirt and Sissy's hair, the killer in other words, or someone who was trying to protect him by blaming the murders on Ménard.

I'm going over now, my father finally said, not able to wait for the tooth fairy to arrive, and probably frightened, like me, at the idea of roasting in hell for not having acted sooner. He'd just got up from his chair when Suzanne Lamar burst into the cottage. She'd looked everywhere for Frenchie, and hadn't found her.

It was seven-thirty on the kitchen clock, seven-thirty-three on Sissy Morgan's watch, and my father now had two good reasons to get Stan Michaud out of his La-Z-Boy.

In too dark a mood to be enjoying his first day off for ages, Stan Michaud was mowing his lawn behind his house and thinking about Gilles Ménard, who must have been monitoring the progress of a spider on his cell's ceiling, or who maybe was lost in contemplation of a crack in the yellowed plaster, when Fred Crosby, who was replacing Anton Westlake that night, phoned him. Dottie took the call, hoping that it was one of her co-workers at the library, or maybe Stan's sister, uncle, or aunt, or a vacuum cleaner salesman miraculously doing his rounds in the neighbourhood, anyone at all who had nothing to do with her husband's work.

Seeing Dottie's sombre mien in the doorway, he understood right away that something was wrong, and hoped a living-room wall had collapsed, which would have explained his wife's knitted brows, but all the walls were in place, and, next to the one closing off the sitting room, the telephone receiver was perched on a low table. Freddy Crosby, Dottie said, and she went into the garden. When she came back, she found Stan in the bedroom, changing out of his work clothes into clean pants, and grumbling that he knew, he knew, he knew, *for Christ's sake.* Can you call Cusack, he asked Dottie while pulling on a shirt, but she replied no, she couldn't, Laura would never forgive her.

Another girl has disappeared, Dot, this is serious. So is marriage, she shot back, placing a kiss on his forehead, and suggesting he call someone else. He tried Westlake first, only to hang up after fifteen rings, then Conrad, then Demers, but those two had the best reasons in the world for not being able to go with him, the first all agog because his wife's water had just broken, the second because he'd just fallen in his garden shed a few minutes ago, his wife said, and was bleeding like a pig from his head. If he's bleeding, that means everything's all right, grumbled Michaud, thinking that he'd be two men short the next day, and he had no choice but to call Cusack and risk causing a divorce.

Frenchie Lamar, he sighed when Cusack picked up, and the other also sighed at the other end of the line. Pass me Laura, I'm going to talk to her, Michaud added, faced with his colleague's silence. He, of course, got bogged down in muddled explanations, and Dottie took the phone out of his hands before he made the situation worse. I'm coming, she murmured, then she applied another kiss to Stan's brow, but there was no more smile on her face. She was on the side of women, women who were alive, and who'd had enough of playing second fiddle to death.

While he sprayed himself with eau de cologne, Dottie pulled on a sweater, and Michaud dropped her off at the Cusacks', where Jim was waiting for him, pacing up and down on the lawn, without a thermos of coffee this time, or any snacks for the road. Jim took Dottie's place on the front seat, Dottie took that of Jim in the Cusacks' yard, a cop-style wife-swap, and the car took off.

At the first intersection Michaud mumbled *I'm sorry*, Jim fanned the air with his left arm, as if to say that he didn't have to be sorry, that was the work, the life, his life. When they got as far as North Anson, he told Michaud that he'd cancelled a reservation in a Kennebunkport motel, where he and Laura were to be celebrating their third wedding anniversary. Laura had been talking only of that, of the straw hat she was going to buy, of the shells being sold in little green or yellow nets, of the mother-of-pearl polished by the waves, of the colours at sunrise, those thin pink-and-cream-coloured bands, *you know*, where the sea meets the sky. Michaud, thinking of his own vacation, almost placed a hand on Cusack's shoulder, but there was the road to deal with, and that shoulder was too damned far, he'd never bridge the gap.

The rest of the trip unfolded amid the sea smells Cusack had talked about, in a climate blighted by awkwardness, and regret at not being able to respond to the sorrow concealed behind the smell of seaweed, which dissipated bit by bit as they approached Boundary and Frenchie Lamar, who at that very moment was running through the woods, barefoot, a large cut in her right cheek, a gash in the shape of an M, perhaps, or a W.

There weren't many men in Boundary that day if you considered the fact that some families had already left, that Ménard was in prison, that the Mulligan sons had pulled up stakes that afternoon after closing up the cottage for the winter, but all those who were there, from the oldest to the youngest, answered Suzanne Lamar's desperate call. They were just a handful, Sam Duchamp and his son Bob, Ed McBain, Scott Miller, the son of Gary, Pat Tanguay, who'd been able to drag along his son Jean-Louis, Brian Larue, Conrad Plamondon, the owner of the campground, and Bill Cochrane with his wooden leg, all gathered together behind the Lamars' cottage, where Florence Duchamp draped a shawl over the shoulders of Suzanne Lamar, who was shivering in her near-to-transparent dressing gown, her grief almost indecent, given the state of her dress.

Before the men fanned out, Sam Duchamp asked her where she'd been looking for Frenchie. Everywhere, she'd looked everywhere, on the Loutre trail, that of Belette, at the top of Côte Croche on the woodcutters' road, crying her name, Frenchie, my little Françoise. We'll keep looking, Duchamp promised, responsible despite himself for leading the hunt, since he was the sturdiest, and it was to him that

Suzanne Lamar had run, an honest man, she said to herself, who'd help her find her child.

Duchamp was discussing things with Larue when he saw a few women appear, Stella McBain and Harriet Miller, Madeleine Maheux, Martha Irving, Juliette Lacroix, women who didn't have small children to watch over, and refused to wait behind their windows, pacing up and down, while one of their own was perhaps being sacrificed to some scumbag's fantasies. No, this time they were going to be part of the search, and find Frenchie before it was too late.

Stella McBain and Harriet Miller were already moving off along Turtle Road when Jocelyne Ménard's car almost skidded out of control while taking a curve. She braked in a cloud of dust on seeing the crowd near the Lamars' cottage, and quickly jumped out of the vehicle, her little Marie in her arms, whom she handed over to Florence Duchamp, please, Flo. Now there was proof that Gilles wasn't guilty, and she wanted to be the first to spit in the killer's face. Suddenly she seemed twice as tall as she really was, taller than all the men gathered there, than Sam Duchamp, than Brian Larue, than Scott Miller, her eyes shining like those of a woman in love, with a burning light, and no one doubted that if someone could get on the killer's trail, it would be her, this woman in love.

Then a strangulated wailing was heard in the half-light of Turtle Road, and they saw Flora Tanguay running, too fat to run like that, Flora waving her arms over her head, and she fell and the wailing grew louder, but it wasn't Flora keening that way, no, Flora was moaning, Flora was struggling for breath. Jean-Louis, her husband, rushed up to help her, followed by Florence Duchamp or Madeleine Maheux, maybe both of them, and the source of those cries now surged into view, Frenchie Lamar, wet blood on her forehead and cheeks, her long legs scored by branches, and her feet bleeding, bare, naked as the leg of Zaza Mulligan far back in the woods. She wanted to run faster, seeing her mother throwing herself towards her, arms outstretched, both of them with their arms outstretched and crying, then Frenchie tripped as well, a young girl with long legs whose long blond hair flew in front of her over her face and over her cries, which stopped abruptly as she struck the ground.

In the darkening night, only Suzanne Lamar was still crying.

When Stan Michaud and Jim Cusack swerved into the Lamar yard, riding on their hubcaps, Frenchie was stretched out on the living-room couch, still unconscious, while Hope Jamison, who'd been sent for, was dressing her wounds and applying compresses to her forehead. As for Suzanne Lamar, she was sitting in an armchair next to the couch, her eyes fixed on Frenchie, whose child's soul seemed to be uncoiling in vaporous wreaths over her sullied body. Florence Duchamp had brought Suzanne some tea, then a glass of vermouth, but neither the glass nor the cup had been touched. Stella McBain, on her knees in front of her, tried to comfort her with the few words of French she knew, ignorant of the fact that Suzanne Lamar had been living in English for so long that she was surprised when she wasn't called Susan. *Tout va bien, now*, everything's all right, *la petite is here*, she repeated in her gentlest voice, and she went on in English, *poor thing, poor little girl.*

That was the scene Stan Michaud and Jim Cusack came upon when they pushed open the door to the cottage, after Brian Larue, outside, had brought them up to speed on the facts, four women in a state of shock, one virtually catatonic, the others trying to hide their distress to spare the first, and a young girl lying passed out on the couch, a sleeping beauty scratched raw by the thorns choking off the forest where the castle was falling down.

Faced with those women, Michaud immediately felt like a fish out of water, and regretted being on the side of the men, on the side of death, of not being able, like all the Dotties in the world, to comfort women in distress. He thought again of his awkwardness with Laura Cusack on the telephone, and wanted to take to his heels, so stupid did he feel, faced with this feminine solidarity. Still, he advanced towards Suzanne Lamar, but she was in no state to talk, no more than her daughter, Frenchie, who began to stir, probably because she'd heard his voice deep in her slumber, a voice recalling that of another man or all men. When he asked Hope Jamison if, according to her, the young girl would soon revive, she replied that she didn't know, that he'd have to wait for the doctor. *That's him!* she cried, hearing three knocks at the door, relieved that someone had finally come who could awaken Frenchie and put Suzanne Lamar to sleep with some pills that would dissolve the vitreous screen hanging suspended over her gaze, a wild gaze that was sending chills down her back.

But it wasn't the doctor who'd arrived, it was Conrad Plamondon, come to advise the police that Mark Meyer had fled the campground. Call for reinforcements, Michaud right away ordered Cusack, and step on it! Just at that moment, Bob Lamar, who'd been delayed by engine trouble and had just learned about what had happened to his daughter, started bellowing at everyone in sight and accusing the police of being incompetent. Hearing her father's voice, Frenchie opened her eyes and begged him to help her, *No Dad! No! Help me! Please… Help me!* But Bob Lamar had already roared away, swearing that he'd find Mark Meyer.

I was behind my mother with Millie when Frenchie Lamar appeared on Turtle Road. She was walking stiff-legged, like Bill the robot, like Frankenstein, and she was bleeding everywhere, like one of Frankenstein's victims, with her cheeks that had been black for three days, but on which long red drops were now mingling with her tears. Under other circumstances I'd have taken to my heels, sure that she was going to throw herself at me and clutch me in her long stiff arms, but I was paralyzed, like all the people gathered on Turtle Road, except for Suzanne Lamar, who virtually took to the air in her dressing gown, trailing behind her a white veil in the darkening night. A vampire mother if there is such a thing, an old Transylvanian princess who had at last succeeded in prying open her tomb, hurtling towards her zombified daughter.

What's wrong with the Madame? Millie snivelled. My mother, who'd been in a momentary trance, quickly turned to take Millie in her arms and tell her that the lady had fallen, that it wasn't serious. My mother was getting better where reality was concerned, because just before that she'd been telling Millie that the Lamars were getting ready for Halloween. She wiped her chin, where the ton of butter with which she'd smeared her corn had left trails full of crumbs of corn husk, then Millie was shifted into my father's arms while my mother, along with the other saintly women who were there, went to pick up Suzanne and Frenchie Lamar, not even frightened by the idea that they might be bitten or hacked to pieces. The women then transported them to the Lamar cottage with the help of Brian Larue, my brother Bob, and Scott Miller, who was beginning to look like James Dean, with the blond lock of hair falling over his forehead. Two or three years more, and it was with Scott that Zaza would have been frenching on the Loutre trail, while Sissy would have maybe been leading Bob onto another path, because he had style, my brother, even if there was no one like him to be a pain in the ass, but that would go away along with his last pimples, at least I hoped so.

Still, I felt a pang in my heart at the thought that neither Zaza nor Sissy would ever french anyone anymore, but there was still Frenchie who'd be presentable once she was cleaned up, and would feel the urge again, one day, to put her hand into that of a boy. But as for frenching, that would take an awfully long time, unless Frenchie wore her name deep inside, where hunger could conquer the fear of being poisoned by a bad piece of meat.

I was thinking about what was left of Bob's pimples, through which a thicker and thicker beard was growing, when he came out of the Lamar cottage with Scott Miller and Brian Larue. The women had chased them out, what was going on in that cottage was women's business. The men, at least one among them, had already caused enough damage. They would do without their presence. They would practise their healing among themselves. In that moment I was proud of being a female, one of those who could be admitted to a birthing room, and could care for the wounded, because they knew what that was all about, a woman's wound. I'd just aged several months in one night, to bring me closer to the menstruating half of the planet, even if I was late, as my grandmother said to my mother, asking her why she didn't dress me like a girl.

Still lost in thought, mite, my father said, gently ruffling my hair, and that gesture made me want to cry, because soon my father wouldn't dare pass his hand through my hair that way, for the simple reason that I was less and less of a mite, that I was unbugging at the speed of light, like all those girls who from one day to the next start saying no to their parents' goodnight kisses. He then led me into the cottage with Millie, while Bob stayed with the others, outside, waiting for the police and the next manhunt.

My father had just tucked Millie in after reading her a shortened version of *The Three Little Pigs* when Cusack and Michaud, tires squealing, drove up unshaven through a cloud of fireflies, looking as if they'd just come out of a suitcase. The men surrounded them, Bob a bit outside the circle, not yet daring to assert himself as a member in good standing of the male fraternity, then Michaud passed his hand over his head, relieved to learn that Frenchie was alive, and probably trying to drive away the visions of traps that had been gnawing away at his brain ever since he'd been pulled from his bed, from his La-Z-Boy, from his rocking chair, or from his dark thoughts. His head smoothed, he entered the Lamars' with Cusack at his side.

Ordinarily, my father would have told me to go to bed, it's late, and blahblahblah, but since everything was all upside down, he let me stay on the veranda, to observe the coming and going at the Lamars'. As for him, he sat in the living room, his body bent over, his head in his hands, and I preferred to stay where I was. What can a twelve-year-old girl say to her father when he's broken down and doesn't understand a thing? I didn't want to see my father like that.

I may have been a girl, but I wasn't yet a saint, a missionary, or anything close. I fixed my eyes on the Lamar yard, trying to see through the gathering darkness, and I saw Bob light a cigarette that was certainly not his first, in the company of Scott Miller. He was getting older too. I'd barely have time to turn my back before he'd be driving his own car, Millie would be wearing high heels, and my father would have grey hair.

Fortunately, Conrad Plamondon created a distraction, because I was on the verge of lining us all up in our coffins. Plamondon had left a few minutes earlier for the campground, dragging his feet, as disoriented as my father, but he came running back, his hair flying, to go and pound on the Lamars' door. They'd found another Zaza, another Sissy, that's what I figured, trying to imagine who it was, Sandra Miller or Jane Mary Brown maybe, who I hated, but wouldn't want to see die in a trap. I was going to run to my father when Conrad Plamondon came out of the cottage, wiping his brow just like Michaud, then passing his hand over his shirt, smearing it with his bad thoughts. Afterwards, it was all hands on deck, and I had another spell of paralysis, standing on the veranda, asking myself why the whole world had gone mad. Then Bob Lamar parked his broken-down car in the yard and started to swear like a trooper after going up to Conrad Plamondon, meanwhile Plamondon waved his arms and the others came over, all talking at the same time, then Cusack came wheeling out of the Lamars' cottage, and I couldn't hear a word of what was being said.

It was my mother, come in search of a hot water bottle and to see if everything was all right, who told us what was going on. She went to sit beside my father in the living room and murmured, it's little Meyer, it seems like it's little Meyer.

They found Mark Meyer the next morning in a cabin near Coburn Gore, thanks to a call from a trucker who'd picked him up on Route 27. The young man was haggard, his clothes were torn, and you could see, from the lump in his shirt near his neck, that he had a dislocated shoulder. The agents who caught him had tried to make him talk, but Meyer just kept repeating two words, *fucking bastard*, which were perhaps addressed to one or the other of the agents, or a phantom in pursuit of Meyer, who was locked into an anger that hardened his gaze, turning his eyes into two black pearls whose brilliance conveyed all the violence behind his silence.

After having contacted Michaud on a staticky radio, the police handcuffed Meyer to the cast-iron stove rusting in the cabin, because Michaud was adamant, stay there, I'm not far away, I'm coming. Still, it took more than an hour for Michaud to arrive with his men, during which time the two agents took turns guarding the prisoner, going outside one at a time to breathe the morning's fresh air or smoke a cigarette so as to escape the cabin's mouldering odour, wherein they detected the presence of a dead rat, fox, raccoon, or perhaps worse. You never knew, with those sickos. Most of the time it was impossible to know how many victims there were, young girls, runaways never found, travelling salesmen who vanished between two villages on a January night, any more than you could figure out what hiding places they'd been able to come up with for the bodies. But the officers, Armstrong and Carpenter, didn't try searching under the cabin. They were ordinary highway cops, and such tasks were not their responsibility. They'd leave that to the guys trained for such work.

When Michaud's car, followed by two other vehicles, came into sight on the bumpy road winding through the trees, Armstrong was pissing beside an old fence, thinking that he'd have no scruples beating up on Meyer with his fists or a truncheon, in memory of those murdered girls, adolescents barely older than his little sister, who'd as yet seen nothing, known nothing in their lives other than a few thrills. He zipped up his fly, told himself that if anyone dared to touch his sister he'd torture him until he was begging to be killed, then he walked towards Michaud and his men, a bunch of guys with tired eyes, all of whom could have used a shower and a shave.

Michaud insisted on doing the questioning alone with Cusack, whom he asked to keep silent, *you watch, that's all*, but he took Meyer outside, the cabin stank, and ordered the technical team accompanying him to find the source of the smell, which didn't augur well to him either, recalling the odour of the Salem dump where Esther Conrad's body had been left, where her youthful fragrance had been overwhelmed by the reek rising from the mounds of rotten vegetables and sodden cardboard boxes and canned goods cooking in the sun.

He led Meyer into the shade, where there were a few logs set up around what was left of a blackened fire, and had him sit facing him, his hands cuffed in front given the injury to his shoulder, they weren't brutes after all, while he brought his notebook and pen out of his pocket, but slowly, to stop himself from leaping at the young man's throat and strangling him then and there.

*Why*, he asked, but Meyer, gone crimson from clenching his jaws, just bored his eyes into those of Michaud, defying him to extract a single word. Michaud sighed, it wasn't the first time he'd dealt with a bastard whose need to justify his acts came close to farce. *Why?* he shouted, then he leaped up so fast that Meyer, taken by surprise, fell off his wobbly log, cried out himself, feeling the pain run through his shoulder, and crawled backwards, unable to use his arms to get up, while Michaud moved in and loomed over him, a giant with an ugly face who'd had no breakfast and would kill for a raw piece of meat.

*You'll talk, you son of a bitch*, and Michaud opened the floodgates to talk to him about Zaza, *so young, so beautiful*, her whole life before her, describing to him softly, taking his time, omitting no detail, the agony a trap's jaws can inflict, ripping to the bone, tearing skin and muscles to shreds, the intolerable burning, then with the flow of blood and the progressive loss of consciousness, the realization that death was approaching, death, *for Christ's sake!* He talked about the mud in Zaza's wound, the nocturnal insects, then went on to Sissy, *sweet and lovely Sissy, so young, so bright*, then Frenchie Lamar, *poor little Franneswoise*, who'd never get over her shock, never get rid of the bold scar defacing her cheek, and many other scars as well, less visible, but how much deeper. Just now Michaud had tried to question her, with no success. *Why, Meyer? Why?* Why was Frenchie not talking? Why was she protecting a scumbag's ass?

During Michaud's long soliloquy, Meyer didn't move, but the sun had shifted, casting Michaud's shadow over the left side of his face, then shining on the black pearl deep in his right orbit, which seemed to sink in deeper still and to dilate when Michaud mentioned Françoise's name, Françoise's wounds, and Meyer cried *no! not Frenchie, you're lying, you're a fucking liar!*

Those words echoed through the treetops, *you're lying, you're a fucking liar*, then into Michaud's head as a blackbird sang out behind Meyer's moaning, *no, not Frenchie!* Something was awry, the blackbird was whistling off-key and the rustling of the leaves was deafening. Michaud couldn't think straight so he struck again, spelling out Frenchie's every wound, however unsightly, however many there were, while Meyer kept tossing about, swearing that the story was a pack of lies.

After a few minutes, Michaud went silent and looked Cusack straight in the eyes: Meyer wasn't lying. Meyer didn't know that Frenchie had been attacked. Meyer was not their man.

# AFTER FRENCHIE

It took several hours to make Mark Meyer spill it all out, he wouldn't talk because he wanted to protect Frenchie, because Frenchie had asked him not to and he loved Frenchie and her smile, a smile that would never betray him.

It had all begun early in the summer, when Zaza Mulligan and Sissy Morgan agreed to listen to "A Whiter Shade of Pale" in Frenchie's room. After, Frenchie thought they'd become friends, and had trailed after them, that's what Sissy and Zaza claimed, letting her follow them just the same because they could look down on her, laughing at her accent, her clothes, her tan, even though it was perfect.

It had all begun when Frenchie Lamar fell in love with him, Mark Meyer, and became horribly jealous of Zaza Mulligan. That was when she'd made off with Millie Duchamp's doll, which the child had left on the beach near a sandcastle that was crumbling in the sun. She took advantage of the fact that the Duchamps had gone in for supper to take a closer look at the bundle of rags that Millie was carrying around everywhere. A dirty doll whose grey cheeks were dotted with freckles. *Éphélides*, her mother would have corrected her, but she didn't care, *éphélides*, freckles, brown spots, bits of bran, or whatever, because the doll had hair as red as Zaza Mulligan's, and wretched little green eyes that she right away wanted to bury in the doll's soft head. Without a thought for Millie Duchamp, she grabbed the doll and took it home. Into the semi-darkness of her room, she pulled out one by one its long long eyelashes, one for Zaza, one for my love, and one for me, then kicked it again and again, *take that, Zaza, and that, and that, and this.*

*What are you doing with that doll?* her mother asked when she went in, but Frenchie slammed her bedroom door, and Suzanne Lamar only heard *take this, and this, and that.*

When he got home, her father found her in tears, the doll at her feet. He sat down with her until she told him everything, the humiliations, the anger, Meyer, jealousy. Then he got up, walked over the doll, and promised Frenchie that he'd take care of everything, that she wouldn't have to worry about it anymore. That's where it all began, when Bob Lamar saw his little Françoise suffering, his own doll, his angel. *Nobody will ever hurt my wife, my daughter, my father, my dog.*

It was only at the end of the day, Friday 18 August that they got on Bob Lamar's trail. They'd checked all the highways, set up roadblocks at the border crossings and just about everywhere the State of Maine had drivable roads, but Lamar had taken to the woods, back where it had all begun. His car was spotted by a State Police helicopter right near Boundary, hidden in a clearing screened off by brush.

Michaud arrived on site with his team and took the path Lamar had beaten into the grass, only to lose track of him once he got into the trees. He split his men into three groups that entered the woods to the north, east, and west. Michaud chose to head east, following his hunch. If his sense of direction was right, he'd soon join Otter Trail, but as he advanced, an overpowering sense of urgency pushed him to hurry his steps, to angrily sweep aside the branches barring his way, forcing Cusack to dodge the whiplashes that stung in the humid air. But Cusack didn't mind, he shared Michaud's fears. He took branches full in the face, wiping away the sweat running on his brow while rubbing at the soreness caused by the thrashing he was receiving.

They turned onto Otter Trail and began to run towards the site of the first murder, that of Zaza Mulligan, Cusack faster than Michaud, who had to slow his pace and stop so he wouldn't pass out. He leaned down, rested his veined hands on his knees, and counted to twenty-five, a number that seemed high enough for him not to collapse, a magic number in which he wanted to believe. At twenty-six, he was still huffing like a bull. But he started off again at a trot, following the white patch, far in front, of Cusack's shirt, stuck to his back like a second skin.

Everything happened too fast, everything always happened too fast, as if he'd been stupid to the point of not being able to foresee the death at the heart of the carnage, nor to anticipate the impact of the projectiles so he could heave himself at Latimer, or the force of the insults so he could help Pete Landry, so he could throw Latimer to the ground and breathe by his side in the mud. When he saw his little Françoise, *my daughter, my love*, heading into the woods barefoot, two or three miles from Boundary Pond, he almost hit a tree, and left his car in the ditch to run towards Frenchie, his daughter, his angel.

*Wait for me! Wait for me, baby doll,* but Frenchie started to run too, too fast, faster and faster, with her bare legs and feet, *don't, don't touch me, Dad*. And coming over a stone, she tripped like Zaza before her, like Sissy, what did it matter, like Sissy in the mud, her hair streaming down her back like an endless, luminous wedding veil, so much beauty, *my love*, a long and vaporous pale silk dress catching the shimmer of the setting sun. *Don't!*

When he knelt down beside her, he saw Latimer's fear in the eyes of his daughter, then Sissy's fear, *don't...* while a thin thread of blood came into view on her right cheek. *My girl*, he murmured, stroking her brow, kissing her brow, but Frenchie drew away, pushed herself away from him, but Frenchie got up, *why?*, cuts on her feet, and took off in the opposite direction, towards Meyer's arms, her veil swirling behind her, towards the arms of her mother, her veil catching the dying light, endlessly.

Lamar remained there, on his knees on the moss, staring at the blood fallen from Frenchie's cheek onto a white stone, *a tear, a drop of red rain.* Without thinking, he then headed back towards the cottage, where the men were gathered, where his daughter was lying on a couch. Hearing someone, Plamondon or Cusack, speak Meyer's name, Bob Lamar saw red, as red as Latimer's blood on the dark sand of Omaha Beach. He'd go right now to have the head of that bastard Meyer, because this war, this massacre, this carnage, all began with him. He leaped into his car and found Meyer at the West Forks crossroads, where he was waiting for Frenchie in the black night.

There too, everything happened too quickly. The kid got away and his nightmares caught up with him, Latimer, Landry, the dead bodies behind which Françoise was slowly walking, blood on her black cheek. The blood came from him. He was the cause. And so he did what he had to do. Night was falling when he hid his car and made his way towards Otter Trail, there where it had all begun, Zaza, the war, his friendship with Landry. At the end of the path, he knelt down for one last prayer: *no one, not even me, will from now on hurt my only child.*

In the silence of the forest Michaud heard only the sound of his breathing, hoarser at each step, and the beating of his heart pounding heavily from his breast to his skull. The light began to fail, and the trees all around were darkening visibly. He switched on his flashlight, whose beam jolted with every one of his steps, casting light only on the awkwardness of his progress, the clumsiness of his body, too heavy. Then he spotted Cusack's light, shining on the still forest a hundred feet away, but illuminating only death, dead leaves, dead needles, rotten wood. With one last push Michaud increased his pace, bounding over obstacles with his light. When he caught up with Cusack he found him crouched at the foot of a tree, in contemplation of the silence and dead leaves.

The men had arrived too late. Before them swayed the legs of Bob Lamar, who was hanging from a grey maple whose leaves had reddened before their time.

# AFTER LAMAR

After Bob Lamar's death, some people said the nightmare was over, but a nightmare of such scope cannot end so quickly. The rumours surrounding it continued to make their way from one cottage to another, sowing pain and confusion in their path. You just had to prick up your ears to hear people whispering that it was madness that had acted that way, madness brought on by the war, and then hatred, hatred and anger, pride, a boundless vanity. You put all those feelings together and you could line up the seven deadly sins against a wall and fire on them full force to soothe your own rage, to forget your own sins. To this rumour was added another, which made its way through the woods and ended up at the lake. At the start of Otter Trail you could hear the cries of Zaza Mulligan, muffled by the heavy treetops, or turning themselves into a kind of pagan chant, a phantom melody recalling funeral prayers or supplications echoing down the viscid corridors of hell. Then to this voice there was added that of Sissy Morgan, leaping from the clearing to the path, setting the trees ablaze as it passed, triggering storms and violent winds in those parts of the forest where no one, for a long time, dared to venture.

The nightmare had carried off the dream, and Bondrée was no more than ruins. As soon as Bob Lamar's body had been found in the woods, the mothers decided that was enough, the fathers stowed away the chairs, the barbecues, the awnings. Within a few days Bondrée was shut down for the winter, and perhaps forever.

Over at the Lamars' there was a constant coming and going around the cottage, unfamiliar cars parking in the yard, friends or family members come to comfort Suzanne and Frenchie, though nothing could erase the marks made by Bob Lamar on the body of his daughter, though nothing, it seemed, could persuade Suzanne Lamar to remove the old negligée in which she wandered like a lost soul, dragging herself in her pink slippers down to the lake, asking herself how she came to be at this lake, then climbing up towards the garden to be greeted by the helplessness of a sister-in-law who dared not take her in her arms for fear that the simple stroke of a hand might turn Suzanne into a harpy who'd claw her cheeks.

Out of a sense of decency people tried not to pay attention to the doors opening and closing on bewildered whisperings and the cries of Frenchie reaching out for the arms of Mark Meyer, but the cottage was weighed down so heavily that you couldn't ignore the fact that it was sinking into the earth, and that soon men muffled in thick scarves would come to set it ablaze, as others long before had put to the torch Peter Landry's shack, so there would be no hint left of that heaviness, which yet would go on pressing down on what was there until all memory of that summer would be wiped away.

As for Stan Michaud, he handed in his inspector's badge three days after having found Bob Lamar's body. He then jumped into his car to head out to Portland and the Evergreen Cemetery, where there lay, side by side, in death as in life, the remains of Zaza Mulligan and Sissy Morgan.

Crouched down among the tombstones, he sought in the gathering dark the names carved into pink granite where a tree cast its shadow, then he murmured *sorry, Elisabeth, sorry, Sissy*, as Bob Lamar's body swayed to and fro in the setting sun.

After having deposited two roses on the still-fresh earth, one red for the redhead, one white for the blonde, he tried to think of what he could say to the young girls, since he had no more questions to ask them, no *why, Zaza*, no *who, Sissy. Rest in peace*, that was all, and he crossed himself. He was in total darkness when he turned his back on the gravestones and looked across to the glow hovering over the city.

Contrary to what he'd promised Laura, Jim Cusack, for his part, didn't have the courage to quit his job, as Zaza Mulligan and Sissy Morgan had against his will become his Esther Conrad, boomerangs whose targeting he wouldn't be able to escape just by hiding himself as far away as possible from violence. Before slamming shut the police station's door behind him, Michaud had nevertheless forced him to take a few days of vacation he didn't know what to do with. Stretched out in his yard, he tried to lose himself in pictures that smelled of the sea and cut hay, images where Laura ran and made the bottom of her dress rise up, or dared him to follow her into the icy water, *come on, you coward*, but Bob Lamar's rigid face kept coming back to him, and the shadow of old shoes grazing the bark of the tree from which the body was dangling. Those visions obsessed him, just like the smell of the urine-soaked shoes. He tried in vain to replace that persistent scene with Laura's joy, Laura spinning her skirt, Laura biting into an ice cream cone with two scoops, one yellow and one orange, sun and fruit melting together in the light of day, but the ground always gave way with an avalanche from on high that buried Laura and her smile, leaving at the surface only a long lock of red hair that sank into the earth as he was trying to drag it out. Cusack woke from his nightmares every time, crying out his wife's name: Laura! Laura! But no voice ever answered him.

I never gave Sissy Morgan's watch to her parents. Either I was too timid, or I was afraid to face their pain, or I felt the object was mine, that it was Sissy Morgan's gift passed on to the *littoldolle* who had survived her. I have it still, in a small box covered in green velvet, forest green, the deep green of Bondrée. When I open the cover, I feel as if I'm opening a music box out of which drift the airs of the summer of '67, and on the top of which two figurines in brightly coloured clothes turn round and round. I wear the watch rarely, except when I want to live in the time of Bondrée and force the past to remember itself. Then there are dozens of figurines that appear in the midst of the plashing of fresh water, the whispering of the waves and the wind, the chirping of crickets.

I've never gone back to Bondrée. The following spring my parents sold the cottage, unable to imagine that the sound of the waves might one day cover over the anguished moans coming out of the forest. With the money from the sale they bought a tent trailer and a new car, with which, from one July to another, we navigated the roads of the Beauce, of Mauricie, or Abitibi, never stopping for more than a week in one place, never more than a week in a place where a remembrance of beauty might wound one or other of us. As the years passed, my new treasure chest doubled in size, filled with black pebbles and cormorant feathers, but never did it equal the magic of that of Bondrée. Once the chest was forgotten, I met an improved version of Mark Meyer, whom I left behind me along with the chest when we were back on the road, then I encountered one or two Zaza Mulligans, one or two Sissy Morgans, whom I saw from afar swinging their hips as I exhaled the smoke from my king-size Du Maurier.

I've never gone back to Bondrée, but I learned from Emma, whom I see two or three times a year, when the sun is shining and we want to lift our glasses to summer friendships, that all the cottages, including ours, have been abandoned, beginning with that of Gilles Ménard, who took it down with his bare hands before turning his back on Bondrée forever with his wife and child, not without having first imprinted within himself a picture of the forest from before the felling of the large trees and the drying up of the pure water. One of the last to leave was Pat Tanguay, fallen from his boat one August morning in 1972, whether struck down by old age or drawn in by the shimmering water. His hat floated peacefully in Ménard Bay, his small craft adrift, then his body washed up on the beach bordering the bay, there where his daughter-in-law, thirty years earlier, had sunk her feet into the mud on her way to visit Pete Landry. After the ambulance come to gather his remains had pulled away, Jean-Louis and Flora, his son and daughter-in-law, got into their car, Pat's old hat on the back seat. The noise from their engine was the last to blend with the birdsong.

Today Bondrée must resemble one of those holiday ghost towns that you sometimes like to think embody the past and the lives of people who once stayed there, where you spread a few coloured garments on the beach, where you imagine some voices, *Michael, Marnie, suppertime, Sugar,*

*Sugar Baby, come on, my love,* where you long for the sweetness of summers that elude us, while picking up a broken toy buried in the warm sand.

Most of the cottages must still be standing, but the paint is peeling and the vegetation has moved onto the terraces, the porches, the verandas with their broken window panes. Here and there a shed has collapsed, a dock has been borne away by the waves, but a few perennials still survive in the overgrown gardens of Stella McBain and Hope Jamison, where the red is dominant, bright red, tanager red. In our yard, under the now-gigantic pine, a rusted tin box is sticking out of the ground, wherein a few unidentifiable feathers lie atop the dust of some ancient snakeskins. An old transistor radio sits under the Mulligan porch, as well as a faded record album, *Sgt. Pepper's Lonely Hearts Club Band.*

Up Otter Trail however, the last vestiges of Pete Landry's shack have disappeared, and no one could tell that a trapper once lived there, and dreamed, while singing to himself *sweet Maggie, Tanager of Bondrée.* In a few decades the same fate will have befallen the cottages built in Landry's Eden, the stone and wood will have gone back to the earth, and the trees will have moved in to obscure the road, a foreshadowing of those days when man will be gone from the surface of the globe. Nature will have asserted its rights, its proper place, waiting for other hunters to arrive, other families that will cut down trees and erect dwellings from new wood, opening onto the beauty of green shades, oblivious to the fact that Bondrée is a forest strewn with traps, a domain where the wavering of the light can easily plunge you into darkness.

I've never gone back to Bondrée, but I've kept intact a vivid memory of it that brings me near to a tenuous happiness each time a rustling of wings stirs up a scent of juniper, and a fox bolts, alive, at the edge of a path.

# A NOTE AND ACKNOWLEDGMENTS

I've borrowed the words, "arg, argul, gargul," which appear on page 111, from a friend I deeply mourn, Jacques Hardy, who wanted to put them into the mouth of one of the characters in a novel that he sadly never finished. Thank you, my good friend.

As always, I must thank Pierre, my companion, for being there, for his patience and precious help, as well as Jacques Fortin, the mainstay of the publishing house Québec Amérique, for, as ever, his staunch support. I thank as well everyone at Québec Amérique who worked to produce this novel, especially Marie-Noëlle Gagnon, Mylaine Lemire, Nathalie Caron, and Isabelle Longpré, who initiated the publishing process. Thank you to Yvette Gagnon for her linguistic counsel. Thank you to Donald Winkler for his excellent work in translating this novel.

Thank you, finally, to all those I have forgotten, to all those who were there by my side during the three years I spent in Bondrée, among whom I must include my mother, and also my father, who passed away long ago, much too long ago, and made it possible for me to know that place which marked my childhood, and, by that token, was bound to become a setting for my fiction.

Many thanks, also, to the team of No Exit Press, in UK—Geoff Mulligan, Clare Quinlivan, Frances Teehan, Claire Watts, Ion Mills and Nick Rennison—, and to the team of Biblioasis in Canada—Dan Wells, Natalie Hamilton, Stephen Henighan, Chris Andrechek and all the others—for their impressive work and for having followed me in the paths of Boundary.

## ABOUT THE AUTHOR

Andrée A. Michaud, author of ten novels, is a two-time winner of the Governor General's Award for Fiction. Her novel *Mirror Lake*, winner of the Ringuet Prize from the Quebec Academy of Letters, inspired the feature film *Lac Mystère*. In addition to the Governor General's Award, her most recent novel, *Boundary*, won the Arthur Ellis Prize for best French-language mystery novel, the Saint-Pacôme Prize for mystery novels, and the Quebec Arts Council Prize for best literary work from Quebec's Eastern Townships.

Andrée A. Michaud lives in the village where she was born, St-Sebastien-de-Frontenac, in a house surrounded by trees and animals.

## ABOUT THE TRANSLATOR

Donald Winkler's previous translations for the Biblioasis International Translation Series include Mauricio Segura's *Eucalyptus* and Samuel Archibald's Giller Prize–nominated *Arvida*. A Montreal-based literary translator and documentary filmmaker, he is a three-time winner of the Governor General's Award for French-to-English Translation, most recently in 2013 for Pierre Nepveu's collection of verse, *The Major Verbs*.